D0786845

# OPEN SEASON

# OPEN SEASON

## MARYANN MILLER

**FIVE STAR**
*A part of Gale, Cengage Learning*

GALE
CENGAGE Learning

Detroit • New York • San Francisco • New Haven, Conn • Waterville, Maine • London

**GALE**
CENGAGE Learning‾

Set in 11 pt. Plantin.

LIBRARY OF CONGRESS CATALOGING-IN-PUBLICATION DATA

Miller, Maryann, 1943–
   Open season / Maryann Miller. — 1st ed.
    p. cm.
   ISBN-13: 978-1-59414-915-3
   ISBN-10: 1-59414-915-1
   1. Policewomen—Fiction. 2. Police—Texas—Dallas—Fiction. 3. Serial murderers—Fiction. 4. Serial murder investigation—Fiction. 5. Racism—Fiction. 6. Dallas (Tex.)—Fiction I. Title.
PS3613.I545O64 2010
813'.6—dc22                          2010036695

First Edition. First Printing: December 2010.
Published in 2010 in conjunction with Tekno Books and Ed Gorman.

Printed in the United States of America
1 2 3 4 5 6 7 14 13 12 11 10

*To our son, David, the best research assistant ever.*

# ACKNOWLEDGMENTS

It is with much gratitude that I acknowledge the officers at the Dallas Police Department who shared their experiences and expertise with me, with a special thanks to the late Tim Huskey, a former police officer and a wonderful writer. He introduced me to other officers who were willing to talk about the difficulties of working in a city and department filled with racial tension. Tim, and all the others, also helped me get all the procedural material correct, and if there is a mistake, it is mine, not theirs.

# PROLOGUE

Sarah took a deep breath and faced Quinlin in the stuffy cubbyhole of an office. The room was hot and musty. Dust motes floated in the slivers of sunshine that had penetrated the haze of accumulated grime on the windows of the old building. The scent of his cologne hung heavily in the still air. Chaps. Rich, masculine, and too easily a distraction.

Dressed in a dark, somber suit, Quinlin didn't speak. He watched her with the careful scrutiny of a snake considering a field mouse. A trickle of perspiration ran down Sarah's back and dampened her white T-shirt. Shifting in the wooden chair, she contemplated the wisdom of taking off her jacket, then decided against it. He would interpret it as a sign of weakness.

She thought she was prepared for this. She'd rehearsed it a million times, remembering the images, nailing down the sequence, readying herself for his opener, "Detective Kingsly, tell me what happened that night."

She recalled the moon playing tag with a few heavy clouds, casting weird, disorientating shadows on the crumbling buildings. She remembered wishing the clouds would give way to rain, anything to relieve the oppressive heat that had pounded the city relentlessly for weeks. She remembered thinking the heat made people do crazy things.

Maybe that's why it had happened.

The rest of it flashed through her mind like a sequence of freeze frames.

*Franco and the boy turn.*

*A glint of metal in the moonlight.*

*John pushes her away, reaching for the gun tucked in
his waistband.*

*The clasp on her purse sticks.*

*A flash of gunfire.*

*The sharp report of return fire.*

*Struggling to get her gun.*

*Franco is down.*

*The kid swings his gun toward John.*

*She fires the same time the kid does.*

*The coppery smell of warm blood.*

*Hers?*

*No.*

*Goddam it, John, get up!*

*Why is everything so quiet?*

*Where is the kid?*

*There's a big gaping hole in the cheap sequined
evening bag.*

Every time Sarah played the scene in her mind, she hoped for
a different ending. It never came. Her purse always had the hole
in it. John was always dead. And so was the kid.

"And you're sure you had no choice?" Quinlin's officious
voice rankled with unspoken insinuations.

Sarah suppressed a surge of anger as he walked behind her
chair. *The son of a bitch is not going to trip me up. No way.*

"Yes." She didn't trust herself with more words.

"That's pretty easy to say since everyone else who was there
is dead."

The comment jolted her, and she clenched sweaty fists in her
lap to keep herself in the chair. *Don't dignify that with a response.*

Quinlin came up beside her and paused. Sarah didn't look at

him for a long moment, then turned and met his insolent gaze with steady gray eyes. *Go ahead. Give it your best shot.*

They maintained the visual standoff for a moment that seemed to drag into eternity, and Sarah breathed a silent sigh of relief when he broke contact first. It had been a minor skirmish in the overall war, but the small victory shifted the balance of power slightly in her favor.

Quinlin walked around his desk and sat down in his chair. "Have you scheduled your appointment with Doc Murray?"

"No."

"Why not?"

The question was accompanied by a sincere smile she knew was calculated to disarm her. *Fuck him and fuck his pseudo-compassion.* "I thought it might be nice to bury my partner before I start putting my life back together."

Quinlin pushed wire-framed glasses up and let his finger rest on the side of his nose. Sarah never knew if it was a pose designed to exude wisdom, but she recognized another familiar tactic. He could sit there like that forever, hoping the strain of the silence would open some verbal floodgates.

It wasn't going to happen to her. Not here. Not now.

She clamped her lips tight and turned the nervous flutter of her hand into an acceptable gesture of tucking a strand of blonde hair behind her ear.

"The visit's mandatory before you can be reinstated," Quinlin said, his voice chilling her like a douse of ice water.

"I know. I'll take care of it."

Apparently satisfied with that response, he leaned back in his chair. "Did you have any suspicion the bust might go bad?"

"No."

Silence stretched between them like a guitar string tuned too high.

"You're going to have to talk to me," Quinlin said. "I have to know what went down that night."

"Read the report."

"Why the resistance, Detective? You know the drill." Quinlin gently rocked in his swivel chair, creating a sound track of rhythmic squeaks. "I don't make decisions based solely on reports."

Sarah broke away from his intense scrutiny and clenched her jaw so hard her teeth hurt. Why couldn't he back off? Just for a couple of days. He couldn't be that much of a prick not to see she wasn't ready to talk. Not until the words could come without the tears.

But then again, it was his job to be a prick. To catch people at their most vulnerable moments. Dig and probe and push until he was satisfied nothing was held back. He did this to every officer who used deadly force. Not just her. But the realization offered no consolation.

"Detective." His voice called her to attention. "Did you know the kid was going to be there?"

"No." She took a deep shuddering breath. "Can I have a drink of water?"

"Certainly." Quinlin rose and went to the water cooler in the corner.

Sarah used the time to compose herself. She had to at least appear willing to comply. Answer some of the questions. Otherwise . . .

She didn't want to think about otherwise.

She accepted the paper cup and took a soothing swallow of the cool water. Quinlin reclaimed his seat and she met his penetrating gaze again. "When we set up the meet, it was just supposed to be Franco. We'd been working him for a couple of months."

"Why didn't you abort the bust?"

"No chance." Sarah balanced the empty cup on the edge of

his desk. "The action started almost immediately."

"You think they made you?"

She shook her head, remembering the meets to set up the buy. "Franco was a punk. He wasn't smart enough to make us. He just thought he was smart enough to take out a rich guy and his broad."

"That's the way you figure it?"

"Yeah." Sarah wiped a clammy hand on the smooth fabric of her jeans, hoping to still the tremble of muscle that could quickly become jerky spasms. If Quinlin noticed, he gave no sign.

She waited out another silence.

"That's all for today." Quinlin sat forward abruptly and picked up a file from his desk, effectively dismissing her.

Rising, Sarah fished her car keys out of her jacket pocket and headed toward the door.

In the quiet hallway, she leaned her forehead against the cool cement of the wall and took an angry swipe at the tear that had dared to trickle down her cheek.

# CHAPTER ONE

Mel unlocked the door to the maintenance room and flicked the switch on the wall for light. He still had fifteen minutes until his shift ended at midnight, but he didn't figure anyone would notice if he bugged out early. There was only one other person left in the whole mall anyway. And by the time the security guard made his pass through here, it would be well past clock out time anyway.

He pushed his tool box into its designated place on the dented metal shelves with a harsh scrape, thankful that he'd had a light workload tonight. Wouldn't have to lose time with a shower. He could just zip out of here and head straight to his favorite watering hole. If he was lucky, he could pick up some good shit on the way. And Rita would be there with some good stuff of her own.

After locking the door to the storage room, Mel set off at a brisk pace, his boots thumping hollowly in the empty corridor.

*He stood in the shadowed doorway down the hall, watching. He'd watched unseen before, waiting for the right moment. He'd long ago quit worrying about the wisdom of what he'd planned. It was the only choice he had left.*

*He eased the door closed and listened to the thud of footsteps draw near, then pass.*

*It was time.*

*A rush of adrenaline sent his heart on a wild, erratic riff, and a*

15

*sudden storm of panic threatened to overwhelm him. It was no simple act he was about to perform. All kinds of things could go wrong.*

*Maybe he should leave. Forget the whole crazy scheme.*

*No.*

*The sound from the hallway ceased. He cracked the door open and saw the man stooped over the water fountain.*

*Go! Now!*

Mel whirled at the unexpected creak of the men's room door opening behind him. Who the hell was skulking around down here at this hour? He relaxed when he recognized the man standing a few feet away.

"You scared the piss outa me." Mel wiped drips of water from his chin. "What're you doing sneaking around here, anyway?"

The man didn't answer, and the lure of Danny's Grill finally overcame Mel's curiosity. If the guy didn't want to talk, so be it. Bastard never was very friendly. Not even when Mel offered to share some of his best shit. If anything, the guy had been downright unfriendly since then. So screw him.

*The decision to act was made somewhere deep in his subconscious. He lunged, whipping the weapon around Mel's neck in one fluid move and pulling it tight.*

*The man's feet scrabbled for purchase on the slick tile as Mel's full weight fell against him. He had to stay upright. Couldn't let the wild, grasping hands break his hold. Had to finish it.*

*It took forever for the crescendo of harsh gasps to recede into a soft gurgle. As if orchestrated by the sounds, the thrashing slowly subsided to a few involuntary twitches.*

*Was it over?*

*The throaty rasp of his own breathing was the only sound the man heard now, but he kept his straining muscles tight for a few more mo-*

*ments. Had to be sure. Wouldn't do to let go too soon.*

*A sour taste of bile filled his mouth as the finality of the act hit him. Was he no better than the rest, deciding who should die to suit his purposes?*

*No matter now. It was done. The crusade was launched, and the ending was no longer up to him.*

Sarah stirred her drink with the plastic straw, the ice clinking against the glass. She tried to remember if it was her fourth or fifth Rob Roy. Not being sure was maybe a good sign that she should stop. Wouldn't do for one of Dallas's finest to be stopped for a DWI.

"Shit," she muttered, taking a big swallow of her drink. "Doesn't matter anyway. If SIU doesn't get me, the Review Board will."

Normally, Sarah shied away from going to bars alone, especially in the late hours before night turned into day. She hated the mating ritual that was often triggered by a woman walking in alone. It created a veritable frenzy of anticipation, playing out in postures and expressions that said, "Maybe I'll get lucky tonight."

She wasn't a virgin, or a prude, but she couldn't reduce sex to the same level as buying a lottery ticket.

Tonight, however, was not a normal situation. The second week of her enforced exile had driven her to the point of near madness. Lieutenant McGregor had told her she needed the time away from the job for herself. Time to deal with losing John. Get her head on straight about the kid. But she also suspected that he wanted her away from the controversy. If she wasn't accessible to the protesters lined up outside the Municipal Building, they couldn't lynch her.

The waitress, who wore a tight, leather mini-skirt that restricted her movements to short, bouncy steps, paused by

Sarah's table and set a fresh drink on the scarred wooden surface. Sarah looked at the petite brunette, puzzled.

"From the guy at the bar." The waitress nodded a mass of curls toward a man who raised his glass in salute when Sarah caught his eye. Ford truck ads with rugged cowboys flooded her mind, tempting her to rethink her position on the lottery.

Ignoring her usual caution, Sarah accepted the drink and waited, trying not to be too obvious about watching him.

Finally, he pulled his lanky frame off the stool and walked toward her table. Two things caught her attention. Well, actually, three. A dimple at the corner of his crooked smile, wisps of curly black hair escaping from the neck of his red cowboy shirt and tight blue jeans defining well-muscled thighs and . . .

"May I join you?" His voice was as smooth as rich leather.

Sarah blinked, wondering if he was just a drunken illusion. But he didn't disappear. He didn't sit down either. He shifted his weight to his outside foot, and she realized he was waiting for permission. Maybe he really was a cowboy. The gallantry was a nice endearment.

Before she could respond to the man's question, a large, beefy figure loomed behind him, and the voice of Lieutenant McGregor broke into the moment. "You're a hard woman to track down, Kingsly."

The sight of the men eyeing each other like junkyard dogs brought the first smile to her face in a long time. She offered an explanation before one of them drew blood. "This is my boss."

After a moment's hesitation the other man extended his hand to the Lieutenant, "Paul Barnett."

"Thomas McGregor." He accepted the handshake. "We just need to talk here a minute."

Paul turned to Sarah and the depth of his eyes, the color of a midnight sky, held her. Then she gave a slight nod. He fished a card out of his shirt pocket and pushed it across the table to her. "In case you ever need help with your taxes."

McGregor slid his considerable bulk onto the bench across from Sarah. "A casual bar pick-up? You?"

"Never had a chance to find out," she mused, watching Paul stride back to the bar.

"Disappointed?"

"I'm not sure." Sarah dropped the card into her jacket pocket, then turned her attention back to McGregor. "How'd you find me, anyway?"

"Simple deductive reasoning." He motioned for the waitress. "After a couple of weeks of waiting to hear if I had a job or not, I'd try to ease the tension with a few belts. And I'd do it close enough to home that I could walk if I needed to. So I did a little legwork that paid off."

"You come just to commiserate?"

McGregor paused to order a Johnny Walker Red, straight up. "No. I heard from SIU this afternoon."

Nerves sent her heart on a wild drumbeat. "And . . . ?"

"They ruled it a clean shoot."

Her sigh of relief came out in a loud whoosh. The Special Investigative Unit, what some still referred to as Internal Affairs, could have stripped her of her badge forever. "What about the Review Board?"

"They don't run things at the station. They just like to think they do."

"What if they decide the shoot was racially motivated?"

"Was it?"

The question slammed into Sarah like a freight train. "I thought you knew the answer to that."

"I do." McGregor leveled deep brown eyes at her. "I just want to make sure you do."

The waitress stepped up and set a glass down in front of McGregor. Sarah lifted her own and took a quick swallow.

"When do I get to come back?"

McGregor eyed her over the edge of his glass. "What does Doc Murray have to say?"

"I thought you made the decisions."

"I do." He paused and drained half of his drink. "Just gotta make sure I don't have any loose cannons around."

Sarah twirled her glass on the table, concentrating on the intricate design of wet circles. "Murray said I'm coping."

"And what do you say?"

She raised her eyes to his, gauging how much he wanted her to say. Did he want to hear about the nightmares that plagued her restless sleep, or the nauseating, heavy feeling in her stomach each time she saw that kid's face in her mind?

No, she finally decided. McGregor had two shoots on his record. He already knew.

"I can do the job."

"Okay." He tossed the rest of his drink down, then set the glass on the table with a satisfied sigh. "I'll put you on the schedule tomorrow."

"Thanks, Lieu."

McGregor stood and dropped a ten on the table. "I never doubted you for a moment."

Sarah savored his reassurance. Maybe if she focused on that, it would help keep the demons at bay. Despite what the shrink had said, she wasn't always so sure about the coping business. Her grief and her guilt hovered in separate corners of her consciousness, coming out and facing off like boxers responding to the bell.

Only she never knew when it was going to clang.

In desperate attempts to avoid the bout, Sarah had given in to silly impulses, including falling victim to the plight of a stray kitten. When the pathetic little thing had scooted through her open apartment door, she hadn't been heartless enough to throw him out on an empty stomach. But that was all she'd planned to do. One meal, then he'd be history. She'd never wanted anything to depend on her for life. Not even a houseplant. But the feel of prominent ribs poking out of a ragged orange coat had touched some soft spot in her that she usually kept well-protected.

Now, she was actually contemplating letting the cat grow up before she gave him the boot.

*Boy, wouldn't John laugh himself silly over that.*

The thought stopped her rambling mind cold. She hated having to remind herself that John wouldn't laugh anymore.

Searching for a distraction, Sarah let her gaze travel back to the now empty barstool. Had the guy been real or just a player in some wide-awake dream? Dropping her hand into her pocket, she fingered the edge of his very real business card. She pulled it out, recognizing Bordowsky, Smithers & Payne as one of the largest accounting firms in Dallas, but her eyes faltered over the title neatly embossed under Paul's name.

No.

It couldn't be.

No CPA ever looked like that.

# Chapter Two

*God, it feels good to be back.*

Sarah thrust her hands deep in the pockets of her jeans and surveyed the large room housing the Crimes Against Person's division. It was an ugly, old place supported with cinder-block exterior walls that were only slightly drabber than the gray interior walls. Early-Salvation Army desks and chairs did little to brighten the place up but, hey, it was home. The jangle of phones and the buzz of voices were as comforting as long-ago memories of family picnics. Back when she had a family.

Grabbing a cup of coffee, she descended the few steps into the Homicide area, relieved that her fellow officers held to tradition. No one made a big deal out of her return, and no one mentioned John's name. His desk, cleared of all papers and personal effects, stood in sharp contrast to the clutter on nearby desks. Seeing it brought an ache to Sarah's heart she didn't want to feel.

Walking past the desk, Sarah pushed the pain away and headed toward the briefing room. She opened the door and glanced around, finally spotting an empty seat at a table halfway into the room. She pulled out a chair and sat down, nodding to the woman in a smart, tailored suit across the aisle from her.

Must be fresh out of the uniform, Sarah thought, remembering her first week in civvies six years ago. The professional image had seemed important then, but quickly bowed to practicality. Socks lasted longer than nylons. Reeboks were easier to run in than heels. And there wasn't a perp alive who cared diddly about whether you wore jeans or a skirt.

The woman turned to give Sarah the briefest of nods, and she recognized the mass of tight curls haloing a creamy mocha complexion as belonging to a former patrol officer. Angel?

Couldn't recall her last name, but the woman had been at a couple of crime scenes with Sarah. Other than being a little too eager to prove herself, Sarah remembered her as more than capable. It wasn't surprising that she'd made detective.

Sarah's attention was drawn to the front of the room as Sergeant Murphy hitched his belt over his ample stomach and started outlining the on-going cases. "Simms and Burtweiler, you're still on the Highland Park B&E case." Murphy pulled another paper from the podium. "Frankfurt and Aikins, you pulled a cush one. Crime-watch meeting over at SMU"

"Can I go, too, Sarge?" Another officer called out. "My date book's getting a little thin."

A wave of laughter swept the room, and Murphy waited it out without even breaking a smile. When the last chuckle subsided, he continued, "Kingsly and Johnson, you've got the big one today. Homicide over at Northwood Mall. Call just came in from patrol."

Sarah turned sharply to look at Angel, and the elusive last name clicked. Something else clicked, too. An attitude that Angel wielded like a sword, heralding the proclamation, "Don't think that the only reason I'm here is because I'm a woman and I'm black."

Sarah hated attitudes, especially ones that might be honed to a new sharpness by recent events. She held the other woman's gaze, trying to get a read. It wasn't friendly. She expected judgments from people like the Reverend Billie Norton and the crowds he managed to assemble for public outcry. He didn't have a clue what it was like on the streets. But Angel knew.

Everyone who ever wore a badge knew. So where were her loyalties going to fall?

Murphy's voice cut into her thoughts. "You two might want to hustle your butts over to the crime scene before the corpse decomposes."

Sarah stood and led the way to the door as another thought fell into place. It probably wasn't a coincidence that she was partnered with a black woman. The longer she considered it, the more she was convinced. She stopped halfway down the hall.

"Go out and grab us a car," she said to Angel. "I've got something to take care of."

Without giving the other woman time to respond, Sarah strode in the opposite direction. She pushed through the door to McGregor's office with so much force it rattled the window. She leaned against the front of his desk. "Since when did you start listening to Price?"

McGregor pushed his chair back and made a steeple with his fingers. He rested his chin on the tips and regarded her with a level gaze.

"Come on! This new partnership reeks of good press."

"You know me better than that."

"I thought I did."

McGregor sighed. "Nothing changed while you were gone. I still make decisions for the same reasons I did before."

"Oh, really? And the public outcry over a poor, innocent, black child being shot by a big, bad, white police officer didn't enter into it at all?"

"I don't give a good goddam what the public says."

"That's not the way—"

"We're not having a debate here," McGregor cut in. "You've got a job to do. Either you're ready for it, or you take a permanent leave."

"How the hell can I do my job when you've set us up to be hounded by the press?"

"I'm going to pretend there was no insubordination happening here." McGregor's voice was soft, but his deep brown eyes flashed a harsh warning. Sarah reined in her anger, turned and walked stiffly out of the room.

The tight lines of tension she saw on Sarah's face wiped any trace of doubt Angel had of where her new partner had gone. There was also no doubt that the effort had been fruitless. Why was that such a surprise?

Yesterday McGregor had told Angel that her promotion hadn't been moved up to satisfy any public relations effort to placate the black community. As much as Angel wanted to believe that—as much as she needed to believe it—she knew the official city reaction to any incident. Throw a bone to the angry dogs in the street.

The teeth marks were starting to hurt.

Should she just end it right here? Refuse to partner with this woman who so obviously didn't want it any more than she did?

No. They had a job to do, and, by God, she'd do it. She'd worked too hard to make detective to throw it all away.

"You drive," Angel said, walking around to the passenger side of the plain, vanilla Buick. "That way people won't think I'm the chauffeur."

Sarah slipped into the driver's seat, snapped her seatbelt in place and pulled out of the motor pool. After driving several blocks in thundering silence, she sighed. "It'll be easier to work together if we at least speak now and then."

"Doesn't matter." Angel glanced out the side window. "I figure this partnership's short-term anyway."

"How's that?" Sarah eased the car into a break in the traffic on the expressway.

"I'll make my own visit to the Lieutenant. He's bound to listen to one of us." Angel turned to face Sarah, and her expression left nothing to doubt.

"It wasn't personal," Sarah said.

"Right."

"What does that mean?"

"Whatever you want it to."

Sarah transferred the surge of anger to the gas pedal, and the car lurched around a slow Cadillac with a screech of rubber. Her eyes went quickly to Angel who appeared to be once again enthralled with the scenery. *Fuck it. She can think whatever the hell she wants.*

Swinging over to grab the next exit, Sarah dodged through the heavy traffic, feeling like she was in the middle of an amusement park ride. Finally, she pulled up behind the patrol cars at the east entrance of Northwood Mall.

It stood like a relic compared to newer, glitzier malls, but it still clung to a certain level of classiness, sort of like a dowager queen who merits respect by means of association. It didn't hurt to associate with Neiman Marcus.

Sarah got out and slammed the door, looking over the roof of the car to Angel. "Can we do this?"

The other woman held her gaze for a long moment, then nodded.

"Good." Sarah pushed off, and covered the distance to the entrance in quick strides, the soles of her shoes slapping the concrete.

The long corridor bustled with activity as Sarah and Angel walked up to the crime scene. A couple of patrol officers held a crowd of mall employees behind the yellow tape, and Sarah recognized members of the forensic team working the area.

She *didn't* recognize the small, wiry man who danced around like water on a hot griddle, but she pegged him as some kind of manager. Managers always danced under pressure.

A tall, scruffy-looking patrol officer approached Sarah. "Detective?"

Sarah didn't recall ever seeing the officer before, but his nametag read, TIM HUSKEY. "Sarah Kingsly," she said by way of introduction. "You call this in?"

"Yeah."

"Got an ID yet?"

Tim pulled out his notebook. "Mel Halsley. Manager ID'd him. A maintenance worker."

"That the manager?" Sarah motioned toward the small man who was now wringing his hands with anxiety.

"Yeah." Tim shook his head. "What an asshole. All he's worried about is how inconvenient this is. Could we maybe be done before the shoppers show up."

"Did he find the body?"

"No. The rent-a-cop did." He inclined his head toward a rail-thin young man wearing a mall-security uniform. The guy looked no more than sixteen, and the shock was still apparent in the tinge of green around his mouth. "Found the body when he came on shift at eight."

"Did he know when the last security check had been done?"

"We'll have to verify," Tim said. "But the usual routine includes a pass at midnight."

"Okay, thanks. That'll help nail the TOD." Sarah walked toward the body sprawled on the pale tile. If she tried, she could pretend it was just a mannequin. Depersonalize it. It was a tip John had passed on to her at her first murder scene. But it didn't work. The cold, lifeless eyes of each murder victim tugged at the soft spot inside her that no amount of experience had been able to firm up.

Pulling down the shade of professionalism, Sarah concentrated on the facts. Male. Caucasian. Mid-thirties. Timex watch. Blue uniform shirt stretched over an abundant middle. The guy obviously hadn't been concerned about the latest reports of the dangers of obesity.

The police photographer stepped carefully around the splayed legs of the corpse to shoot another angle, and Sarah held out her shield. "Let me know when we can poke around."

"Sure thing, Detective."

*This one's going to be a forensic bitch.* Sarah glanced around. Not many surfaces even worth dusting for prints. God knows how many people passed down this hall in a given day. No way could they do eliminations. But they'd plow through the routine anyway. Being able to place a suspect at the scene would carry a lot of weight with the DA. *If* they got lucky enough to catch whoever had decided that Mel Halsley didn't deserve to live.

Seeing Angel talking to a tall man in a food-service uniform, Sarah walked over. The man could have been a study in brown, with hardly a hesitation in the flow of color from fabric to skin. Hints of gray in his close-cropped hair dispelled Sarah's first impression that he was young. As she approached, he nodded to Angel and slipped away.

"What'd you get?" Sarah asked.

"Nothing. None of these people saw anything."

"How about that one?" Sarah motioned to the food service guy who was striding away. "What did he have to say?"

Angel took a few steps away from the crowd. "It was mostly personal."

"Oh?"

"He's a friend. We were catching up."

Sarah held back a sarcastic remark. It would be unnecessarily pissy to ask why she didn't catch up on her own time. Unless she *did* harbor some belief that Angel was only the product of affirmative action.

"What did he have to say about this?"

"Knew the victim slightly. Met him after he started working for food service. But they never moved beyond a nodding acquaintance."

Roberts, the head of the forensic team, stepped up. He wore his usual tweed jacket; his red bowtie big enough to hide the second fold of his double chin. "This'll introduce a whole new element of fun into your life," he said, holding out a plastic evidence bag that contained what looked like a page torn out of a dime-store notebook.

Sarah fingered the plastic, looking closely at the words scrawled on the paper in crude block letters:

THEY WON'T GET AWAY WITH IT ANYMORE

"Great," Sarah said. "Just fucking great."

"It was stuck in the dead guy's pocket," Roberts said, as Sarah passed the bag to Angel.

"Guess we can't pretend it wasn't put there on purpose." Angel said.

"No." Sarah let a sound of frustration slip between her lips, then turned to Roberts. "Can we have a preliminary report this afternoon?"

"And what do I tell everyone else who's waiting?"

Sarah smiled. "Just tell them you got a better offer."

"I would," Roberts said through his laughter, "if I thought you really meant it."

The mall manager scurried over and reached across the crime-scene tape to pluck at Sarah's sleeve. "We're supposed to open in a half an hour." His voice carried an edge of desperation.

"Oh, right. Let's not lose sight of the bottom line."

The manager frowned at her and Sarah realized her sarcasm had blown right past him.

"Walt's here," Roberts said, and Sarah turned to see the coroner striding toward the body. Walt was a tall, angular man who took a wild, Impressionistic approach to color and fashion. Sarah had once threatened to arrest him for visual assault.

"We're about finished," Sarah called over her shoulder to the manager as she and Angel joined Walt.

"Hey, Kingsly. Glad to see you back."

Sarah allowed the sentiment. Walt wasn't officially part of the fraternity so his comment broke no unofficial code.

Setting his brown canvas bag down beside the body, he pulled on a pair of surgical gloves then hunkered down to begin the examination. Lifting the dead man's chin, Walt revealed a thin bloody line encircling the neck. "Ho, boy," he said. "Don't see this too often."

"What?" Angel asked.

Using his gloved fingers to pull on the puckered skin along the wound, Walt peered inside. "Wire."

"Wire?" Sarah's stomach lurched and she averted her eyes.

"Yeah. Piano wire, I'd guess."

Sarah sighed. "I'm beginning to like this case less and less."

"You and me both, sister," Angel said.

Sarah smiled wryly. At least that was one thing they could agree on. She turned back to Walt. "What about TOD?"

"Looks like ten, twelve hours at the most." Walt rolled the body to check lividity. "But you know the routine. The best indicator's going to be when he was last seen alive."

"Security says everything was okay down here at midnight." Sarah checked her watch. "It's only nine-thirty now."

"See. I was right." Walt stood up and peeled his glove off with a snap. "That's why I got into medicine. It's such an exact science."

Sarah rewarded his joke with a smile. "When are you going to do the post?"

"Take a number and stand in line."

"Could you perhaps put me somewhere in a ballpark?"

"Okay. I'll try to schedule him for tomorrow afternoon. But you know how well schedules work."

"Appreciate anything you can do."

Walt nodded. "I'll get him bagged up and out of here."

Back at the station, Sarah grabbed an available computer console and called up the National Crime Information Center system. If Halsley had ever been even remotely connected to a crime, his name would be somewhere in this computer web.

Waiting for the data bank to do its magic, she glanced over at Angel who had pulled up a chair and was now threading a pencil through long, thin fingers.

They had to do something about the issue that stood between them like a surly child. But what? Would it go away if they ignored it? Not likely. But maybe they could just continue to work around it until they couldn't avoid it anymore.

Sarah jumped when the printer clattered to life beside her.

"Halsley have a sheet?" Angel nodded to the page Sarah ripped off the printer.

"Mostly small stuff." Sarah scanned the information. "Misdemeanor possession. A couple of thefts. One B&E. And a possession with intent. Served two years in Seagoville. Paroled last year."

"Maybe we should check with his keeper. See if he was walking the straight and narrow."

"It's a good place to start." Sarah paused, waiting for some response from Angel, a move that would eliminate the necessity of telling her what to do. Shit. Working with someone new was like screwing without foreplay.

"Do you want to split the legwork?" Sarah asked.

"Sure."

31

"Okay. You see what his parole officer has to say. I'll check out his digs."

Angel had a quick tae kwon do workout instead of dinner. Their list of useful information had stopped with the last click of the printer spitting out Halsley's rap sheet. The PO had nothing useful to offer and Halsley didn't seem to have any friends they could check out. Sarah was still trying to make contact with parents who lived somewhere in the Midwest.

A whole lot of nothing.

Watching her reflection in the mirror to see if her moves looked as sharp as they felt, Angel concentrated on her field of motion, listening for the whoosh and snap of cotton with each kick.

If she was honest, she'd admit that her need for release wasn't just the frustration of the case. McGregor had firmly refused to entertain her objections to the partnership. Said it had nothing to do with the visit from the PR guy shortly before the promotions were announced. And if she didn't like it, he'd be glad to put her back on patrol.

*Right. Like I'd tell him in the face of that threat.*

Losing her place in the pattern, Angel padded back to the edge of the mat to start over. She bowed to her reflection in the mirror, then assumed the starting position.

Holding herself firmly in Chimbee, she tried to focus on the meaning of the moves before she began again, but her life kept intruding.

The worst part wasn't *how* she felt about working with a white cop who'd killed a black kid. It was *how* her father was going to react. Gilbert Johnson held to the belief that all white folks were as bad as the worst. That belief was fueled by the Reverend Billie Norton, pastor of Trinity Baptist Church, where her father sat in the same pew every Sunday morning.

Norton had probably convinced her father what she was doing was not only traitorous, it was sinful as well.

Realizing she'd blown her concentration all to hell and lost any chance of doing a clean pattern, Angel moved to the edge of the mat. She bowed, then stepped off, grabbing a towel to mop her face.

"Hey, Angel. You want to spar?"

Angel turned to see Danielle, a petite, blonde college girl who was also working toward her black belt. "Can't," Angel draped the towel around her neck. "No time."

Turning to head toward the locker room, Angel admitted the lie in her response. She had plenty of time. And she shouldn't have been so short with Danielle. It wasn't the girl's fault she looked like a younger, smaller version of Sarah, but Angel didn't want to take the chance of any latent frustration slipping out and creating her own racial incident.

# CHAPTER THREE

The harsh buzz of the alarm finally penetrated Sarah's consciousness. She fought her way out of the tangle of sheets to smash the OFF button. It couldn't be six o'clock already. Hadn't she just gone to bed an hour ago?

Opening one eye to verify the obvious, Sarah groaned. Going back to the bar last night had been stupid.

At first, she'd just had a couple of drinks to calm her nervousness in case Paul did show up. Then she'd had a couple more to drown her disappointment when he didn't, staying until well after midnight. She could have called him and made a normal date like a normal person, but that would have been too . . . what . . . normal?

The temptation to close her eyes for just a few more minutes tugged at Sarah, but she resisted the lure. She needed her morning run to clear the cobwebs, and she knew she'd better do it now before the sun started to fry the concrete and anyone dumb enough to be on it.

Slipping her trim figure into blue spandex shorts and a white tank top, Sarah pulled her hair into a ponytail and put on a bright yellow sweat band.

A blast of heat and humidity greeted her when she stepped outside, so she limited her run to two miles, walking the last few blocks back to her apartment to cool down. What a joke. She tugged at her damp shirt, fanning herself. *The only way I'll cool down is in a tub full of ice cubes.* Pausing to grab the newspaper, Sarah talked herself into believing a shower might work instead.

Twenty minutes later, she padded barefoot into the kitchen, her green silk shirt protected from her damp hair by a towel. The room lived up to its designation as an efficiency. It hosted a small rectangle of carpeting that could accommodate a table and perhaps two chairs, if she had them. In the work area she could reach the refrigerator, stove and sink without having to take more than three steps. Turning on the hot water tap until it ran steamy, she grabbed a jar of instant coffee from the windowsill and leveled a teaspoon into the cup on the yellow Formica counter. Then she held the cup under the running water, watching the coffee foam to the top.

She owned a coffeepot for the occasions when she had company, especially those of the morning-after variety. But since those moments were rare, she relied on instant gratification. It worked until the real thing came along.

A plaintive meow drew her attention, and Sarah looked down to see the kitten regarding her with unblinking, amber eyes. "You hungry, Cat?" She scooped him up and set him on the counter next to her coffee. He sniffed the cup and turned away with a sneeze.

"What? Coffee not your drink of choice?"

He cocked his head and watched her pour milk into a bowl, then delicately started lapping at it, giving himself a little white mustache. "Maybe I should sign you up for commercials. Then you could make me rich."

He ignored her.

Sarah took another sip of coffee, then leaned one hip against the counter and opened the paper, pulling the Metro section out. She preferred to start reading at the front page, but rarely had the luxury of enough time to indulge that preference. A glance through Metro, however, sometimes turned up interesting tidbits of information relevant to an investigation.

Once, a veiled reference to a prominent surgeon seen at a Dallas nightspot with a redhead who wasn't his wife had given Sarah the grounds to vigorously pursue her inclination that he wasn't entirely innocent in the tragic demise of said wife.

Laying the section flat, a headline halfway down the page caught Sarah's eye—USE OF DEADLY FORCE STILL IN QUESTION. She scanned the story, then set her cup down abruptly when she came to:

*City Councilman, Hank Darby, said that the public should never have expected a fair ruling from the departmental investigation of the shooting incident. "They protect their own," he said. "Even when an innocent boy is brutally killed."*

Sarah slammed the paper down. "Innocent, my ass!" The outburst startled the kitten who skittered across the counter, splashing a trail of milk as he went. Sarah moved quickly to grab him before he fell off the edge.

"I'm sorry, Cat." She smoothed his ruffled fur. "You need a Valium or something?" He snuggled into the hollow of her neck and the low, soothing rumble of his purr vibrated against her. Maybe the experts were right. Having a pet could lower your blood pressure.

Reluctantly, she put the kitten down and cleaned up the mess, rinsing the bowl and her coffee cup before setting them back on the counter. Then she hurried to her bedroom, threw the covers up toward the headboard in a half-hearted nod toward orderliness and grabbed her favorite brown suede jacket off the doorknob.

Her mood improved by the time she arrived at the station but soured again when McGregor buzzed to tell her he wanted a briefing as soon as Angel got in. At least she could console herself that it would be a short meeting. It wouldn't take long to brief him on nothing.

Settling down at her desk with a cup of freshly brewed coffee, Sarah dialed the forensic department to see if Roberts had anything yet.

"What do you want from me, Kingsly? Working the crime scene was like vacuuming a section of Grand Central Station. We could still be sifting through shit six months from now."

"I take it there's nothing out of the ordinary?" Sarah grabbed a quick sip of her coffee, scalding her lip in the process.

"Not so far."

"The Lieutenant's gonna love that."

"You want a magician? Try the yellow pages." Roberts broke the connection.

Sarah pushed the phone away and glanced up to see Angel enter the squad room wearing stone-washed jeans and a tailored, navy jacket over a crisp, white Oxford shirt. Woman's a quick study, Sarah thought.

Resting a small cardboard box against her hip, Angel paused. "I was told to use that one." She motioned to the only empty desk in the room. "I just want to be clear on that."

Sarah glanced at the vacant chair, then back to Angel. The explanation hadn't been necessary. No one would take over a dead cop's desk unless specifically told to. Everyone knew that, and the act of thoughtfulness stood in stark contrast next to the simmering hostility of yesterday.

Unable to get a read from her partner's unfathomable dark eyes, Sarah finally nodded, then stood up. "McGregor wants us to bring him up to speed on the case."

Angel shifted the box on her hip. "I'll just dump my stuff."

"Sure." Sarah shrugged into her jacket to avoid having to watch Angel. As long as the desk was empty she could pretend that it was just waiting for John to come back. Denial wouldn't be so easy with someone else's family pictures filling up the emptiness.

Frank Simms touched her shoulder as she started to pass him in the aisle. Obviously, he'd seen the exchange between her and Angel and his stark, black eyes swam with sympathy. From him, Sarah found the gesture acceptable. He'd lost a partner too, but he'd handled the aftermath with a quiet dignity that seemed to elude her.

Even when his wife had died last year and everyone thought he would crumble, he'd just doggedly plowed through each day, appearing to keep one step ahead of the pain.

Maybe it was his Navaho heritage that gave him an edge on accepting the normal course of life and death. Sarah didn't know. Whatever it was, she would give her left nut, if she had one, for an ounce of his stoicism.

Simms broke the moment first, sinking into his chair and picking up a case-file as if nothing significant had just happened.

Finding a measure of comfort in his understanding, Sarah lifted her chin and walked toward McGregor's office. Angel caught up with her just as she opened the door and entered.

McGregor's office looked like a storage room. Sarah moved a pile of folders from a chair and stacked them on boxes in the corner. Angel followed her lead and cleared another chair. McGregor concluded a phone call, then faced them. "Okay. What do you have?"

Sarah deferred to Angel who gave her report clearly and concisely without once referring to notes. "Medical examiner put time of death at shortly after midnight. That was based in part on a statement by the rent-a-cop that there was nothing out of the ordinary when he made his customary swing through the lower hall at twelve sharp.

"The victim worked in maintenance for the past year following his parole. According to the PO, Halsley reported in pretty much as required. The PO thought he might have done a little dope, but never could prove it. Doesn't think he moved into dealing, but wasn't sure about that either. Otherwise, he was keeping himself pretty clean, so the PO figured he wouldn't go looking for trouble."

Angel shifted in her chair, re-crossing her legs, apparently using the pause to retrieve the next bit of information from her mental data bank. "No complaints from his boss at work," she continued. "The guy did his job as well as could be expected for minimum wage and no career path. He was kind of a loner, so no one got to know much about him."

Angel turned one palm up in a dismissive gesture. "So far, we have a lot of nothing."

McGregor sighed and turned to Sarah. "Any hope you've had better luck?"

"Not a lot. Finally tracked his parents. They live in a small town in Iowa. He left home after barely squeaking through high school, and they haven't seen him since. They pretty much wrote him off after he started going bad, as his mother phrased it. They didn't know anyone he might have associated with and made it clear they didn't want to."

"Anything from the lab?"

"Nothing any more encouraging." Sarah resisted the impulse to pull out her notebook, which she had previously considered a sign of thoroughness. Angel had been damn thorough.

"Not that I expected something helpful from a public place like that." Sarah didn't fight the edge of frustration that crept into her voice. "Forensic pulled enough prints to start their own national comparison file, and we can't do a damn thing with them. Couldn't even get a break with prints from the paper."

"Damn." McGregor tapped a pencil on the top of his desk in

a soft, staccato rhythm. "The twenty-four-hour clock just ticked away."

Sarah and Angel exchanged a knowing look. "A lot of homicides *are* solved after the clock stops," Angel said.

"I know." McGregor sighed again and directed the next question to Sarah. "So how's it starting to shape up to you?"

"We can look real hard at the drug angle. But I find it a pretty big stretch to think he'd be doing business inside the mall. And dissatisfied customers aren't known for garroting their dealers, no matter how pissed they are."

"The note doesn't fit their usual MO, either," Angel added.

McGregor leaned back in his chair. "I hate when this happens."

The comment was so uncharacteristically juvenile; Sarah wondered what else he had on his plate. Did it have anything to do with that item in the paper? Contemplating his petulant expression, she decided she didn't want to know. "Anything else?" she asked.

McGregor rubbed his face with thick fingers and shook his head. "Just catch me a bad guy before my ulcer eats a hole clear through to my back."

"We'll try, Boss." Sarah stood up and opened the door, letting Angel step out before her.

"Did he expect us to have more?" Angel asked once they were in the hallway.

"He knows we're not miracle workers." The corner of Sarah's mouth turned up in a grin. "Maybe it's PMS."

Her smile faded when Angel didn't laugh. "Lighten up," Sarah said. "It was a joke."

"Sexual harassment is never funny. Even from another woman."

"Oh, brother!" Sarah turned and stomped back to her desk. Releasing a deep sigh, she sat down, wondering at the walking contradiction Angel was. Didn't the woman even *want* to make the partnership work?

Swiveling in her chair, Sarah pulled her mind away from the impossible to the nearly impossible. At least she had a place to begin with the case. She picked up the phone book and looked in the yellow pages for piano tuners, her finger stopping on an ad that boasted thirty years experience in the business. Propping the phone receiver between her ear and her shoulder, she dialed the number.

Experience counts.

"Good day." A British accent clipped the words. "Precision Tuning."

Sarah identified herself, then paused, not sure where to begin.

"How may I be of assistance to you, Detective?" the voice prompted.

"What can you tell me about piano wire?"

"Strings."

"Pardon?"

"They're called strings." The man chuckled. "But not to worry. Most people make that mistake."

"Oh." Sarah leaned back in her chair and put one foot on her desk. "Are they distinctive?"

"How do you mean?"

"From one piano to the next. Between a Grand and a Kimball, for instance."

"No."

The man followed his one-word answer with the beginning of what Sarah suspected could be a lengthy explanation of how wood and craftsmanship creates the unique sound of each instrument. She used her next question to cut him off.

"How about age? Can you determine how old a string is?"

"That would be almost impossible. Strings have been made the same way for over a hundred years."

"So a string from a piano made last year wouldn't be any different from those in a fifty-year-old piano?"

"The old bass strings might be a little dull after so many years. But otherwise, no. The basic elements would be the same."

Well, that was an abrupt dead end, Sarah thought, hanging up after thanking the man for his help. The only good thing to come out of it was that she could correct Roberts the next time he talked about the piano *wire*.

Turning her head to pop the stiffness out of her neck, Sarah glanced over at Angel. Maybe it was time to go shake a few trees to see what might fall out.

"Come on," Sarah said, striding over to Angel. "Let's go talk to Halsley's boss again."

"You don't think I did it right the first time?" Angel regarded Sarah with a defiant tilt to her chin.

Sarah bit back an angry response and leaned over to rest her palms on the desk, speaking in a deceptively neutral tone. "Let's get something straight here. Just because I make a suggestion or ask a question, it's not an indictment of your ability. It's the way people talk to each other when they're working a case together."

A tic in Angel's cheek testified to the cost of her restraint, and Sarah fought an impulse to just let the eruption happen. But caution held her back. *Maybe another time. Another place. Away from here.* Pulling herself upright, she whirled and headed toward the door.

## CHAPTER FOUR

Skirting around a young mother who wrestled with a stroller while clinging valiantly to an exuberant toddler, Sarah and Angel followed the maintenance supervisor down the corridor.

During the ride over, Sarah hadn't said a word and that was just fine with Angel. Put the hostilities aside and concentrate on the job. So far it was the only arena in which they could at least be civil.

Herb Crenshaw led the detectives past the restrooms, deeper into the hall where the air was stuffy and carried a faint trace of mildew. Unlocking a door marked MAINTENANCE, Herb flicked a light switch and motioned the women inside. "Don't know what you expect to find," he said. "But you're welcome to it."

Floor-to-ceiling metal shelves lined two walls of the room, with shorter freestanding shelves clustered in the middle. A workbench, cluttered with tools and the remnants of a recent repair, took up most of the third wall. Just to the left of the door, a desk and two metal filing cabinets attempted to create a small office space. Angel moved into the center of the room, noting several well-used toolboxes. Then she turned back to Herb who was lounging in the doorway with one shoulder against the metal jamb. "Does every worker have their own box?" she asked.

"Not exactly." Herb pulled himself upright and walked over to Angel with Sarah following. "A couple of boxes are set up

with an assortment of tools needed to handle routine maintenance needs." He tapped a couple of lids. "But while a guy was
on shift he could consider it his own, I guess. Those other ones
are for tools we don't use very often."

"Mel would have used one of these?" Angel asked.

"Yeah."

"How did he account for his time?" Sarah asked.

"He had work orders," Herb said. "I made one up every day
and posted it. He had to sign off on the jobs before he could
leave."

"Can I see the one for the night he was killed?"

"Sure."

Angel watched Sarah follow Herb to his desk, then turned
back to the shelves. The faint aroma of oil carried a pleasant
reminder of her Uncle Joe's garage where he'd introduced her
to the inner workings of a combustion engine when she was a
child. Now, whenever her car broke down, she wished she'd
paid more attention.

When Angel raised the lid of one of the boxes, two trays
swung out over a larger bottom bin. The upper tray held an assortment of small tools, and Angel carefully moved a dirty rag
to see some larger wrenches and screwdrivers in the lower section, along with scraps of wire and cable. Digging through the
odd collection, Angel remembered how her uncle had used his
toolbox for a trash can until it got so cluttered he had to clean
it out.

*Must be a common trait.*

"Any way of knowing who this belongs to?" Angel held up a
matchbook, smudged with dirt and grease.

Herb ambled over to look at the matchbook that carried an
advertisement for Danny's Bar & Grill. "That place is just over
there on Greenville Avenue. Anybody could've brought it back."

"What do you think?" Angel asked Sarah.

"It's worth a look-see." She turned to Herb and handed him a business card. "You think of anything that could help, give us a call."

Herb nodded and led them out of the storeroom.

A moderate lunch crowd filled most of the tables at Danny's, the clientele an eclectic mix of suits and service people. Bar stools were sparsely populated with customers who preferred to drink their lunches.

The tempting aroma of barbecue reminded Angel that she'd skipped breakfast this morning. She didn't suppose her partner would consider lunch first. One of the few things she'd figured out about Sarah was her single-mindedness. The woman didn't even pause for a pee if she had a lead to follow.

Threading their way around a couple of tables, Angel noticed four young executives, napkins strategically placed to protect white shirts. An explosion of laughter from one of them joined the general din of people who were obviously relishing this midday respite from the drudgery of work.

Angel sidled up to the bar next to Sarah and raised a finger to the bartender who was a dead-ringer for Denzel Washington.

"What can I get you?" The flash of white teeth in an off-center smile solidified the impression.

"The answer to a couple of questions." Sarah dropped her shield on the bar and his friendly smile slid into a frown.

"Hey, we're in the middle of a lunch rush here." He turned pleading brown eyes to Angel for support.

"We certainly respect your right to make a buck," Angel said, glancing down the row of customers. "But everyone looks real satisfied right now. So why don't you stop wasting your valuable time."

"If it's about that robbery last week, I told—"

"What's your name?" Sarah interrupted.

"Cal." His eyes flicked nervously from Sarah, to Angel, then back again. "Cal Thompson."

"Okay, Cal. Do you ever work the night shift?"

"Yeah. Sometimes."

"What's the matter, Cal?" Angel gave him a hard look. "You're about as jumpy as a kid caught with his hands in his pants."

"Nothin'. Nothin's wrong. I just don't like being rousted."

Angel leaned on the bar. "Believe me, if this was a roust, you'd know it."

Cal shifted his gaze back to Sarah, and his expression invited her next question.

"You know about that guy who was killed over at the mall?"

Cal nodded.

"Ever see him in here at night?"

Again Cal nodded. "He used to come in pretty regular."

"Who'd he hang with?" Angel asked.

"No one in particular." Cal shifted his attention to Angel. "He was friendly enough. Kind of a buddy to everyone, but he didn't zero in on any one person, unless Rita came in."

"Rita?" Sarah prompted.

"Women like that don't need a last name." Cal smiled when his comment met with laughter from a couple of guys a few stools down.

Angel shot them a look that pushed them into silence, then glanced back at Cal. "Did she run her business here?"

"It wasn't anything like that." The man wiped a large hand across his cheek. "She just likes to have a good time. Sometimes if the mood was right, they'd leave together."

"What does this Rita look like?" Sarah asked.

"I don't know. Average." He glanced at Angel. "Sort of like her, but white."

"You mean my size, short, curly hair?"

46

"Yeah."

"Does she live around here?" Sarah asked.

"I don't know."

"You don't know a hell of a lot, do you, Cal?" The menace was back in Angel's voice.

"Yeah I do. I know she works over at the Coca-Cola bottling plant," he said, a note of triumph in his voice.

"See how painless that was." Sarah slipped her badge back in her pocket. "Remember that next time."

Out on the sidewalk, Angel paused and glanced back at the building where a Miller Lite sign blinked in bright yellow neon in the window. "We should find out who's on that robbery. They need to take another look at our friend, Cal. He sure was sweating about something."

"Good idea," Sarah said, leading the way back to the car.

After snapping her seatbelt in place, Sarah eased into a break in the heavy noon traffic, the air conditioner pulling in the acrid aroma of exhaust. "By the way," she paused to change lanes, joining the stream of cars flowing toward the entrance to the expressway, "you handled yourself pretty well back there."

There was no response, so Sarah glanced over at Angel. "That was a compliment. In case the concept escapes you."

"Let's get something straight here." Angel carefully chose the same tone and words Sarah had used earlier. "Just because it might end up that we make a good team on the job, that's all it will ever be."

"Fine!" Sarah turned on the radio and let Travis Tritt tell her how he could love her.

Twenty minutes later Sarah pulled into the employee parking lot for the bottling plant, then glanced up as a jet screamed in a take off from Love Field. When the roar of noise subsided, Sarah turned to Angel, hoping for some indication of her state of mind. Angel merely opened her door and got out.

Shaking her head, Sarah released her seatbelt and followed her partner inside the building. They walked up to a cluttered information desk that dominated the small reception area and inquired about an employee named Rita.

"You got a last name?" The young blonde tucked a wad of gum into her cheek to ask the question.

"No we don't," Angel answered. "We need to talk to the personnel manager."

"I'll ring to see if he's in." The girl reached for the phone. After a brief conversation, she looked back at the detectives. "He'll be right here."

"Does *he* have a name?" Sarah asked.

"Oh. Sure." The girl giggled. "Mr. Edwards."

Sarah decided not to bother the girl for the first name.

The detectives moved away from the desk and waited for a few minutes before a door to the right of them opened. A man, who was as average looking as his name, strode toward them. He offered his hand. "Rob Edwards. What can I do for you ladies?"

"Dallas PD." Angel held out her shield. "We'd like to talk to one of your employees. Rita. We don't have her last name. But she's thirtyish. Average height. Short, curly hair, probably dark. Likes to party."

A moment of silence followed, during which Sarah watched the man lose his charming smile, then readjust it again. "That could be Rita Malcolm," he said. "She's my day-shift supervisor."

"She here now?" Sarah asked.

"Should be. Unless she called in sick."

"Could you take us back there?" Angel gestured toward the opposite door that was muting the unmistakable hum of machinery.

"It might be better if I brought her to you," Edwards suggested. "It's awfully noisy on the floor."

The detectives nodded their agreement, and he led them into a small meeting room. It was only slightly larger than the reception area, but it did have tables and chairs. Framed stills that chronicled the evolution of Coca-Cola ads over the years decorated the walls.

"I'll go find Rita," Edwards said, leaving the door slightly ajar as he slipped out.

The absolute quiet of the room grated on Sarah's nerves. "Think we ought to point out to Edwards that the bimbo at the front desk hardly gives a good first impression?" she asked when the silence became too much for her.

Angel shrugged.

Holding back a flare of anger, Sarah forced a neutral tone. "You want me to take the lead on this?"

"Fine."

The return of Edwards was a welcome respite, especially since the woman with him matched the description Cal had given them. Edwards introduced Rita, then looked like he wanted to hang around.

"Thank you," Sarah said, hoping he'd pick up on her dismissal.

He did.

"What do you want?" Rita pulled a chair away from the table and sat down.

"Did you know Mel Halsley?" Sarah asked.

"Yeah." A flicker of some emotion Sarah couldn't name passed across the woman's face. "Terrible thing him getting whacked like that."

Sarah took a seat opposite the woman and Angel chose a chair at the end of the table. "The bartender at Danny's said you two were pretty friendly," Angel said.

"What of it?" Rita pulled a crumpled pack of cigarettes out

of the breast pocket of her blue uniform, then put them back. "Can't smoke nowhere now'a days."

"When was the last time you saw him?" Sarah asked.

"A week or so. I don't know."

"Be a little more specific," Angel cut in.

"Okay." Rita thought for a moment. "It was a week ago Friday. I took him back to my place. We had a little smoke. A little sex and a little more smoke. That's the last I saw of him."

Sarah pondered the attraction for a moment. Rita wasn't a bad looking woman. Why would she have to settle for a guy like Mel? Unless he wasn't the only one. Could be another boyfriend got jealous of good old Mel. "Anyone else you've been dating?"

"We didn't date, Detective." Rita smiled. "We fucked." The woman eyed Sarah as if daring her to react.

She decided not to. "You know about any trouble he had recently?"

Sarah watched the woman process the question and her possible answers. She was trying to look seriously thoughtful, but Sarah recognized the little flickers of evasiveness in the woman's eyes.

Angel must have recognized it, too, because she jumped in with another question. "Where did Mel score?"

"Score?"

"Come on," Angel said. "You know what I'm talking about."

"Am I going to get in trouble?"

"That depends," Sarah said. "We're not interested in any penny-ante shit. Just trying to find anybody who wanted Mel dead."

Rita fidgeted with her cigarettes again, the crinkle of cellophane the only sound in the room for a moment. "Well, Jimmy got pretty pissed at Mel a couple of weeks ago."

"Enough to kill him?" Angel asked.

Rita shrugged.

"Why was this Jimmy upset?" Sarah pulled out her notebook and pen.

"Cause Mel stiffed him. Mel said Jimmy sold him some bad shit. So the next time, Mel took the stuff but wouldn't give Jimmy the money." The words poured out as if once Rita decided to talk, she couldn't wait to get it all said. "Jimmy tried to make Mel pay, but he didn't have any muscle with him. He threatened to come back."

"Did this incident happen at Danny's?"

Rita gave Sarah a look. "Hell no. Jimmy's just a kid."

"This kid have a last name?" Angel asked.

"Not that I ever heard."

"We need a description," Sarah said, and wrote down the details as Rita related them. "And where can we get in touch with you if we have any more questions?"

"Are you gonna cut me some slack? I'm not into any big-time dope stuff. Just smoke a little weed now and then."

"Depends on your level of cooperation, Rita." Sarah leaned into the woman's space. "You've got to make me want to look the other way."

# CHAPTER FIVE

Most of the next day was an exercise in futility. Sarah tried to generate some information based on the description Rita had given them of Jimmy, but her efforts turned up zilch. None of the narcs could peg him, and without a last name, there was little hope of picking him up on any data banks.

Perhaps, if Rita was right, Jimmy wasn't high enough on the drug chain to have come to the attention of the guys in narcotics. That being the case, Angel and Sarah would need more than a little luck to track him down, and they decided to try their luck on the streets.

Angel chose to drive and Sarah offered no objections. She wasn't about to say or do anything to set the other woman off again. After the morning briefing, Angel had been almost friendly, and Sarah wanted to keep it that way.

"How about we take a swing through South Dallas?" Angel asked. "I know a couple of kids there who could maybe give us a lead on this Jimmy character."

"Fine by me."

As the car sped across the highest ramp of the mix-master, Sarah's eye was caught by the breathtaking expanse of sky painted in varying tones of mauve and gold as day gave way to the approach of night. The sky had been the first thing she'd noticed when she'd moved to Texas what seemed like a lifetime ago. It was so endless here, much different from the patches of blue scattered between trees and mountaintops in Tennessee.

"If we don't find anything in a few hours, I vote we wrap it up and try again tomorrow night," Angel said.

"I'll go for that." Sarah pulled her eyes away from the scenery. "The overtime's great but it's killing me."

Angel took the State Fair exit off the expressway. The neighborhood they cruised through was as poor as it could get—the houses slumped under a desperate need for paint and repairs. Sarah didn't like to look at them. They reminded her too strongly of the shack she'd lived in with her mother before coming to Dallas. From her childhood perspective, her grandmother's brick, three-bedroom house in Mesquite had been a mansion. If only her mother—

"Good thing there's nothing going on at the fairgrounds," Angel said, turning the car up a narrow street. "Otherwise we couldn't get through here."

Sarah welcomed the distraction. "You going somewhere in particular?"

"Yeah. There's a little store a couple of blocks up. That's where Tavin hangs out."

"Tavin?"

"Met him when I patrolled here. He's basically a good kid trying not to let it show."

"You think he knows Jimmy?"

"Could. If Jimmy really is only into small-time stuff." Angel slowed the car as they approached a gas station-convenience store. "That might be him there."

Angel made a quick zip into the parking lot of the 7-Eleven. The group of teens clustered at the end of the sidewalk pulled away as if some internal radar told them: *cops*. Sarah reached for the door handle, and Angel detained her with a touch. "I'll go. They see you coming, they'll run like hell."

It made sense, Sarah realized. There wasn't another white face in sight, and too many kids still believed that the combination of "white and cop" spelled automatic trouble. She watched as Angel approached the group of kids, maintaining her safety zone and singling out a tall, gangly boy of about fifteen.

Sarah didn't spot any gang colors, but she wasn't sure if she could distinguish them from the wild array of clothes kids wore all the time. Maybe she needed more time with the narcs. Angel was talking to a boy wearing baggy jeans, the crotch hanging halfway to his knees. His leather vest was perhaps another badge of defiance, this one for the weather.

When it started to happen, it was like the world went into slow motion. In one frame, Angel and the boy were just talking, but the next had him towering over her, his face contorted in anger and his hand in a pocket that bulged alarmingly.

Activating the line to the Dispatcher, Sarah gave the location and request for immediate back up. Then she jerked the car door open, pulling her weapon. "Everyone stand easy," she called out.

Panic almost robbed her of reason when one of the nearest kids turned. It was like being in that dark alley with John again, and past tangled with present as adrenaline jangled her nerves. Her breath came in short gasps.

"Sarah! Don't!"

Angel's command jerked Sarah into the present, breaking her free from the hold of panic. She released the pressure of her finger on the trigger but continued to point the gun while darting quick glances around.

"Sarah!"

The shout focused her attention on her partner. Sweat rolled in waves down her back, yet fear chilled her to the bone. She swallowed the rising bile as the realization of what she'd almost done flooded her senses.

"Lower your weapon, Sarah."

Some objective part of her mind registered the fact that Angel took a step forward, the kids frozen in place behind her. Tension crackled in the air like electricity, and Sarah looked at the gun in her hand. It felt good. Powerful. Monstrous.

The wail of an approaching siren grew in volume like a rising crescendo of orchestra strings. One of the kids pushed forward. "That's the bitch that shot our bro'."

His statement ignited the others. They surged toward Sarah and she felt the cold venom of their hate slice through her.

"Stop!" The command, reinforced by the presence of the steel-blue .44 Magnum in Angel's hand, halted the kids for a moment.

A patrol car pulled to the curb, rubber whining against concrete. Two uniformed officers jumped out, unsnapping their holsters.

The boys took a step back, looking wildly from the patrol officers, to Sarah, to the end of Angel's gun still pointed at them.

"Let's do this so nobody gets dead." Angel's voice carried a note of calm authority, and the tension dissipated like air slowly seeping out of a balloon.

"You want us to take them in?" One of the officers asked.

"It's okay." Angel holstered her weapon. "We've got it under control."

Through a fog of shock, Sarah watched Angel speak to the kids who shot hateful looks in her direction. She couldn't remember lowering her weapon, but it now hung heavily at her side. God, she never wanted to come that close again.

She stood, immobile, as the boys shuffled off, their postures shouting insolence. The officers got back in the black-and-white, but they stayed, watching to make sure the situation remained under control. Sarah wanted to return to their car, but her feet wouldn't accept the message to move.

"What the hell were you doing?"

The harsh words shocked Sarah out of the numbness as effectively as a blast of cold water. She looked at Angel in disbelief. "What do you think I was doing? That guy was going to be all over you in about two seconds. I—"

"Nothing was happening." Angel's entire body twitched with anger and sweat glistened on her dark face. "You got that? The kid was just posturing for his friends."

"And how was I supposed to figure that out?"

"You're the one with all the fucking experience."

"Yeah." Sarah took a step forward. "And that experience told me you might be dead if I didn't act."

"Are you sure that's all it was?"

A bright flash of headlight bounced off the plate glass window catching the women in a stiff tableau. Sarah could count the passing seconds with every tick of her heart. Finally, she sighed. "We don't have to turn this into a pissing contest."

"You're the one who pulled a gun and almost got us killed."

Angel turned abruptly and stomped back to the car. Sarah slowly slid her weapon into the holster at her side and followed.

Inside the car, the silence hurt. Sarah leaned back against the seat and closed her eyes. Now that she didn't have to look at Angel, she could admit to the possibility she'd acted too soon. But what else could she have done? She played the scene again in her mind, looking at every move, every nuance until she convinced herself there was no way in hell she could have known there was no threat. Would it do any good to try to convince her partner of that?

Angel's voice came out of the darkness. "I guess we can consider tonight a bust."

The sarcasm stirred Sarah's anger, but she clamped a lid on it. She didn't want to go there with Angel anymore. "Let's just go home."

"Fine by me." Angel put the car in reverse and backed away

from the store with a loud squeal of protest from the tires.

Cat greeted Sarah at the door with strident yowls. She recognized the call of hunger and smiled as he continued the serenade, following her into the bedroom where she tossed off her jacket and holster, hanging them on the closet doorknob. With his insistence encouraging her, Sarah quickly scrounged through the pile of dirty clothes until she found a tolerable pair of shorts. Then she traded her work shirt for an oversized T-shirt that frequently turned into a nightgown when she fell asleep in her lounge chair.

That was a distinct possibility tonight. No way was she going to bed where the nightmares waited for her. And she didn't want to think about what had really happened out there on the street tonight. Or what it could possibly mean about her state of mind.

In the kitchen, she filled Cat's dish with dry cat food. His expression seemed to say, "You've *got* to be kidding."

"I told you not to get spoiled."

His amber eyes followed her every move as she took a package of popcorn out of the cabinet and put it in the microwave to cook. "That's not going to work," Sarah said, as kernels started to explode in a stutter of pops. "This is for me."

Her resolve lasted all of five minutes into the video. It was her movie of choice when the job was all fucked up. Eddie Murphy made it look like so much fun to be a cop.

# CHAPTER SIX

"I might have something for you."

Sarah glanced up when a shadow fell over her desk. Burt-weiler, looking every minute of his sixty-plus years, met her gaze. His bulk, wrapped in a rumpled gray suit, always reminded her of the character Fish on the old Barney Miller sitcom, and Sarah had often marveled at the odd pairing of Burt and Simms. On the surface they were the least likely to succeed as partners. Looks and age difference aside, how they ever handled the dichotomy between Orthodox Judaism and Native American philosophy was beyond her. Was there a lesson on the strength of difference she could learn here?

"We finally closed those Highland Park burglaries," Burt said, leaning a hip on the edge of her desk. "It was driving me nuts trying to figure how the perps knew when people were gone. Then one day we go out there. I tell Simms to see what the Great Spirit has to say. And damn if he doesn't get an idea."

Sarah raised an eyebrow. "The Great Spirit?"

"He don't mind a little joke now'n then. Breaks the tension." Burt paused to take a peppermint toothpick out of his shirt pocket, unwrap it and stick it in his mouth. "Anyway, we're sittin' there and he sees the paperboy. 'What if it's him?' he asks me. 'No way,' I says. 'He's just a kid.'

"Simms just gives me one of his looks. So we check it out." Burt paused again. He loved to play with his audience. That's what made him so good in the box. "And damn if Simms ain't right. It's the freakin' paperboy. Kid's eleven with a brother fifteen. The two of them planned the whole thing. When a customer stops the paper for vacation, the kids pay a visit."

"And you came just to share your success with me?"

"No. Thought you might want to take a look at the kid what was working with them."

"Any particular reason?"

"He fits the description of the one you was looking for. And . . ." True to his craft, Burt saved the best line for last. "His name is Jimmy."

Sarah jumped up and followed Burt, pulling her jacket on as they walked. She tried not to hope too much, but sometimes they *could* get lucky.

Burtweiler opened the door to the interrogation room, and a fist of anger grabbed Sarah's chest when she saw the kid, wearing a muscle-shirt draped with several gold chains, sitting at the table. He was so young. Thirteen? Fourteen? They were all so goddam young. Too young to have roles in this R-rated world.

Sarah fought an urge to jerk that tough-guy costume off him and walked to the other side of the table. He gave her an insolent look, and she returned the favor.

Burt loomed his bulk over the kid. "You stepped in some deep shit here, Jimmy."

He shrugged.

"What? You think cause you're a juvie you ain't gonna do time?"

The kid wrapped himself up in his attitude.

"Wrong answer, asshole." Burt grinned. "You got a rap sheet that'll stretch clear down to the Rio Grande. And old Judge Watkins. He don't like all you punk wise guys cluttering up his courtroom. He's gonna send you away until you're too old to be a grandpa."

"What do you want from me?" Jimmy asked.

Burt nodded at Sarah who stepped forward. "We want to know about the trouble you had with Mel Halsley."

"Who?"

"Come on, Jimmy. Don't try to play mind games with me." Sarah used her pen like a drumstick on the table. "You've got about five seconds to cooperate or we forget all about telling the judge what a nice guy you are."

Jimmy licked his lips, then nodded. "Okay. I knew Mel."

"And he stiffed you, so you decided to teach him a lesson."

"No. I mean . . ." Jimmy's eyes darted from Sarah to Burt, then back to Sarah. "Yeah I had a hassle with him. But I never iced him."

Sarah paused her drumming. "And we're supposed to take your word for that?"

"I wasn't anywhere near the mall that night. I can prove it. I was . . ." Jimmy swallowed whatever else he was going to say.

"You were what, Jimmy?"

The kid shifted his skinny buttocks on the hard chair and remained silent.

"Guess that's it," Sarah said, turning to face Burt. "He doesn't want to talk. I'm not wasting any more time here."

Sarah took a step toward the door before Jimmy called out, "Wait. What about our deal?"

Sarah turned to see Burtweiler stride over to the table and put his big, fat nose an inch from the kid's. "Get this straight, asshole. We don't make deals. Only the DA can do that. But you talk and maybe you can escape a murder rap."

Jimmy sat absolutely still for a moment, only the furtive darting of his eyes revealed his inner tension. "We were doing some jobs in Willowbend the night Mel bought it."

A sinking feeling settled over Sarah. The flash of good luck had just played out. Perps lie about everything, except when it's saving them from a bigger rap.

Damn! She left the interrogation room, slamming the door behind her.

Angel was at her desk when Sarah got back to their department. Sarah stopped for just a beat to consider what her partner's mood might be after last night. *To hell with it.* She walked up to Angel. "I just met our elusive friend, Jimmy."

Angel's face registered surprise.

"Burtweiler brought him in and remembered we were looking for someone like him."

"Finally we get a break."

Angel's voice carried no hint of the previous trouble, and Sarah relaxed. "It isn't time to celebrate yet," she said. "He's got an alibi."

"What punk doesn't? Never leave home without one. Isn't that their motto?"

"Yeah. But this one's pretty solid."

Sarah watched her partner's excitement fade as she filled her in on the details. They'd check the alibi. They had to. But she didn't hold out much hope.

# CHAPTER SEVEN

Walter liked to hear the sharp click of his leather heels on the concrete as he walked out into the parking garage. The sound could almost make him believe he was still a young, trim Marine performing with the drill team, fifty pairs of boots creating their own cadence in a smart staccato of precision moves.

Those were the days when he'd thought he'd amount to something, the time before he'd been shipped over for the last hurrah in Desert Storm. The brass could've waited a week. Then he wouldn't have ended up with his foot damn near shot off. The fact that he'd done it himself didn't make any difference. No one knew about it stateside, so he could tell whatever story he wanted, his heroic efforts growing proportionately to how many beers he drank. Might as well get some benefits out of it, right?

Pausing in the halo of a ceiling light, Walter lit a cigarette, pulling the smoke deep into his lungs then blowing it out in a grey cloud.

Boss wouldn't let him smoke on the job. Said it was a smoke-free environment, just like every place was, but who the hell would ever know. Damn place was deserted, and by the time the shoppers showed up in the morning, there'd be no trace of second-hand smoke for them to bitch about.

The rebel inside tempted Walter to tell his boss to go screw himself. He'd smoke when and where he wanted. But he knew he couldn't afford to take any chances. This job was the only security he had. Such as it was. Then the absurdity of finding security working as a security guard struck him funny, and he laughed out loud.

A soft shuffle of sound overlapped his laughter, and Walter turned to discern the source, tensing as he saw a figure emerge from the shadows shrouding a pillar. "What are you doing here?" he called out.

The man didn't answer, but Walter relaxed as the man stepped into the circle of illumination and he could see who he was talking to.

"Kind of late to be out and about, ain't it?" Walter asked.

Still silent, the man passed him, and Walter shrugged. No big deal if the guy didn't want to be sociable. He didn't have any more time to waste anyway. As he started to turn, a sudden swift movement startled him, and he dropped his cigarette to grab at whatever was cutting into the soft flesh of his neck.

Walter's chest heaved as his lungs struggled to draw air beyond the constriction. Panic rising, he bucked against the man, trying to dislodge the iron grip. Momentarily, a sense of unreality overcame him, as if he were an observer watching the dance of death.

Then the memo about that guy who'd bought it at Northwood flashed frantically through Walter's mind. The possibility that the same thing could be happening to him didn't register until that one stark moment when he had to acknowledge the chasm of black yawning before him.

Before he lost consciousness, Walter wished he hadn't ignored the warning to tighten security.

*Panting, he let the body slump to the cool concrete. The fight had caught him unaware and he'd almost lost it, surprised by the strength of the man's will to live.*

*Swallowing the stream of bile that rose in his throat, he took a few steps back, trying to disassociate himself. The long-ago memory of the chopping block on his grandfather's farm washed over him in revulsion. It was hard to tell if the warm, coppery smell of blood belonged to then or now. His stomach roiled in protest.*

*Maybe he should make this one his last.*

Sarah watched the pale ribbon of smoke slowly spiral toward the ceiling fan where it was sliced by the endless, hypnotic revolutions of the wooden blades. She didn't even know why she was here.

No. That wasn't exactly true.

She was here because she finally had the courage to call Paul at his office, and his eagerness to meet her for a late drink had erased any misgivings about picking up the phone. But now that he was due to walk in any minute, the misgiving had returned, along with a major case of nervous perspiration and a long-forgotten urge for a cigarette.

Get a grip, woman. It's not like this is your first date. Sarah hastily stubbed out the cigarette when she saw Paul step inside. He wasn't dressed like a cowboy this time, but the black Dockers and hunter-green golf shirt didn't alter her earlier impression. She tried to calm the steady drumbeat of her heart as he scanned the room, then walked over to slide into the booth.

He glanced at the ashtray.

"I don't do that very often," Sarah said, surprised at her compulsion to explain.

"I'm glad." A slow smile worked its way up from his lips to his eyes, the blue even darker in the dim lighting. "I'd hate for anything to happen to you just when we're getting to know each other."

The warmth of a blush moved across her cheeks, and Sarah hoped the shadows would prevent him from noticing.

"Are you really an accountant?" Sarah again surprised herself.

Blurting was about as alien as explaining.

"It's a dirty job, but someone's got to do it."

Sarah laughed, relieved that he hadn't taken offense. The appearance of the waitress to take his order gave Sarah a moment to study his profile. Square jaw lightly tinged with the shadow of a beard that had been recently shaved but was pushing for recognition again. Crooked nose. Probably acquired in a sporting injury. He didn't look like a fighting kind of man.

"Did you want another?" the waitress asked. Sarah checked the level in her glass and shook her head. It was enough.

After the waitress left, Paul regarded her across the table. "I've been speculating a lot since the other night, but I'll be honest. It's got me stumped."

"And the mystery is?"

"What line of work you're in that calls for night meetings with your boss hosted by your friendly, neighborhood tavern."

"That was a little out of the ordinary."

Paul's smile faded into a slight frown. "Is there some reason you're avoiding the question?"

"No, uh—"

The strident beep of a cellular phone interrupted their conversation, and Sarah found the source of the intrusion in her purse. "Sorry," she said, grabbing the phone.

Paul made a small gesture of understanding, and she could sense his puzzlement as he openly listened to her end of the conversation. It was brief. "Yes . . . Uh-huh . . . I'll be right there."

Snapping the phone shut, Sarah gave him a weak smile. "I have to go to work."

A shadow of disappointment crossed his face, but his voice betrayed more. "Another meeting?"

"No." Sarah didn't want it to be this way. She'd even hoped she could save it until at least the second date. Some guys really freaked when they found out about her job. But she didn't have time to debate the wisdom of just blurting it out now. If she didn't ease his suspicions, she'd never see him again. "I'm a detective."

"Oh." Paul raised an eyebrow in surprise. "Private?"

"No. City."

"I've never felt this friendly toward a cop before."

She regarded him thoughtfully for a moment. "Will you still be interested if I have to leave to go to a crime scene?"

"Yeah." He flashed his incredible smile again. "It'll give us something to talk about on our next date."

Pulling out one of her cards, Sarah slid it across the table. "Next time, you call me."

Two black-and-whites blocked the entrance ramp to the parking garage, their roof-flashers emitting space-like lasers of color that cut across the night sky. A small crowd of curious watchers gathered as close as they could, their faces reflecting eerily out of the edge of darkness. Sarah pulled up behind the squad cars and doused her headlamps just as the lights from a van swept the area. The side door of the van bore the announcement, WXVA-TV-Channel 9 News.

"Goddam vultures," Sarah muttered, slamming her car door and pushing her way past Bianca Gomaz, a familiar face in everyone's living room on the evening news. She was a rising star in broadcast journalism, attributed with bigger balls than most of her male counterparts in the field of investigative reporting. Her many talents included an incredible recall of names and faces.

"Detective Kingsly!" Bianca strode forward, a cameraman hustling to keep up. "Can you spare a comment?"

"I don't think so."

"Give me a break."

Sarah continued past and nodded to the uniformed officer who was standing at the edge of the ramp. "Keep them out of here," she said.

"Bitch!" Bianca called after her.

"Yeah," Sarah said to the bleak, cement walls. "Sometimes you gotta be."

Trudging up the paved incline, Sarah pulled her jacket close against a sudden gust of chill night air that swept down from the upper levels. In the dimness, she could barely make out the arrows directing her to the third parking tier. As she drew near, the murmur of activity grew louder until she finally arrived at the crime scene. The body of a rent-a-cop rested on the gray concrete, sporadically illuminated by a sudden flash of light as the crime-scene photographer recorded the moment for posterity and evidence.

"What have we got this time?" Sarah asked, sidling up to Angel who turned from the uniformed officer she'd been talking to.

"I'm hoping it's not, but it looks a lot like the poor slob at Northwood." Angel held up a plastic evidence bag hosting another note. "Unless we've got another perp who likes to write letters."

"What does this one say?"

Angel smoothed the plastic so she could read. "THIS ONE'S NOT GETTING AWAY WITH IT."

"I don't suppose the doer was kind enough to elaborate on what 'it' is?"

"Nope."

"Damn." Sarah leaned over to look at the body, then pulled herself upright. "It couldn't turn out to be something as simple as an unhappy shopper?"

"Only in our dreams." Angel laughed, and the sound rang pleasantly in Sarah's ears. She glanced over to watch Roberts and his team begin a methodical sweep of the area and then turned back to Angel. "Who called it in?"

"The head of security." Angel nodded toward a tall, lanky man in a jogging suit standing with a patrol officer. "He came down here to check things out when his guy didn't respond to a page."

"Name?"

Sarah felt a perverse twinge of pleasure when Angel had to refer to her notes. "Tom Franklin."

"You talk to him yet?"

"No. I only beat you here by a few minutes."

"Okay. I'll see what he has to say. You find out if Walt's on his way yet."

Sarah sized up the man as she approached. Pretty young looking to be the head of security, and she dreaded the possibility of having to deal with some kind of hotshot. But a steady gaze from aquiline eyes reassured her. "Mr. Franklin, I just have a few questions for you."

"And you are?"

The tone of the question was more cautious than challenging, and the reassurance settled deeper. "Detective Kingsly." She showed him her shield.

Franklin took careful note of her badge number, then offered a firm handshake. "Anything I can do to help."

"What time did you get here?"

"Ten forty-five."

"You're sure?"

"Yes. I paged Walter at ten-fifteen. When he didn't respond by ten-thirty, I came right over. I live close."

"Do you routinely contact your employees during their shifts?"

"Only since the incident at Northwood. We're all trying to tighten security."

"What can you tell me about the victim?"

"Not much. To be honest, I didn't much care for the guy. He was hired before I came on, and he treated the job like a joke. Resented the hell out of it when I moved up."

"So there was bad blood between you?"

Franklin shook his head and the hint of a smile tugged at the corner of his full lips. "If you're trying to make a case for motive, it'd make more sense if I was the one lying on the concrete."

Sarah acknowledged his point with a nod. "Did Walter know the Northwood victim?"

"No. None of my people did. We had a special briefing right after it happened. They all said they'd never met the guy."

"So you can't think of any connection between the two?"

Franklin shook his head again. "Sorry."

Sarah closed her notebook and slipped it in her pocket. "We'll need to come by tomorrow and look at his employment records."

"Any time. Just call. Your patrol officer has my number." Franklin nodded toward one of the men in blue, then shifted his weight from one foot to another. "You think I can go home now? My wife is going to be worried. I told her I'd be right back."

"Sure. Go on."

Watching Franklin disappear into the darkness outside the perimeter of light, Sarah became aware of something that had bugged her since she'd first arrived at the scene. How had the press latched on to this one so quickly? If she hadn't run that amber light at Preston and Belt Line, the television van would have beaten her here.

Sarah walked to the edge of the wall and looked over. Vans from two other network stations were lined up behind the first one.

"Don't you find that strange?" Sarah asked Angel who had stepped up beside her.

"What?" Angel took her own look. "The news-hounds?"

"Yeah."

"I don't know." Angel shrugged. "This is news, isn't it?"

"Yeah. But it's a damned fast response considering the call is less than an hour old. Makes you wonder how they knew. Unless . . ." Sarah let the thought trail and looked back at the reporters and camera operators vying for their two minutes of airtime.

"What are you thinking? That they got a tip?"

"It's a possibility." Sarah turned. "Might be interesting to have a little visit with Ms. Bianca Gomaz."

# CHAPTER EIGHT

Sarah opened the door to the interrogation room and let Bianca and Angel precede her. One of them left a trail of exotic perfume that was about as pleasant as stepping into a spritz of air-freshener. Sarah wrinkled her nose. It had to be the reporter. For a moment Sarah regretted taking the lead in this interview. She'd rather be across the room where Angel, wearing jeans and a chambray shirt, leaned casually against the wall.

"We appreciate you coming in this morning," Sarah said, closing the door with a loud thud.

"You were very persuasive last night." Bianca's voice dripped with sarcasm, and she pushed her sunglasses up into her luxurious mane of dark hair. "Kind of dingy in here, isn't it?"

Sarah glanced around the room, noting the dull, gray walls soundproofed with cloth that looked like it had been bought for a buck-ninety-eight a yard at a carpet outlet. A solitary wooden table, decorated with the scars of countless nervous smokers and the stains of spilled drinks, stood in the middle of the room surrounded by metal and vinyl chairs cracked with age and use.

Otherwise, the room was bare, and Bianca was right. It was dingy as hell.

Sarah motioned Bianca to one of the chairs. "We thought you'd prefer doing this away from a room full of guys who'd like to see you up-close and personal."

"How considerate." Bianca sat down, crossing long legs sheathed in royal-purple silk pants that she wore with a matching jacket. The color provided the perfect backdrop for the woman's Castilian legacy of light skin and shimmering black hair.

Appraising the reporter, Sarah felt like an indentured servant in her jeans and red T-shirt. But it was a new T-shirt.

Bianca pulled a slim, brown cigarette out of her purse. "Can I smoke?"

Sarah glanced at Angel, who shrugged, then back to Bianca. "It's your life."

Bianca lit up and blew a stream of smoke that hung in a flimsy gray cloud between them. "I don't do this often," she said. "Only under certain circumstances."

A weird sense of déjà vu hit Sarah, and she steeled herself against feeling any affinity with this woman. Making that kind of personal connection had proven disastrous in the past, and Sarah knew she had to protect any advantage she might have over someone who knew all the plays of the interview game.

"Think I'll go scrounge up something that resembles an ashtray," Angel said, striding toward the door.

Bianca blew another stream of smoke at the ceiling, watching Angel slip out. "Interesting partnership you have here."

"Nothing all that novel about it," Sarah said, pulling up a chair to sit opposite the reporter.

"Oh, really?" Bianca laughed, but the mirth didn't reach her ebony eyes. "Given the current atmosphere in the city, I'd guess it's more than just a random pairing."

For the second time, Sarah found herself disconcerted and broke eye contact before she gave anything away. The reappearance of Angel, bearing a Styrofoam cup with a little water, saved Sarah from having to make a response. She waited quietly while Angel set the cup down on the table before leaning against the wall again.

Bianca broke the ensuing silence first. "So, what can I do for you?"

"We were just curious about the extent of coverage last night at Prestonwood," Sarah said.

"News is our business, Officer. Surely you haven't overlooked that."

Sarah declined to enter the verbal sparring match the thrust invited. "Who decided this one should get more attention than the kid who was shot in Oak Cliff?"

"Gang killings are old news." Bianca lit another cigarette with the glowing end of her first one then dropped the butt into the water where a brief hiss pronounced it dead. "People are tired of youth violence. They want to hear about something different."

"Bullshit!" Angel pulled herself off the wall and stepped closer to the table. "You didn't just pick this up on the police scanner and decide to cover it on a whim. You got there too goddam fast for that."

"How interesting." Bianca eyed Angel carefully. "I didn't think you were allowed to speak."

Sarah could feel her partner's anger rise, and she turned to give her a warning look. Angel responded with the briefest of nods, then faced the reporter with a steady gaze and an uncompromising set to her jaw. "I'm disappointed." Angel's voice was as hard as her expression. "I thought someone like you would know the value of a straight answer."

The statement found a vulnerable spot in the reporter's brassy armor, and Sarah pressed the advantage. "Were you acting on a tip?"

Bianca glanced from one detective to the other, tapping a long ash into the makeshift ashtray.

"A simple yes or no will suffice," Angel said.

"Yes." The word came out in a long sigh. "It was anonymous of course."

"Of course." Sarah didn't even try to eliminate the sarcasm.

"It was." A flare of anger narrowed Bianca's eyes. "Most of our tips are. If people want to be on TV, they call a talk show host."

"Tell us about this caller," Angel prompted.

"I didn't speak to him. Kurt, our news director did. The call came in over our NEWSTIPS line. Then he contacted me and told me to meet the crew out there."

"And what time was that?" Sarah asked.

"Shortly before eleven. He wanted me to hustle over, so he didn't waste time with details."

"And after?"

"After what?"

"After you got back to the station," Sarah said. "How many details did he give you then?"

"That the caller was a man. He'd delivered his message slowly and deliberately. Told Kurt there was an *interesting* dead body in the parking garage at Prestonwood."

"Were those his exact words?" Angel asked. " 'Interesting dead body'?"

"I don't know. I never listened to the tape."

"There's a tape of the call?" Sarah asked.

"Yes." Bianca gave them a look that suggested they were stupid not to realize that. "We tape all the calls that come in on our hotline."

"We'll need a copy," Angel said.

Sarah watched Bianca hesitate, study Angel for a moment, then turn her gaze back to Sarah. "I'll tell you what, Detective. Maybe we can both get something out of this deal."

Sarah eyed the reporter silently, and Bianca pushed on as if she hadn't made a sale in a week. "I'll help you get the tape and you give me an exclusive on your partnership?" She flashed a smile that must have cost a thousand bucks. "It'll be good for the department."

"You seem to have overlooked one tiny detail, Ms. Gomaz. We don't need you to get the tape." Sarah paused to play the smile game. "And if you sincerely want to do the department a good turn, try a story about Burtweiler and Simms. They've got the best arrest record on the books."

"But nobody's ever heard of them." If Bianca harbored any irritation, she covered it well with her professional veneer. "And a story showing how willing you are to work with a black cop might put you in good light with the Review Board."

"Screw the Review Board."

"Can I quote you on that, Detective?"

Sarah bit her lower lip until it screamed in protest, mentally kicking herself.

"I think we have enough for now," Angel said, giving Sarah a moment to push her chair back and move away from the table. Then Angel turned back to the reporter. "We'll send an officer to pick up the tape."

"Fine." Bianca dropped her cigarette into the water then, made one fluid motion out of grabbing her purse and standing. "But you might find our reports of the department more complimentary if we had a friendlier relationship."

"We'll pass the word along," Sarah said, anger giving the words a cutting edge.

Bianca paused in the doorway and gave Sarah a knowing look before stepping out.

*Damn! I let the bitch get to me.*

Sarah hung back while Angel walked out with the reporter. Secretly, Sarah could excuse her loss of control. She still hung precariously over an emotional abyss, ready to topple with the slightest provocation. The mental picture stirred a shred of manic laughter that rang hollowly in the empty room. Wouldn't Doc Murray like to probe that scenario with his diagnostic questions.

Unable to shake the image of herself teetering on the edge of a dark pit, afraid to look over, Sarah wondered if she'd ever be on steady ground again. And the real bitch of it all was that she had no one to turn to.

John should have been there to help her sort through this mess of guilt. That's what partners do for each other. And part of her was damned pissed that he'd left her so alone. But she had a hard time looking that one square in the face. Seemed pretty callous to be mad at someone for dying. And she knew that some of the anger was just because there was this great big void in her life that no one had stepped forward to fill. Angel may have taken his desk, but she was a long way from taking his place.

Perhaps that's why the reporter's request for the story had struck such a chord. How could they talk about a partnership that behaved like many marriages, fine on the outside, but don't open the door too wide. Someone might see the truth.

Shrugging off the dismal thoughts, Sarah picked up the Styrofoam cup and dropped it in the trash outside the door. Then she went to her desk and called Lieutenant Grotelli to have him send a Patrol officer over to get the tape. Maybe they'd pick up a break with it. God knows they needed one. As soon as this second murder created a media blitz, they'd have city hall all over their asses.

Why the Commissioner and the Mayor thought pressure helped solve cases was beyond her. Experience should have enlightened them to the fact that pressure caused mistakes, and mistakes let perps walk. Despite that fact, the boys at the top all reacted like wooden men, jerking on a political puppeteer's string whenever a case made screaming headlines.

Venting her frustration in a deep sigh, Sarah leaned back in her chair and reviewed what little they had on the latest victim. Walter Durham had lived just one month past his forty-eighth birthday and had a checkered work history. A run of his name through the system had turned up a few minor busts for drug possession, but no serious criminal charges.

Beyond the fact that they both worked at malls, what else the two victims had in common eluded her. It wasn't a question of what they MIGHT have shared. There had to be a common denominator to attract the killer because, even though it hadn't been said yet, the possibility that this was the work of a serialist loomed. And it had to be for more than just the coincidence of employment.

Sarah was also convinced that the perp had made that phone call to the TV station. But why? Most serial killers contented themselves with letting the gruesome acts of murder garner the publicity, especially in the beginning. Contacts with the press usually came later, triggered by an unconscious need to be found and punished.

So what desperation drove this guy to break the pattern?

She made a note to check with McGregor about sending copies of the messages and the tape to the FBI. The Behavioral Sciences Department might be able to use their magic to tell them what kind of perp they were dealing with.

"You've got to give the lady credit. She doesn't quit easily." Angel paused at Sarah's desk. "When you didn't jump on her offer, she must've figured I'd be a softer touch. Tried the 'best friend' routine, extolling the benefits of showcasing a successful black, woman cop."

Angel smiled. "She seemed to take some offense when I suggested she was more interested in ratings than my image."

Sarah returned the smile, relieved as her uncertainty about the partnership rearranged itself into a more comfortable position. "I guess that's something else we can agree on, then."

Unsaid words drifted between them like soft billows of fog, and Sarah gratefully accepted the slight reprieve from her turmoil. "Well," she finally said. "Are you ready to find out what a fine upstanding citizen Walter Durham was?"

"Who's first on our list?" Angel asked. "The boss?"

"Yeah." Sarah grabbed her notebook and pen, stuffing them in the pocket of her khaki safari jacket.

# CHAPTER NINE

Franklin wore his navy and white uniform with understated authority, and Sarah lost some of the disdain she normally held for rent-a-cops. Franklin was more like a fellow professional.

He led the two detectives to a small but tidy office, equipped with a computer centered on a large desk. A printer stood on a metal stand next to it. A desk organizer held an assortment of pens, paper clips and small notepads, and on the other side of the computer a smiling brunette was framed in an eight-by-ten frame. Sarah assumed it was the wife he'd referred to last night. A standard office chair was in front of the desk and two wooden chairs bracketed a small table on the other wall.

Franklin walked over to the desk and punched a few keys on the computer, making the screen flash in a quick progression of functions. "I'm trying to eliminate the necessity for paper files," he said, letting the monitor settle on one picture. "But I can print you a copy of Durham's work record."

"Could you print two?" Angel asked.

"Sure."

Franklin keyed in some commands, and the laser printer came to life.

"Have you thought of anything since last night that might have a bearing on the murder?" Sarah asked.

He shook his head. "Wish I had."

"We have to consider it might be someone associated with the mall."

"Yeah." Franklin grabbed pages as they settled in the tray. "I went over everything I could remember about the guy and nothing popped."

"Do you have records on all mall employees?" Angel asked. "Something we could dig through to try to make a connection?"

"God, no. With the turnover rate at some places, that would be a nightmare to set up and maintain."

"What do you do if you're not sure about someone who says they're a new employee?"

"We have telephone access to all store managers. If there's a doubt or suspicion, we check it out."

Sarah understood the inherent problems in trying to develop a database of the entire mall's employees, but it sure would have helped to have records to check. "Any possibility Durham was involved in something illegal? Maybe setting up inside jobs?"

"I don't think so." Franklin handed a set of pages to each woman. "Durham was something of a blowhard. Liked to strut his stuff. But basically, he was honest. That's why I couldn't find a way to fire him even though I didn't like him. He did the job adequately."

"What about his life outside the mall?" Angel asked.

"As I already told Detective Kingsly, we weren't very friendly."

"I'm not asking what you felt. What do you know?"

Sarah was surprised at the edge in Angel's tone, but it didn't seem to bother Franklin. "Not much," he answered without losing his friendly tone. "Parents are dead. He wasn't married. Never had been as far as I know. And I never met any of his friends."

"Anybody on your staff know him better?" Sarah asked.

"I don't think so. Most of my employees are loners. But some of the folks at the food court might be able to help. Durham did like to eat."

"Did he favor any place over the others?"

"Yeah. He was partial to barbecue." Franklin glanced at his watch. "The manager should be there now setting up for lunch. Want to meet him?"

"Sure."

Franklin led the women up to the second floor where the food court was strung along most of the north side of the floor. At a section hosting the sign "Freddie's BBQ" a squat, balding man was stirring a large stainless steel tray full of chipped beef in barbecue sauce. Heating coils glowed under the pan, releasing a pleasant, tangy aroma. Franklin got his attention. "Freddie," Franklin said. "These detectives want to talk to you about Walter Durham."

Freddie rested the spoon against the edge of the pan and eyed the women carefully.

Franklin turned to Sarah. "This is Freddie Mills. You need anything else, call me."

Sarah nodded, then turned her attention to Freddie, who still considered her with a careful scrutiny. "What do you want to know?" he finally asked.

"Were you and Walter friends?"

Freddie shrugged. "We knew each other."

"You don't seem too broken up about his death," Angel commented.

"Don't start getting ideas. I liked Walter well enough. I'm just not an emotional guy."

"Did you ever see him outside of work?" Sarah asked.

The man resumed stirring, sending up tantalizing whiffs of tomato, red pepper and hickory. "Some."

"Would you care to elaborate?"

"Walter liked an occasional poker game."

"Was it always the same players?"

Freddie shook his head. "We'd just usually pull it together at the last minute. Grab whoever was available. Other security guys. Or some from food service."

"Any of those people friends with Walter?"

"Walter was too irritating to have friends. You know what I mean?" Freddie halted his actions to look up at Sarah. "His favorite subject was himself and his favorite voice was his own."

"So why'd you hang with him if you found him so obnoxious?"

"I didn't say I did. He irritated other people. Wore them out after a while."

"And he didn't bother you?" Angel asked.

"Nah. I just blew it off. Figured the guy was hungry for attention. Seen it plenty of times before."

"You do anything else with Walter besides play poker?"

"Sometimes."

Sarah let her gaze invite him to be more specific.

"Walter liked to party. Or go barhopping. I went with him a few times." Freddie pulled a large plastic bag filled with small bags of chips from under the counter and lined them up in a basket.

"Did you ever go to Danny's over on Greenville."

"Not that I recall."

"Think about it," Angel prodded.

He paused and shot her an irritated look. "Don't have to think about it. I never been there."

Sarah recognized the subtle shift in his manner as a prelude to losing him, so she shifted gears. "Did he have a girlfriend?"

"Yeah. Never met her, though."

"Name?"

"Francie something. Don't know where she lives, either. But I got her number here somewhere." Freddie wiped his hands on a dingy white apron and dug out his wallet. "We could call him there when we were trying to set up a game."

Sarah wrote the number in her notebook, then nodded to Freddie. "Appreciate your help."

He turned without responding, and Sarah wondered if his evident relief was based on a desire to get back to work or away from them. It wouldn't hurt to run his name and see what popped out.

"He was a veritable fountain of information," Angel said as they walked away.

Sarah smiled. "It wasn't a total bust. At least we got the girlfriend out of him."

After a quick lunch at KFC, they went back to the station. Sarah called the number Freddie had given her and reached a woman whose first responses seemed drenched in sleep. She hated to do it this way over the phone, but didn't see any option. After verifying that this was the Francie who knew Walter Durham, Sarah told the woman as gently as she could about his death.

"Oh my God . . . How did . . . ?" The question faded into silence on the other end of the line.

"It would be better if we finished this in person."

"Yes. Of course."

Sarah noted the address Francie gave her, then stretched and stood, bumping into McGregor who'd come up behind her. "Uh, sorry, Lieu."

"What did you and Angel get this morning?"

Apparently it was going to be all business today.

"Not a hell of a lot. We should know more after we check out his digs and talk to his girlfriend."

"Okay. I want a verbal report at five o'clock sharp, and all written reports filed before you go home."

Definitely all business today.

Sarah found Angel in the restroom and relayed McGregor's mandate. "Let's split the legwork. That way we'll be more apt to actually get something to placate the monster when we get back."

Angel nodded, and Sarah wished her partner would at least smile. A little humor would go a long way toward relieving the tension.

A disquieting mood kept Sarah company the rest of the afternoon. It was never a pleasant experience to have to talk to someone about the death of someone they cared about, but the woman's dismal circumstances had made it even worse. She was a divorcee with two young boys, a deadbeat dad and a night job waiting tables at Denny's. Not much of a life, and she'd made it clear that she'd staked a lot of hope on the late Walter Durham.

She had no idea why anyone would want him dead.

Back at the station for the late briefing, Sarah found out that Angel had been equally unrewarded at Durham's place. The landlord had offered nothing more illuminating than the brief report he'd given to the uniformed officer who'd talked to him last night. A search of Durham's sparse belongings turned up nothing to tie him to the first victim or shed any light on who killed him.

"The only good thing is that it didn't take long to look around his place," Angel said. "For all the personal touches, it could have been a motel room."

"We haven't found a connection to drugs on this one yet, either," Sarah said. "His military records show he was wounded in Desert Storm, so it's possible he brought a habit home with him. Lots of guys did. But he'd have had to be drug free to be certified as a security guard."

McGregor rubbed his temples in slow circles. "So it comes down to the audio tape."

"Yeah." Sarah leaned forward eagerly, glad that he'd chosen to focus on the positive instead of chewing them up about the negatives. "We got it copied and taken over to our guy at the studio. See what he makes of it."

"How long will that take?"

"Could be a couple of days. When I called he said he was swamped." Sarah paused, anticipating a burst of anger at the delay, but McGregor surprised her by merely nodding. "It'd be a good idea to contact Sanchez, too. See if we've got enough for the Behavioral Science Department to take a stab at a psych profile."

"Yeah, do it."

Leaving his office a few minutes later, Sarah wondered at McGregor's unusual behavior. When a case was going poorly he was more apt to rant and rave than sit in quiet contemplation. She wondered what had happened in those few hours that she'd been away from the station. Should she go back and ask?

She hesitated, halfway down the hall, then shook her head. If it was something she needed to know, he would've told her.

At nine-thirty Sarah dragged her weary body home and was greeted by Cat who was eager to play. He pounced on her feet as she crossed the living room, and when he scampered up her leg she was glad her jeans absorbed most of the impact from his claws.

"Bad kitty," she said, disengaging him carefully. "I am not a tree."

Cat wrapped himself around her forearm and nipped at her wrist. Not sure of what else to do, Sarah cradled him against her and rubbed his ears with her other hand. That action triggered a rumbling purr, and he ceased all hostilities.

"You're not so fierce after all," Sarah said. "At the first offer of love you roll over."

The blink of the message light on her answering machine caught Sarah's attention and she pressed the PLAY button.

"Sarah, this is Jeanette . . ."

The voice stopped Sarah's steps toward the kitchen, drawing her back to stare at the machine.

". . . Listen. I know you're probably busy. But the thing is, the kids miss seeing you around here. We'd love to have you come for dinner. Call me some—"

Sarah stopped the painful message and sank down on the sofa. She didn't realize she was crying until Cat climbed up her chest and licked the tears from her cheek. She'd forgotten to think about Jeanette and the kids in the weeks since the funeral. Well, maybe not forgotten exactly. Refused might be more like it. And she wasn't even sure why.

In the three years of their partnership, Sunday afternoons had frequently found Sarah at John's home. Jeanette had never seemed to mind the intrusion, and the kids had been delighted with another body to share a game of touch football.

Remembering stirred a wrenching combination of sadness and yearning. Her head told her it would be good for her and the kids if she went over. They all needed some good times in their lives. But her heart still ached with the pain of losing John, and she didn't know if it would allow her to play yet.

What good would it do to go over and cry?

The soothing rasp of Cat's tongue on her face turned into a nip, reminding Sarah that supper was long overdue. She pushed off the sofa and padded toward the kitchen, ignoring the telephone on her way past.

Dropping Cat on the counter, Sarah perused a couple of cabinets, then the open refrigerator, before deciding she didn't have the inclination or the energy to cook. She finally poured a bowl of raisin bran.

She contemplated fixing one for Cat, too, then decided she'd better not set a precedent for future discipline problems. As a concession, she added a little milk to the chows in his dish and set him on the floor. "Exercise your imagination, Cat. You can pretend you're eating what I am."

Despite the distraction of routine, Jeanette's message kept tugging at Sarah's consciousness. She didn't have to respond tonight. Or even tomorrow. But she couldn't ignore John's family forever, even though the scaredy cat in her wanted to run and hide.

# CHAPTER TEN

McGregor eyed the impassive faces of the members of the Board staring back at him from behind a table. Thirteen people, one more than a jury, and he wondered if that was accidental. Some of them looked about as enthused as the average Joe who hopes for an exemption when his random summons for jury duty appears in the mail.

Of course McGregor couldn't blame these people who'd volunteered their time for this community service. Not when the City Council was still split over the appropriateness of some of the appointments. The Review Board, which wasn't such a bad thing in McGregor's mind, could hardly be effective without the solid backing of city leadership. That would be like hobbling a fine cutting horse then expecting him to be able to work the cattle.

The first wind of the proposed board that had blown by a number of years ago had raised his hopes for easing some of the animosity between John Q Public and the department. When a complaint against an officer was investigated, who could question the findings of an impartial panel?

It could have worked, too. If it weren't for the piss-ant politicians who couldn't keep their personal agendas out of it. The beauty of the concept had been lost in political maneuvering for advantage that, as usual, left the general public to wonder if anybody cared about them.

McGregor didn't have to read the nameplates strung along

the table to recognize some of the biggest names in Dallas law, and nerves rumbled in his stomach the same way that they did in court. Like most cops, he was out of his element on the stand, sweating through each cross, fearful that he would inadvertently open some small hole for the defense to charge through.

"Lieutenant McGregor, in making a determination in the actions of Detective Kingsly on the night of twelve July of this current year, your seasoned experience would be of considerable benefit in ascertaining the culpability of said party." Larry Holcomb's delivery was as uninspiring as his dark, somber suit, and only the barest flicker of life crossed his carefully controlled expression.

The guy must not handle the public side of litigation very often, McGregor thought. Any jury member who wasn't put to sleep by the lawyer's droning monotone would have to be able to process data like a computer in order to glean the point out of the jungle of words.

"What do you want to know?" McGregor asked, resisting the urge to pull at his tie.

"According to the written report from your Special Investigation Unit," Holcomb picked up several typed sheets of paper which were stapled together and flipped through them. "And I quote, 'After careful review of all factors leading to and contributing to the use of deadly force by Detective Kingsly, the official ruling is that the action was justifiable.' "

Holcomb looked at McGregor. "Do you agree with that, Lieutenant?"

"Yes."

"And how long are you going to pretend that racism doesn't exist within the department?"

McGregor followed the question back to a trim, black woman who wore a dark suit brightened by a coral scarf at her neck. "I thought we were here to discuss the shooting incident," McGregor said. "We can take up the issue of racism at a later date."

"Very adroitly put, Lieutenant." The woman graced him with a placating smile. "But according to a report filed by the Reverend Billie Norton, black youths die in a disproportionate number during arrests and attempted arrests right here in this city." She paused for effect. "And you really want us to believe that racism is a separate issue?"

McGregor curbed a flash of anger, forcing himself to respond in a level tone. "And how long are you going to ignore the evidence just so you can call this a racial incident?"

"Lieutenant. I hardly think—"

"No!" McGregor held up a hand to stifle the protest from Holcomb. "You dragged me here for this exercise in futility, so, by God, you'll listen."

Eyeing each of the Board members in turn, McGregor continued. "I'm not overlooking the fact that we have a problem in race relations. Nor am I trying to pretend that the attitude of a few in the department hasn't contributed to the situation. But you have to learn how to separate reality from outrage. We lost one of our finest officers that night. And we would have lost two if Detective Kingsly had stopped to consider the backlash from having to shoot that boy."

"Wounding him would have kept both of them alive," Holcomb said.

"Yeah." McGregor shook his head. "And Santa Claus still comes down my chimney."

"Unlike your mythical example, we do have proof of the existence of racially provoked actions by your officers." Holcomb sifted through some papers for emphasis. "Our investigation will determine if that was the case for Detective Kingsly."

McGregor shifted his bulk in the unyielding wooden chair and waited for the barrage of questions. As a bead of perspiration trickled down his back beneath his suit coat, he reminded himself that he had the easier part. He didn't envy Sarah her turn in the witness chair.

Sarah glanced at the clock and sighed in frustration. The afternoon was almost gone with little to mark the progress of the investigation. The forensic team faced the same nightmare created by the Northwood crime scene, and the preliminary medical report only confirmed her worst fears: Cause of death: Ligature Strangulation. The rest of the report could have been a copy of the one from Halsley, and Sarah knew better than to hope that the sifting and sorting that Roberts and his crew were knee-deep into would produce some anomaly.

The shrill clamor of her phone was a welcome intrusion, and she picked up the receiver with an automatic response. "Kingsly."

"Ah. I'm impressed. You sound so authoritative." The familiar baritone voice momentarily chased away her frustration.

"Paul. I'm glad you called."

"After reading the paper this morning, I almost didn't," the voice told her. "I figured you'd be up to your neck in alligators."

"It's a slow process."

"Slow enough that we can get together tonight?"

"I don't know." Sarah leaned back in her chair, contemplating the waves of sleepiness she'd been fighting for the last hour. "I've been a little short on sleep the last couple of nights. Perhaps a date with my bed is all I should consider."

"That offers some interesting possibilities."

His implication awakened a sensation she thought her weary body incapable of, and she almost changed her mind. But she knew in her current state, she could do little more than play the fantasy in her mind.

"I'm afraid the reality would hardly live up to your expectations," she said.

"What about Saturday, then? I'll even go all out and spring for dinner."

"You do tricks, too?"

A soft rumble of laughter rolled across the line, and Sarah decided she should work hard at finding ways to keep this man amused.

"Can I assume that's a 'yes'?" Paul asked.

"It definitely is."

"Good. I've got a place in mind, but I'll have to check on reservations. I'll let you know as soon as everything's arranged."

"Great." Sarah cradled the receiver, savoring the warm feeling of contentment the sound of his voice had given her.

"You look like you just got some good news." Angel leaned one hip against the edge of Sarah's desk. "Are we ready to break the case?"

"No. It was personal."

"I see."

A chill shroud descended between them, and Sarah realized that Angel had misinterpreted her response. For a moment, she considered letting her partner stew if she was going to be that touchy. But then she reconsidered. It wasn't fair to leave the woman adrift.

"I didn't mean personal as in I didn't want to tell you." Sarah waited for a slight thaw in Angel's attitude. "It was just that it had nothing to do with the case."

"I see." This response was only slightly less cutting than the previous one, and Angel strode away.

Sarah shook her head, then turned back to the file on her desk. *To hell with her. You can't make this work by yourself. She has to at least try.*

Walking into the Lieutenant's office with Sarah right behind her, Angel's attention was caught by the young man rising quickly from one of the chairs. She didn't think anyone younger than her father stood when a woman entered a room, and the gesture was endearing. So was the smile that creased his smooth mahogany face.

McGregor quickly came around his desk. "This is Chad Smith. From narcotics."

"We've met." Sarah offered her hand to the tall detective. "Nice to see you again."

Chad acknowledged Sarah's greeting then turned to Angel. "I don't think I've had the pleasure."

Angel stifled a groan, reassessing the charm of his smile. Did he think he was as smooth as his line? "Detective Johnson," she said, keeping her handshake as impersonal as her introduction.

Chad took her hand in a firm grip and eyed her with an amused crinkle around his eyes. Was he mocking her? No, Angel decided, trying to ignore the tickle of response to his touch. *It's a dare.*

Angel pulled her hand free and glanced at Sarah who wore an impassive face. Either she hadn't noticed the exchange or chose to ignore it.

McGregor motioned for them to be seated, then sank into his swivel chair. "I've asked Chad to work with us until we get a handle on these Mall Murders."

"They have a title now? With capital letters and everything?" Sarah straddled a chair and rested her elbows on the back.

"So far only in the Commissioner's office," McGregor said. "But don't be too surprised if you see it in tomorrow's headlines."

"And what exactly is Mr. Smith going to add to our investigation?" Angel asked.

The Lieutenant shot her a sharp look and she wondered if she'd stepped over the bounds.

"Maybe I'll let the detective explain that himself," McGregor said.

Giving a slight nod, Angel recognized the subtle reprimand couched in his emphasis on Chad's title. Message received loud and clear.

Angel turned her attention to Chad, who gave no outward sign of even being aware of what had just transpired.

"There've been some significant changes in the drug business here in the city." Chad stretched long chino-clad legs in the space between his chair and the desk. "Some of the Asian gangs are trying to take over territory held by the blacks and Chicanos."

"What does that have to do with our murders?" Sarah asked.

"Surveillance tapes show your second victim, Durham, bought stuff from members of the Bloods who control most of drug business in the city."

"So I guess we got our drug connection," Sarah said to McGregor, who nodded.

"Are you suggesting that the Asian gang is killing off the customers?" Angel didn't even try to mask the fact that she found the possibility ludicrous.

"I'm suggesting we investigate it."

"But it's an awful big stretch." Sarah swiveled in her chair to face Chad directly. "And it doesn't reach to the first guy. His drug source was so small, there's no way he could be a marketing threat."

"Not to mention the fact that the way these victims bought it hardly fits the usual profile of turf wars," Angel added.

A slight current of tension passed through the room, and Angel wondered if she should have just kept her mouth shut, been more of a team player. But Chad's theory was just so thin. She was relieved when McGregor broke the uncomfortable silence.

"I'm not saying this is the only avenue you should walk down," he said. "It's just one that has a little ray of light."

"Aren't we overlooking something more obvious?" Angel asked.

McGregor's expression asked "what?"

"Where they were killed. Even the Commissioner nailed it with his title."

"But we have nothing to pull them together," Sarah reminded her. "We read the same reports and talked to the same people. Halsley and Durham worked at two distinct jobs at two different malls. They probably never even met."

"They didn't have to know each other to have been killed for some reason other than drugs." Angel underscored her statement with a firm thrust of her jaw.

"Perhaps insisting it wasn't drugs is as dangerous as insisting it was." Chad leaned forward with his elbows on his knees. Angel found his nearness disconcerting and eased back.

"I hate to break up this interesting little debate," McGregor said. "But I'd suggest you three go out and prove your theories instead of beating them to death in my office."

Chad and Sarah laughed easily at the Lieutenant's remark, and Angel felt a pang of envy. She wished she could share in the camaraderie, but she still felt the restraints of being the new kid on the block. She belonged by virtue of having moved into the neighborhood, but she wasn't part of the history and traditions that bound the rest of them together like a family.

McGregor held up a hand to Sarah. "I need a word with you before you go."

Sarah nodded as Angel and Chad moved toward the door. McGregor waited until it was closed behind them before speaking. "I had to give my statement to the Review Board this morning."

The words hit her like a heavy fist in the stomach. But at

least it explained his sour mood yesterday.

"They're determined to turn it into a racial incident," he continued.

"I'm sure you set them straight." Sarah tried to be flip, but she couldn't get past the dread deep inside.

"I tried."

The quiet resignation in his voice made her feel like the pep squad had just given up with the home-team behind by ten points. Until this very moment she hadn't really been afraid of the Board. She'd considered its presence more of a nuisance, like a pesky fly that she could skillfully swat whenever she chose to.

"What can they do?" she asked, not really wanting the answer but knowing she needed it.

"Worst case?" McGregor's expression seemed to ask if she was sure she was ready to hear it. She nodded. "They could push for your dismissal."

Anger brought her out of her chair. "They can't do that."

"I told the Commissioner it would be over my dead body," McGregor said. "He suggested I reconsider."

"Oh, Christ." Sarah paced, beating one fist against her thigh. "The suits are going to leave me out in the cold."

"I haven't taken the Commissioner's advice yet."

It took a moment for his words to penetrate the whirling rampage in her mind. Then Sarah stopped and faced him. "You'd risk your job for me?"

"Before you get your ego out of joint." McGregor made a big show of rolling a pencil in his thick fingers. "I wouldn't be doing it just for you. I've got a whole department to look after."

Sarah slumped back in the chair, her panic treed for the moment. "Any advice for the poor unsuspecting lamb?"

"Just tell your story. And try to keep a handle on your anger."

"I take it that last bit comes straight from experience?"

McGregor nodded. "They're going to push. That's what they want. To get you mad and see what tumbles out. Don't give them the opportunity."

"No problem." Sarah tried to exude more confidence than she felt. "I'll treat them like a whole room full of Quinlins."

# CHAPTER ELEVEN

Neon glittered against the black backdrop of sky as Chad's lumbering, maroon Cadillac rolled in a slow crawl down the street. In the backseat, Angel was thankful for the steady hum of the air conditioner that kept the car a good twenty degrees cooler than the outside air, which still hung heavy with heat and humidity. The steady, cool breeze from the side vents made it to the back seat and nibbled around the neckline of her magenta silk shell. Still, tiny beads of perspiration dotted her face.

Chad didn't look nervous at all, one hand gripping the steering wheel and the other thrown casually across the back of the seat behind Sarah. If Angel were honest, she'd admit that part of her discomfort was due to the picture they presented. A pimp out with his girls, favoring the white one because that gives him more street cred.

The purist in Angel wanted to remind him that he was merely perpetuating the worst of black stereotypes. The Cadillac. The gold chains. The white woman. The insolent attitude.

"Shit."

Angel didn't realize she'd spoken aloud until she caught Chad's reflection eyeing her in the rearview mirror. "Yo, Mama. What you say?"

"Save your jive for the street." Angel's voice was as frosty as the air-conditioning. "There's nobody to impress in here."

Chad laughed, and it irritated Angel that he didn't even have the good sense to be insulted. She glanced back out the window, ignoring Sarah who'd turned to give her a puzzled look. *Honky bitch is probably enjoying the hell out of this, too.*

If Sarah had known what Angel was thinking, she might have laughed at the irony of it. She didn't have a clue what her partner was all riled up about. Dressing like a whore and driving around the mean streets wasn't her idea of a good time, but it was part of the job. Angel had better get used to it.

Sarah stifled a yawn and glanced at Chad. He looked like he could go all night, but despite the quick nap she'd grabbed before he picked her up, she could feel her reserves draining. She wasn't even sure if she could remember half the information he'd given them about the gangs operating in the areas they'd driven through for the past hour.

"It doesn't do for my women to look bored." Chad gave her a sidelong glance. "Spoils my image."

"Consider it an endorsement of how good business is. No time to sleep."

Chad laughed, and Sarah was glad that at least he was in a good mood. The stiff silence from the back seat was beginning to wear on her.

Pulling to the curb, Chad doused the lights, letting the engine idle in an uneven rumble. Then he nodded toward Danny's Bar & Grill across the street. "You were right about that bartender being nervous about something. But it wasn't the robbery."

"What was it?" Angel asked, leaning forward and resting her arms on the soft leather of the seat.

"There's a back room in there where certain business transactions have been known to take place," Chad said. "Our guess is that the robbery wasn't as straightforward as it looked. It could have been a message for Jamel."

"Jamel?" Sarah asked.

"The main man around these streets."

Sarah studied the endless parade of bars and restaurants lining both sides of the street. "But there aren't a lot of gangs in this area."

"No. Think of it as the suburbanization of the drug business. You don't have to live where you ply your trade."

"Okay. So if this Jamel controls this area, how did Jimmy get to 'ply his trade' here?"

"Just because Jimmy says he's small time, doesn't mean we have to believe him. He could be connected," Chad said.

"That's all very enlightening, but what does it have to do with our case?" Angel asked.

Angel's voice carried the same challenging tone she'd used earlier, and Sarah admired Chad's restraint. He leaned casually against the door so both women were in his line of vision. "Okay. Fact: The Asians are putting pressure on the locals. Fact: Anything goes in the intimidation game. Murder. Robbery. Whatever. It's not so unbelievable that the crimes could be related."

He paused as if giving them a moment to absorb what he said, then continued. "It's even possible that the open homicide on that kid in Oak Cliff could be connected. The one that went down the same night as Durham."

"Aw, come on." Sarah shook her head. "You can't just paste a gang-killing into the picture and put a nice tidy frame around it all."

"But it wasn't just another gang killing." Chad smiled, looking like the kid brother who finally pulled one on the elder and gotten away with it. "It couldn't have been."

"Why not?" Angel asked.

"Because there was a hush-hush gang summit going on that night."

"You're shitting us." Sarah couldn't hide her surprise.

"Nope." Chad paused, a glint of humor in his soft brown

eyes. "I found out from Hendricks this afternoon. The summit started at ten, and the cease-fire covered the whole night from eight o'clock on."

"What prompted you to talk to the head of the gang unit?" Angel asked.

"Just covering all possibilities. I'm not closed to the idea that the killings may not be drug related. I just want to make sure we don't overlook anything in our hurry to move on."

A car cruised past them, a pulsing rumble of bass straining the speakers and vibrating along the concrete. When the intrusion faded, Chad continued. "The best way to find out what these murders are about is by eliminating what they're not about."

Sarah considered his comment. He was right. They had to keep going after possibilities, probing, assessing, then throwing out what didn't fit. Eventually, only one possibility would be left. "I'd give anything to see that back room," she said, diverting her attention to the bar flashing its bright yellow beer sign over Chad's shoulder.

"We've got someone set up in there." Chad turned to face forward again. "It shouldn't be too long before he can tell us if there's any ethnic change in the people who go there for more than a good time."

Chad pushed the button to activate the lights and eased the big car into the flow of traffic. "Anyone besides me hungry?"

The question was met by silence, and Chad glanced at each of the women in turn. "Come on. I'll even let you buy if that'll make you feel better."

"I've, uh, got other plans." The stammer surprised Sarah as much as the lie.

Chad didn't seem affected by either. He caught Angel's eye in the rearview mirror. "What about you?"

Angel's first impulse was to decline. She'd be better off taking her sour mood home to see if it would improve by morning. But she was hungry, and the thought of a cheese sandwich held little appeal. "Only if we do drive-through," she finally said. "There's no way I'll go in someplace wearing this get-up."

Chad's easy laughter rang through the car, and Angel wondered if he was an impostor. No man could be that happy and still be black.

At home, Sarah shrugged out of the tight leather pants, her stomach sighing in relief. She tossed the pants across the ladder-back chair, one of the few pieces she'd taken from her grandmother's house. She could have had it all. There were no other family members to fight for their share. But when the old woman had died, Sarah had felt this great need to divest herself of things.

Not that she'd wanted to be rid of the memories. She'd always treasure the years they had spent together. But Sarah had known that it was time to move on to another place in her life and she'd wanted to travel light.

So she'd sold the house and taken only what she needed. One chair. The big double bed. And the tall, oak bureau with the tarnished brass pulls. Having them around, Sarah felt the comfort of a connection to the old woman who had given her the first taste of normalcy in her life.

Wearing only briefs and the body-molding tank top, Sarah padded into the cluttered bathroom, knowing that her grandmother would have had a lot to say about the mess. *What would she say about the mess you've made of your life?* Sarah pondered the question as she wiped the gaudy make-up with a warm, wet washcloth.

Picturing the old woman, wisps of gray hair pulled free from the twist anchored with shell combs, Sarah could almost hear her say, "Life is not what happens to you. It's what you make of what happens."

If only it were that simple, Sarah thought, dropping the cloth in the sink and heading toward the kitchen.

Cat, delighted at the company, wound his soft furry body around her legs, occasionally pausing to nip her bare ankles while she pulled a package of hot dogs out of the refrigerator. *Why not.*

She threw an extra hot dog into the pan for him. He deserved a treat after being alone all day and half the night.

Assembling the condiments on the narrow strip of counter beside the stove, Sarah wondered why she'd been so quick to pass up Chad's invitation. Right off she could eliminate any warning bell about the dangers of romantic entanglements within the department. If Chad had his sights set on a detective of the female persuasion, it wasn't her, although it didn't appear that he was having any luck with the object of his interest.

Sarah fished one steaming hot dog out of the pan and cut it in small pieces for the kitten. Then as an afterthought, she squirted a dab of ketchup on one of the bits of meat. Who wanted to eat a plain hot dog?

Setting the plate down on the floor, Sarah watched as Cat sniffed, then tentatively touched the ketchup with his little pink tongue. "Come on," she prompted. "It's pretty good stuff."

Cat took another hesitant taste, then nosed the contaminated piece of meat aside and settled back on his haunches to eat another piece.

Sarah recognized her preoccupation with the cat as one of her weak attempts to avoid thinking. As if by concentrating on the mundane, she could convince her mind that there wasn't anything important worth considering. But there was. And its name was Angel.

Declining to continue the evening had been motivated in part by the unease that Sarah felt around the woman. And it struck Sarah as odd that it only happened when they weren't focused on work, as if some unseen force was working to prevent them from ever overcoming the barrier to friendship.

The big question was where did the force emanate *from?* It would be easy to simply blame Angel, and the woman's behavior certainly offered plenty of evidence to uphold that theory. But Sarah wasn't fool enough to think any problem was singularly faceted.

Balancing the hot dog, a diet cola and a handful of carrot sticks she'd grabbed as her nod to nutrition, Sarah went into the living room. She put her food on a TV tray, then sank into the welcome comfort of her beat-up recliner, forcing herself to take an honest evaluation of her attitude. Did any of the difficulty with adjusting to a new partner have to do with the fact that she's black?

Sarah took a bite of her dinner, the tang of ketchup and mustard warm in her mouth, and let her mind chew on the question she'd just posed. Before tonight, she might have been able to answer "no" without a second thought. But now she wasn't so sure. A long-forgotten fragment from one of her college psych classes surfaced—something about everyone having some level of prejudice.

She took a slow swallow of the cool drink, trying to resurrect the rest of what the crusty old professor had told the class. "That prejudice, even if it's buried, will still surface when a person's safety or security is threatened." Or something like that.

Is that what Doc Murray meant when he had warned her about projecting her anger and guilt? "Killing someone is a terrible burden," he had said. "And you need someone to blame. You can't assign that to the kid anymore. He's dead. So you might start blaming a whole group of people."

Recalling his words with such clarity caused a tremor to pass through her body, and she suddenly found she wasn't hungry anymore. During their session she had dismissed Murray's words as so much psychobabble, but they weren't so easy to dismiss in the quiet solitude of introspection.

Frustrated at the endless loop of questions that had no easy answers, Sarah picked up the TV remote and pushed the power button. The sudden blare of a Bon Jovi video tried valiantly to drown the clamor in her mind, but some thoughts refused to succumb.

Not for the first time, she regretted never having made any close friends. She needed someone she could talk to when she was feeling like this, someone who would understand and offer generous doses of comfort and solace. Her grandmother had understood. Even when her advice was too naive. And John had understood. But there had never been anybody else.

Cat wandered into the living room and jumped into her lap. He studiously inspected her plate and her chin before sitting down to stare at her with wide, unblinking eyes. "Well, Cat. Do you want to hear about all my troubles?"

He responded with a deep, rumbling purr loud enough to compete with the latest offering from MTV.

# CHAPTER TWELVE

Angel pulled at the hem of the black mini-skirt and wished she'd taken the time to change before coming to the hospital. But fear had controlled her thinking.

Chad had dropped her off about midnight, and the blink of the message light on her answering machine hadn't been a big surprise. What sent her into a mental tailspin was the clipped message relayed by her father's voice. "There's been an accident. Your mother's at Presbyterian hospital."

*Oh, God! What happened? How long ago did he call? What if . . . ?*

No. Couldn't think that way. Mama had to be okay. And with that thought driving her, Angel had grabbed her car keys and raced to the hospital.

The hours dragged into an eternity as she sat with her father and LaVon waiting for some word. Other than her brother's weak attempt at humor, telling her she looked like a French whore and her asking how he knew what a French whore looked like, they had kept a silent vigil; a distant rustle of activity and the cloying aroma of sickness a constant reminder of why they were here.

Somewhere beyond the door that whooshed open at the press of a button, surgeons were trying to repair the damage inflicted by a drunk driver who'd run a stoplight. Angel clung precariously to a belief that they would be successful.

LaVon pulled himself off the padded chair and stretched.

"I'm going to get some coffee."

"Wait. I'll go with you." Angel jumped up, then looked at her father. "Daddy?"

"You two go on," Gilbert said. "I don't want to be missing the doctor."

Angel wasn't sure which part of the vigil hung the heaviest on her heart. Waiting to hear if her mother would live, or watching her father slump lower in the chair like a scarecrow that's slowly having its stuffing pulled out.

Turning away from the painful sight, Angel stepped into the comforting presence of her brother's arm around her waist. She leaned on his strength as they negotiated the maze of corridors to the vending machines. Despite their numerous, and sometimes volatile, childhood rivalries, they had grown up to be good friends, and Angel never considered blaming him for their father's favoritism. Perhaps because LaVon acknowledged its existence, and even challenged the old man in moments of daring.

"It'll be okay, Baby." LaVon gave her a gentle squeeze, and Angel wished she could be as certain of his reassurance as she used to be when he'd lavished it on a scraped knee. The knee had always healed.

"I don't know what Daddy's going to do if she . . . doesn't make it." Angel faltered over the words. She couldn't give voice to the fear that consumed her.

"Don't you say that." LaVon slapped quarters into the machine then gave it a resounding bang when it didn't immediately dispense his coffee. "She's not going to . . ."

Angel realized he couldn't say the word either. Saying it might make it happen.

Silently, LaVon handed her the Styrofoam container of coffee then poured another. They pulled out chairs at a small Formica table that was sticky with the residue of someone else's snack and sat down. LaVon took three packets of sugar and tore them open, creating a white, crystalline stream that flowed into his coffee.

"How can you continue to do that and not get fat?"

LaVon smiled, and Angel wondered if he found the same relief in mindless chitchat that she did. Watching him stir his coffee with a plastic spoon, she marveled at how handsome he was. Of course, every sister thinks that of her big brother, but Angel knew it went far beyond sisterly adoration. He'd done some modeling to bankroll his education, and numerous people had encouraged him to take his chiseled good looks to the movies.

Today he could have been an actor playing an attorney, complete with a costume right out of wardrobe; cream-colored casual pants, open-necked oxford shirt with narrow gold stripes, and a brown suede sport coat.

Angel hoped he was happier being the real thing. "How's the practice going?"

"Building slowly." LaVon pushed his wire-rimmed glasses up on his face.

"Maybe you should have taken that offer with the firm."

"And be the token black? No thank you."

"Maybe they wanted to hire you for your ability." Angel took a sip of her coffee and made a face as the bitter liquid slid down her throat. "It didn't have to be a quota."

"Right."

Angel leaned back and sighed. "You sound just like Daddy."

"Well, maybe he's right."

"I don't think so."

"Don't tell me you haven't wondered about your promotion?"

His words stung, like being blindsided by a bee, but Angel resisted the defensive reaction of swatting at the offender. "Of course we can make a case for 'tokenism' if we keep applying it to every situation."

Wadding up his napkin, LaVon wiped at the sprinkles of sugar that had missed his coffee cup. Noticing the tic of anger in his jaw, Angel wondered if the better part of wisdom would be to drop the whole subject, but she wanted to put her own conflicting thoughts to rest. Sometimes she hated the fact that she so often wondered about the motivation behind her advancement. She could easily hate the white establishment for the legacy of doubt and mistrust that had put her in that position, but she was trying real hard not to.

"So what has Daddy had to say about it?" Angel asked, demanding her brother's attention.

"About the promotion?" LaVon continued mopping at the table. "Nothing much."

"Then what has he been upset about?"

"This isn't the time—"

"Come on, LaVon."

"Okay." LaVon flashed her an angry look. "He doesn't think you should have accepted the partnership with that white woman."

Angel struggled to keep her anger from matching his. "Assignments aren't made on a democratic basis."

"He still thinks you should have filed a formal protest."

"Why?"

"She killed a black boy."

"Christ, LaVon. She killed a drug dealer. That's part of the job."

"Would you?"

The question caught Angel off guard and she faltered in an attempt to answer it. She honestly didn't know if she could shoot anyone, or whether she'd hesitate if that anyone were black.

Her firing instructor at the academy had reassured her that her doubts were normal. Most cops couldn't answer that question until they were forced to, and the majority of them prayed that the challenge would never be issued.

Angel also realized this was the first time she'd taken a stand on the issue of Sarah's motives. She'd avoided the question, would Sarah have acted differently had that kid been white?

LaVon leaned toward her. "Our boys don't need to be shot," he said. "They need to be helped."

"We're not social workers, LaVon. We're cops." Her simple statement stood like a windbreaker, halting their rollicking emotions, and the ensuing silence was like the calm after an avalanche. Angel wanted to ask him how he could still endorse such a limited viewpoint after all his education and experience, but they needed the calm right now.

Angel stood up and dropped her cup, still half full of coffee, into the trash container. "Come on. I want to get back."

A tall, angular man in bloodstained green scrubs stood in the surgery waiting room talking to Gilbert. Angel hurried to keep up with LaVon who lengthened his stride to close the distance.

The doctor turned to acknowledge their presence with a somber nod. "Your mother made it through the surgery," he said, his voice weary with the ordeal. "We've moved her to ICU."

"Then she's going to be all right." It was half-statement and half-question, and Angel looked from the grim face of the doctor to her father, then back again.

"She's still in very serious condition," the doctor said neutrally. "She has extensive chest and abdominal trauma. Several broken ribs and there was considerable internal bleeding. We had to remove her spleen and repair one of her lungs. If she makes it through the next twenty-four hours, her chances will improve dramatically."

Angel stepped closer to her father and looped her arm with

his, needing the reassurance of contact as much as she thought he might.

"Can we see her?" LaVon asked.

"Sure. Go over to the ICU waiting room. I'll have the nurse get you when they're ready."

It seemed like forever, but it was only a few minutes before a young nurse wearing scrubs came and said they could go into the ICU room.

Angel let her father and brother go in first, and her breath caught in her throat when she saw her mother. When had she grown so old? The skin on her face, normally so firm and glowing with life, hung flaccid, allowing bones to protrude and create a virtual stranger. This wasn't the same woman who'd been mistaken for her sister at the academy graduation.

Moving her gaze from her mother's face, Angel followed the trail of tubes and wires hooked to IV bags and various monitors which measured the strength of the life left in her mother's battered body. Against the low hum of the other machines, the soft whisper of the ventilator dominated, a living thing breathing life into the motionless form. Angel glanced at her father who stood mute at the foot of the bed and wondered if he would muster the courage to step closer.

A ragged sob caught her attention, and she looked at LaVon who stood at the other side of the bed, clinging to their mother's hand. Tears coursed down his cheeks, and Angel averted her gaze. His visible anguish made the possibility they'd been avoiding all too real.

Gently touching her mother's clammy forehead, Angel leaned close and whispered. "It's going to be all right, Mama."

She held that declaration like a shield against the fear that followed her home, but it was harder to believe in a dark and sleepless night.

★ ★ ★ ★ ★

Standing in the warmth of early morning sunlight, Sarah hesitated before pushing the doorbell on the little frame house in the old residential neighborhood just off Henderson. It matched the home address on Angel's personnel file. Before driving over, Sarah had spent a half an hour debating the wisdom of the action. What if Angel didn't want her here?

Silence followed the peal of the doorbell, and Sarah listened for some rustle of movement behind the closed door, while another wave of doubt washed over her. If Angel had been at the hospital most of the night, maybe she wouldn't appreciate being disturbed.

Finally, Sarah heard the click of locks being disengaged, then the inner door opened, and Angel's gaunt face peered through the screen. The sight of the woman's tousled hair and blue terry-cloth robe increased Sarah's misgivings. "Did I wake you?"

"No. I was up."

"McGregor gave me the news." Sarah shifted her weight from one foot to the other, the movement raising a soft squeak from old planks of wood beneath her feet. "Is she okay?"

"They're still being cautious about the prognosis."

Sarah wondered if Angel was purposely reducing her fears to clinical language as she continued, "There's been little change since last night. But at least she hasn't deteriorated."

"That's good." The reassurance stumbled lamely into an awkward silence.

The harsh bark of a neighborhood dog broke the stalemate, and Sarah watched Angel look around like a sleepwalker suddenly awakening to reality. Then her partner's gaze focused on the bag clutched in Sarah's hands. "What's that?"

"Breakfast." Another uncertainty gripped her. "Hope you're not a health-food nut."

Angel's eyes traveled back up to meet hers. "Are you kidding? I'm a cop."

Sarah returned Angel's feeble smile and felt her taut nerves relax. "Can I come in?"

Angel pushed the storm door open, and Sarah stepped directly into a living room cluttered with life. Books, magazines, and newspapers mingled with discarded clothing on every available space. An empty pizza box balanced precariously on the edge of the coffee table. Looked a lot like her place.

Following Angel's lead through the room, Sarah found the respite from the glare of the morning sun a relief. She assumed the drapes were kept closed to conserve the meager output from a small window air-conditioner struggling against the summer heat.

The pungent aroma of freshly brewed caffeine welcomed Sarah to the kitchen.

"Want some coffee?" Angel asked, clearing a stack of old newspapers off the small wooden dinette table.

"Yeah, sure." Sarah put the bag of donuts on the table, then sat down, noting that the kitchen boasted little in the way of homey touches. The room was functional, offering all the essentials, but the window was unadorned and only dirty dishes decorated the counters. Briefly, she wondered if that meant Angel shared her aversion to things domestic.

After pouring the rich, brown liquid into two white mugs, Angel carried them to the table and sank into a chair opposite Sarah. Steam drifted up from the mug, dancing lazily in the air, then dissipating when it reached the level of Angel's unreadable expression.

Sarah suddenly found herself wondering what to do with her hands, her eyes, her mouth. The coffee was too hot to drink. She didn't have a cigarette to fiddle with. And anything she could think of to say sounded too inane. She decided to say nothing, offering Angel a donut instead.

"Mmmm," Angel said. "The dunkers are my favorite."

"Mine, too."

Sarah realized she might have overplayed her enthusiasm when Angel gave her a wry grin. "It's going to take more than that to make us soul-mates."

Angel finished her first donut, then reached for another. "You were the last person on earth I expected to see on my doorstep this morning."

Taking a sip of her coffee, Sarah studied her partner over the rim of her mug. "Something told me you might need sustenance."

Angel chuckled, wiping crumbs from her chin. "I'm glad you listened."

Sarah watched the merriment suddenly drain from Angel's face, as if she found the laughter unsuitable for the moment. The anguish that replaced it cast a pall over the entire room.

"I don't know what to say." Sarah touched the other woman's hand in an awkward gesture. "The dumbest things pop into my head. 'This must be terrible.' Like you need me to tell you that."

Brushing a tear from her cheek, Angel stared out the window. "You never realize how much they mean to you until something like this happens."

"I know."

Angel glanced quickly at Sarah. "Sounds like that's more than just a polite response."

Sarah shrugged. "Don't need to bore you with the saga of my tragic life."

"Why not. It'll help keep my mind off of mine."

Sarah swirled the dregs of coffee in the bottom of her cup, deferring her decision to confide or not.

"Help yourself to more," Angel said. "I'm too tired to play hostess."

Rising, Sarah took both cups and refilled them, then returned to the table. "My mother died when I was twelve."

Sarah appeared as surprised as she was that the words had slipped out, and Angel blurted the first thing that came to mind. "I'm sorry."

"No big deal, you know. Shit happens."

Angel could sense the depth of the hurt behind the flip comment. "I think it's probably always a big deal," she said softly. "Whether we can say it out loud or not."

"You're right." Sarah let a long breath out. "And I shouldn't be so insensitive to what's going on with you."

"You're not. I'm the one who started this whole line of conversation. Remember?" Angel held Sarah's gaze until she gave a brief nod of assent, then asked, "What about your father?"

Angel watched her partner struggle with the answer and almost regretted opening the subject up.

"Ran off the following year," Sarah finally said. "Left me with my Grandma."

A heavy, empty silence followed, and Angel could feel Sarah's hurt reach across the table and touch her. "Did you have any brothers or sisters?"

"No." Sarah took a deep ragged breath. "My mother had her first bout with cancer not long after I was born."

Pain commanded the moment, and Angel controlled her curiosity with an effort. The detective in her wanted to know more, but some instinct told her this was as far as Sarah could go right now.

"What about your family?" Sarah asked, confirming Angel's hunch.

"We're so typically middle class it's almost a joke." She took a swallow of coffee. "Up to and including the boy for him and the girl for her."

"That's nice."

The sincerity holding up the words made Angel realize how right Sarah was. It was nice to have a family, even if they weren't perfect.

"Guess I'd better get back to work," Sarah said, pushing her chair back with a loud scrape across the tile. "What would people think if they found out that I was eating donuts on company time?"

Angel smiled. "I'll be in a little later."

"You probably shouldn't."

"There are lots of things I shouldn't do."

Sarah nodded, and Angel knew she understood. Rising, Angel dusted the donut crumbs off the draped collar of her robe, then walked Sarah to the front door. "I, uh, appreciate your visit," Angel found the sentiment difficult to express. "It was nice."

Sarah nodded again, then turned and walked through the warm sunshine to her car. Watching, Angel wondered about the odd twists and turns of her partner's visit. It was a thoughtfulness she never expected and perhaps didn't deserve. Had Sarah come out of a sense of politeness? Duty? Or was there something else?

Turning to go back into the house, another thought stopped Angel. This was the first time a white person had ever been in her house. Funny. For a little while she'd forgotten Sarah wasn't black.

# Chapter Thirteen

Bianca drummed impatient, red-lacquered fingernails on the table while Jerry forwarded through the rough footage of her last story, explaining where he was planning to edit it and why. She didn't really care. If the guy wanted to play Stephen Spielberg over two minutes of tape highlighting the dispute between an old man and the housing authority that wanted to move him out of the right-of-way for the 191 Loop, he could just have at it.

It was hot and stuffy in the little editing room, and every time Jerry spoke, Bianca wondered if he'd had anything for dinner besides onions. Desperate to escape the sour aroma, she told him whatever he decided was fine and made a hasty exit.

Her current story was a disappointment after the excitement of her last one, and she'd rankled with irritation when Kurt had assigned her to it. She wanted to be available in case something broke on the murders, not stuck on some nothing story that any rookie could handle. Kurt's response had been a cold glare followed by the suggestion that if she didn't like the way things were run here, she could always go back to the little station in Lubbock.

Knowing when to give up the fight, Bianca had gone out with a small crew and taped the interview with the old man. She played for the tears and sympathy, guiding him through a faltering saga of the family he had raised there. A mention of the pets buried in the backyard had been an especially poignant touch, and despite her initial reluctance to do the story, the result pleased her.

Now that she was finished, she could still salvage a little bit of Saturday night. She'd drop by her apartment and trade her suit and high heels for her hip-hugging white denim pants and that spectacular new navy-and-cream western shirt. That ought to turn some heads at Cowboys & Cadillacs.

Eagerly heading down the hall toward the exit, she groaned when she heard her name called. She turned to see Merle, one of the producers, waving to her. "You got a phone call."

Bianca sighed and retraced her steps down the hall as far as the newsroom where the studio crew was already setting up for the late broadcast. She picked her way through the maze of cables leading to the cameras that were positioned to cover the anchor desk on three angles, and dodged the young girl scurrying purposely with a clipboard in hand.

Finally making it to the phone on the back wall, Bianca grabbed the receiver Merle had left to gently sway at the end of the short cord that attached it to the base. "Hello?"

At first she could hear nothing over the murmur of voices in the room directing light and sound checks. Then a man's voice came softly through the receiver. "Miss Gomaz?"

"Yes."

"You've got to let them know."

Bianca sighed. It was another one of those calls, the ones that could take five minutes to figure out if it was a prank or not. "Let who know what?"

"You didn't say anything about my message."

The voice was slow and deliberate and something struggled in Bianca's subconscious for recognition. Whoever had called Kurt the other night had spoken the same way. Could it be . . . ?

A surge of anticipation hit her and she turned away from the hum of activity in the room. "What message?"

"That's why I called. You were supposed to tell them why. But you didn't."

Bianca reined in her racing thoughts, forcing herself to concentrate on one step at a time. "How was I to get this message?"

"It was there."

"Where?" She scrambled to follow the disconnected thoughts. "At that parking garage?"

"Yes."

"But the police didn't release any information about a message."

"They wouldn't," the voice said in quiet resignation. "They don't really care about justice."

Bianca took a moment to absorb the implication of his statement. "Are you . . . ?" She could hardly bring herself to ask the question she knew she must. "Did you kill that man?"

Silence.

"Both of them?"

More silence.

"How can I help you if you don't give me the information I need?"

"Just tell them."

The connection broke abruptly, and Bianca listened to the dial tone buzz in her ear as she stilled her racing heart. This was incredible. It had to have been the guy who called the other day. And he wouldn't have called again unless he was the doer. And he was hers. All hers.

Replacing the receiver with a trembling hand, Bianca checked her watch. Almost nine. She could do it. The story would write itself. Fifteen minutes tops. And she was still dressed from the interview. Make-up could fix her face in ten minutes and she'd be camera ready.

Certainly Kurt couldn't refuse to give her a spot. This was the hottest exclusive they'd gotten since that minister tried to off his wife. And if she slanted the story just right, they could stretch it for several days of the "latest breaking news on the Mall Murders."

Bianca's heart raced as she considered the possibilities this story could create. Move over Diane Sawyer. Smiling, she turned and called out to the harried producer. "Merle. Where's Kurt?"

"What am I? His keeper? Check his office."

Bianca stepped quickly over the snakes of cable and hurried toward Kurt's office. Visions of all the fantasies that would come to life filled her mind, and not one of them included calling the police.

Sarah nosed her Honda behind a shimmering midnight-blue Jaguar and hoped the young valet attendant wouldn't direct her to the back lot for employees. She should have let Paul pick her up. As a successful accountant, at least she assumed he was successful, he probably drove something more acceptable to uptown dining.

If the dark-haired attendant had an opinion, he kept it hidden behind a professional demeanor that included the required dazzling smile and a friendly, easy attitude designed to make her feel special.

It didn't work. Awkwardness engulfed her as she slid from the car and immediately stumbled on the spike heels she wore so infrequently. The young man steadied her with a firm hand on her elbow without losing his poise.

Gathering the shreds of her dignity, Sarah tugged at the skirt of her all-purpose black sheath dress, then firmly told herself to stop fiddling and go in the damn door already.

The Mansion on Turtle Creek was just that, a mansion, and

Sarah felt like she was stepping into another world when the door closed with a mere whisper of sound. Of course it would be quiet. Everything was quiet and dignified and refined, from the liveried staff to the fresh flowers polite enough to emit only the gentlest of fragrances.

Paul stood alone, slightly to one side of the center of the entryway, and Sarah admired the confidence that held him in place. She would have sought the security of melting into the fringes of other small groups clustered closer to the walls.

He strode forward to greet her. "You look stunning."

"Thank you." Sarah noticed a couple of other men giving her appreciative looks, and she was glad she had taken extra time with her hair. Tonight it touched her shoulders in a soft, blonde wave.

She also noticed that Paul hadn't escaped the attention of the women who openly stared at him. In a custom denim jacket with soft, gray-suede inlays cutting across broad shoulders to splay down the front, he looked less like an accountant and more like a rodeo star. The black leather cord holding the exquisite gold and silver bolo served as the required tie.

"When you said you'd spring for dinner, I didn't expect this," Sarah whispered. "You could have gotten away with a sit-down at McDonalds and made me happy."

Her remark garnered a smile, and she felt some of her nervousness slip away.

A thin, smooth maitre d' led them to a table for two in a small alcove that was open to one of the larger dining rooms. "Is this satisfactory, Sir?"

"It'll do nicely."

Sarah managed the seating process with more grace than the parking, and after the maitre d' moved on, she leaned over the table. "You take special classes to talk like that?"

"Like what?"

"All the formality. It's like dialogue out of a classic 40's movie."

"Lest I come across as a snobbish bore," Paul said in a perfect British clip. "Let me assure you that the role is only played in the most posh establishments."

Amusement lingered in his eyes, which had darkened almost to navy in the dim lighting, and Sarah realized she could learn to like this man a lot. The thought scared her, and she unconsciously fingered the rich linen tablecloth.

"Did I overplay the part?" A shadow of concern crossed his face. "My drama teacher always warned me about emoting."

"No." Sarah didn't have to force the smile. "It was just an errant thought. I've chased it away."

"Good." Paul picked up the wine list. "Would you be offended if I made the choice?"

"Please do."

After the wine ritual was completed and a crystal goblet of shrimp cocktail served, Sarah realized this was the first real date she'd been on in a couple of months. It felt incredibly good to enter another world of fun and laughter and pretend for once that life could be a fairy tale.

They stalled the eventual end of dinner as long as they could. The waiter was far too tactful to make an overt gesture to encourage them to leave, but the subtle message rang clear in longer intervals between offering to refill their coffee cups.

Despite how confident he had appeared at first, Sarah noted an edge of nervousness about Paul now. She watched him swirl the deep amber liquid coating the bottom of the brandy snifter and wondered what had broken the spell that had hovered over dinner. The current silence wasn't as companionable as other moments had been.

Abruptly he looked up at her and his smile put her fears to rest. "Would you like to go for a drive?"

"Sure."

His suggestion that she drive so she'd have more control of the situation, though said half in jest, touched her, and she was only momentarily concerned about what he might think of the state of her trusty little Honda. Either he was going to accept her the way she was, or not at all.

His second request was equally touching. "Take me to your favorite place in the city."

"Seriously?"

"Yeah." He folded his tall frame into the passenger seat and fastened the seatbelt.

Twenty minutes later when she pulled into a downtown parking garage, he turned to her with a whimsical smile. "I guess it must be the novelty of having your choice of parking spots that holds the great attraction."

Sarah laughed and fished in the backseat for her extra pair of running shoes. She slipped out of her heels and put her relieved feet into the other shoes. After tying them, she opened her door, then looked at Paul, not giving it a second thought about how she looked wearing the dress with tennis shoes. "Well, come on."

They walked several blocks down Ervay, and Paul wondered if she was taking him to the underground mall. She didn't seem like the shopper type, but his first impressions had been wrong before. Then, instead of turning to go to the mall entrance, she led him across the street to the last place he would have expected, Thanksgiving Square.

Walking down the terraced stairs, the soothing rush of water that was cascading down a brick incline muted the sounds of traffic. It was like entering an oasis. Paul followed Sarah to one of the low cement walls bordering a flower bed.

She sat down, then flashed a smile. "It's a little odd, I know. But sometimes I like to remind myself that some tranquility actually exists in this city."

Paul shrugged out of his jacket and lowered himself on the wall next to her. The quiet was comfortable as they watched the water spill over the bricks and splash into a pool. A light spray of mist cooled the night air, and the black sky was sprinkled liberally with pale stars dueling with the downtown lights.

Sarah leaned back with a deep sigh, and Paul glanced at her.

"Is there something in particular you're trying to forget?" Sarah stayed quiet for such a long time, he prompted her. "I read more of the newspaper than the financial section."

"Monday I appear before the Review Board."

He put an arm around her, drawing her into the hollow of his shoulder. "How they can think you actually wanted to shoot that kid is beyond me. It takes a particularly sick mind to *want* to kill anybody."

Sarah welcomed the comfort of his words and his nearness, very aware of the firm muscle of his chest beneath her cheek. She also became aware of the light touch of his fingertips tracing the ridge of her collarbone to her shoulder and back again. It seemed a random pattern at first, but then she heard the beat of his heart increase in tempo. She moved her head to look up at him.

Without speaking, Paul lowered his lips to hers and her body heard the silent question being posed. Her lips answered without consulting her mind, and after a few feverish moments, she pulled away. "We could get arrested for that."

Paul smiled and brushed a tangle of hair off her cheek, tucking it behind her ear. "We could change the setting."

His tone carried no hint of urgency or pressure, but she saw the passion still smoldering in his eyes. It was so tempting. It had been far too long since she'd been with a man who created such electric excitement, and her body urged her to accept his invitation. But something about this unbelievable man made her curb her raging desire.

As if unsure of what was holding her back, Paul smiled play-fully. "What? Do you find the prospect that horrifying?"

"No." Sarah shook her head. "On the contrary. The prospect is more tempting than you can imagine."

"Maybe not." Paul gestured to the erection that was straining against his jeans.

"You just have the advantage of being able to show off."

Laughter lowered the temperature, and Sarah gave him a thoughtful look. "There's nothing I'd like more than a night of glorious sex with you. And I have no doubt it would be."

When she faltered into another silence, Paul voiced the unspoken word, "But?"

"That would be too casual. Like a great dessert, eaten and then forgotten." She hesitated again, picking her words care-fully. "I think what's trying to happen between us might want to last longer."

Paul averted his gaze, and Sarah wondered if she'd gone too far. She reached up and touched the smooth plane of his cheek, then let her fingers slide into the faint stubble of beard on his jaw.

"One of the drawbacks to no worries about going bald is hav-ing to shave two or three times a day," Paul said.

"You could always let it grow."

Paul gave her a quick smile. "People seem to like their ac-countants clean-shaven."

"So? Dare to be different."

Paul quickly glanced away. "Sometimes I'm not a very daring person."

Watching a leafy shadow move slowly across his profile, Sarah sensed some kind of internal struggle taking place within Paul. The question of what could be causing the struggle stirred her curiosity, but she decided to wait the silence out. It would be fruitless to try to construct reasons for someone she knew so little about.

"It's probably a professional hazard," he finally said. "But I'm more comfortable with slow and methodical."

"We could do that."

He turned and looked at her for such a long time that she wondered if she had scared him off. Then a slow smile crawled across his face. "Yes," he said. "I guess we could."

The blare of the theme music for the ten o'clock news finally roused Angel from her prone position on the lumpy sofa. She rubbed a weary hand over her face, one cheek still numb from resting on the arm where the stuffing barely camouflaged the heavy wood frame. In that brief moment of disorientation, she tried to remember the hours between the eight o'clock visitation at the hospital and now.

When she'd come home, she'd only intended to sit down for a moment before taking a shower then deciding which she needed more, food or sleep. Obviously, the decision had been taken out of her hands, but she still needed the shower. More urgently, she needed to rid her mouth of the sour taste of sleep.

Standing, Angel stretched, then headed toward the bathroom until a smooth, male voice from the TV commanded, "Stay tuned for an exclusive Channel 9 special report on the Mall Murders."

She turned back to see the familiar face of the news anchor looking most sober and serious as he continued the teaser, "Shortly before nine o'clock tonight, this station was contacted by a person claiming responsibility for the Mall Murders. We will hear more details from Bianca Gomaz after this commercial break."

Angel watched the reporter's eager face fill the screen before the broadcast faded to a thirty-second spot promoting the benefits of letting Merrill Lynch plan her future financial security.

What the hell? Angel sank back on the sofa, only half aware of searching in her jacket pocket for the mint she'd picked up in the hospital earlier. It wasn't as good as toothpaste, but there was no way she was going to risk missing a single word of what Ms. Gomaz had to say.

Angel wasn't sure, but it might have been the frustration of waiting that made the ensuing commercials more boring than usual. Finally, the reporter's image returned to the screen, and she related the story with a breathless intensity.

The carefully worded reference to the phone call that could have originated with the killer titillated more than it informed, and even the mention of the "message" was more bothersome than troubling. It was the veiled insinuation that the police were disregarding the safety of the citizens by withholding important information that sparked Angel's anger.

"That stupid bitch." Angel rose abruptly and smashed the power button on the TV, casting the room into darkness and silence. Both were a welcome relief. Then she stormed into the bathroom where she brushed her teeth furiously, trying to think beyond her emotions.

There was no telling how much shit this was going to stir within the departmental hierarchy, and she had no delusions about where most of that shit would land.

Rinsing a washcloth in warm water, Angel held it against the faint throb of a headache.

# CHAPTER FOURTEEN

Sarah banged on her alarm clock several times and still the shrill ringing didn't stop. Then she woke up enough to recognize that the unwelcome blare of noise came from the phone. Fumbling the receiver to her ear, she managed a sleepy hello.

"What the hell are you doing asleep?"

Her bedside clock read just after eight, and Sarah considered asking the lieutenant what had crawled up his ass and died. This was her day off and if she wanted to sleep in, who was he to jump all over her? But then she realized that only something dire could create this monster yelling in her ear.

"What's wrong?" She sat up to better ignore the soft pillow beckoning to her.

"Didn't you watch the news last night?"

"No." A hollow feeling settled in her stomach.

"Our favorite reporter took a few whacks at the hornets' nest and the ones with the biggest stingers are swarming around me."

All thought of sleep chased away, Sarah listened while McGregor hit the high points of the broadcast, ending with, "The Commissioner's already called me. Twice. He wants containment."

She had to stifle an impulse to laugh and resort to worn-out clichés. In his present mood, there was no telling how the Lieutenant would react. The fact that the Commissioner had broken the chain of command and gone directly to McGregor strongly indicated the amount of pressure he must be feeling.

"First thing you've got to do is forget about your day off," McGregor continued. "Then get your ass down here as quick as you can. Price is going to be here at nine to see what can be salvaged press-wise."

Great, she thought, hanging up after the Lieutenant's abrupt disconnect, the PR's going to kill us.

Sarah took the quickest shower in history then pulled on her favorite uniform of jeans and a T-shirt. Price would probably have something to say about her lack of professional appearance, his rationale being that one never knew when the media would catch them, but she didn't really give a good goddam.

Thankful that Cat didn't need a walk like a dog would, Sarah reminded him where his litter box was and gave him fresh water and food before she left. On the way out, she grabbed the rolled-up bundle of the *Dallas Herald* on her doorstep. Since the paper was owned by the same parent company as the TV station, she was sure the story would be repeated in all its vivid detail.

Steering through the light traffic with one hand, Sarah dumped the paper out of its plastic bag. It fell open on the seat to reveal the headline: POLICE SUPPRESS CRUCIAL INFORMATION. She stopped at a red light and managed to read a little more. The sub-head posed the same question the Lieutenant had told her was raised in the newscast the night before: "Is Your Safety Being Compromised?"

A horn honked behind her, and Sarah looked up to see the light had turned green. Punishing her Honda, she floored the accelerator and tore away from the intersection on screaming tires. *How in the hell are we supposed to do our jobs when we have to put up with shit like this?*

Her mood didn't improve when she walked into the conference room to see Price seated across from Angel and Chad.

Price was ten minutes early, and that blew any opportunity they might have had to plan any strategy without him.

As expected, Price gave Sarah a disdainful glance during his less-than-enthusiastic greeting, and she noted with wry amusement that Chad and Angel had both dressed for Price. At least that's what Sarah assumed, not seeing a piece of denim between them. Even the Lieutenant kept his coat and tie on as he paced behind the chair at the head of the table.

"Since we're all here, I suggest we get down to it." Price opened a folder and slid single sheets of typed paper across the table to each of them. "I've already outlined the main areas of concern that we need to address."

Sarah glanced longingly at the full coffeepot on a small portable cart in the corner, catching the Lieutenant in the sweep of her eyes. He didn't look too happy about Mr. Kiss-the-media's-ass acting like he controlled every crevice of the department. She let her expression tell the Lieutenant she understood, then turned back to Price. "How about a fresh cup of coffee first?"

"I don't drink the stuff." Price masked any negative reaction to her interruption with what she supposed was his best effort at a smile.

"But I do." Sarah rose and strode over to the coffeepot where she paused and looked back at the group. "Anyone else?"

Nobody took her up on the offer.

When she returned to the conference table, cup in hand, she could tell that Price was still working hard to maintain his smile. She returned his effort and sat down. "Now, where were we?"

Sarah noted with pleasure that this time McGregor didn't hide his amusement as he settled his restless body into the chair. "We should consider the points with which Mr. Price has so thoughtfully provided us."

"The main issue to be addressed has to do with the messages

and why they were withheld," Price said.

Sarah had to grudgingly admit that he was good. Nothing in his manner acknowledged the shift in control, and he continued as if the script hadn't been rewritten. "The public has to be assured that there was no intent to place anyone in danger as has been implied."

"It wouldn't be an issue if the media hadn't made it one," Angel said.

McGregor motioned for her to be quiet. "We can't just start releasing statements without thinking this through." He turned to Price. "We give information about the messages, we'll have every nut case in five counties doing copycats. Then we'll never solve anything."

"What do you suggest, Lieutenant?"

"Number one: it's a big mistake to have a press conference." McGregor poked a pudgy thumb at one of the items on Price's sheet of suggestions. "We shouldn't even release any information. Give them nothing to report."

"And you don't think our silence on the matter will raise the concerns of the public?"

"Not if you do your job right," McGregor said. "You know we're not in the habit of giving out details of on-going investigations. There are inoffensive ways of saying that."

The barb in McGregor's words found its mark, and Sarah enjoyed watching Price squirm. Then she glanced at Angel and Chad, who were likewise smiling.

"What do you think, Detective?"

She didn't realize Price's question was aimed at her until Angel cued her with a nod.

Sarah met Price's gaze, wondering if he really wanted her opinion or if his solicitation was just an effort to cover his ass, his way of letting the brass know he'd made every effort to get the detectives to see reason. After just a moment, she decided it didn't matter. "I agree with the Lieutenant," she said. "It'll cripple our case to release details."

"You seem to have forgotten about Full Disclosure."

"We should give some other jerk-off a blueprint for murder?"

"That isn't what I'm suggesting."

"There's another point I think we should consider here," Angel said. "The only advantage we have is the fact that only the police and the killer know the details of the messages. If we toss out that advantage, we might as well toss out our shields."

"That's not going to satisfy the Commissioner," Price said.

"Maybe he'll have to lower his expectations," Chad offered.

"That's not your call, Detective."

"If I can be so bold," McGregor said. "It is our call."

Price's lips became a thin, tight line.

"And in case you're wondering," McGregor continued. "I have no plans to change what we're doing here."

Price shot the Lieutenant a meaningful look. "I'll pass that on to the Commissioner."

"I'd be disappointed if you didn't," McGregor said.

Watching them reminded Sarah of the old kids' game of dare, double-dare, and it pleased her to see Price back down first. He quickly gathered his materials, the soft rustle of paper the only sound in the room. Then he pushed his chair aside and stood up. He paused for a moment, as if trying to formulate some great parting shot, but finally just pursed his lips and strode toward the door.

Sarah smiled at the incongruity of a speechless PR guy.

After the door slammed behind Price, McGregor turned to her. "Wipe that damn grin off your face and go out and catch me a killer."

"Is overtime authorized?" she asked.

"It will be by the time you turn in your time sheets."

★ ★ ★ ★ ★

Chad and Angel pulled empty chairs to the edge of Sarah's desk and sat down. The files, which had grown thicker over the past week as full medical and forensic reports came in on the two murders, were open on top of the accumulated clutter. Sarah handed sections of the Halsley file to the other detectives and pulled the autopsy report. She read the first page, trying not to let the tedium that comprised ninety percent of the job get to her.

She knew that in any one of the popular TV shows, the Lieutenant's directive would have sent the detectives out to engineer some kind of visually spectacular breakthrough on the streets. Reality brought them to the boring routine of reading and re-reading the reports and re-interviewing witnesses until something unusual jumped out.

The pretend way looked like a lot more fun.

She sighed and thumbed through the pages, scanning the information to see if anything was different from the preliminary medical determination.

A few minutes later, a notation at the end of the autopsy report caught her attention. "The medical evidence does not support the original TOD estimation of after twenty-four-hundred hours," Walt had carefully written on the bottom of the last page.

Why the hell didn't you call and tell me, Sarah thought, then immediately quelled her irritation. With a record number of homicides in the city, the man was probably swimming in dead bodies. It wasn't fair of her to expect him to have the time to make her job easier.

"What do you make of this?" Sarah tossed the report across to Angel.

"Medical reports have less reason to lie than someone trying to protect their job," Angel said after a few minutes. "But if it only marginally changes the time of death, it probably won't have much impact on the overall investigation."

"But I don't like holes in my cases. Not even little ones." Sarah turned to Chad. "Why don't you track the rent-a-cop down and check his story. Angel and I will see what the sound-man has been able to do with that tape."

At the studios at Las Colinas, Sarah and Angel found Greg Folsom in the post-production area that housed the sound and film editing equipment. It was where most anybody could find him God knows how many hours, seven days a week.

A wizard with a mixer, Greg handled most of the multi-track mix-downs for film and video production, and on occasion, he also contracted his services for the DPD. He'd once told Sarah it was his way of carrying his childhood fascination with "cops and robbers" into adulthood.

Today, his long black hair was pulled back in a ponytail, the tip of which brushed a well-muscled shoulder, bare beyond the narrow white stripe of his tank top. A headset covered his ears. He jumped when Sarah touched him, then held up a finger to indicate he'd be with them shortly. Sarah watched, fascinated, as reels of tape slowly unwound like celluloid snakes crawling through the intricate array of machines.

A low, steady hum followed the thin brown strips on their journey.

Greg pushed a button that halted the tapes, then pushed another button that made them backtrack. Apparently successful in his search, he halted the machine again. After making a notation on a clipboard, he took off the headset and faced the women.

"You sleep here, too?" Sarah asked with a smile.

"I've been known to." Greg's return smile included Angel. "I suppose you're here about the tape."

"Were you able to work on it?" Sarah asked.

"Yeah. Let me show you what I got." He rolled his chair to another machine that resembled a super-sized tape deck and inserted a cassette. "It's not much, but I put everything on separate tracks."

Greg activated the tape player and resumed his monologue, "Here we have some street sounds," he paused so the detectives could hear the hum of tires on asphalt, diesel acceleration, and a horn honking. "Because the volume's so low, I'm guessing the caller wasn't outside. But he was somewhere near a pretty busy street.

"The only other thing I was able to pull out was some fragments of music." He paused again while a faint cacophony of disconnected notes filled the room. "I've really got the volume boosted for this. Otherwise you couldn't hear it. On the original, it's practically drowned by the other sounds."

"Do you have any idea of the source?" Angel asked.

Greg shook his head. "There's just not enough to be sure. My first thought was that it was an organ. But it could just as easily be an accordion. The caller could have been near one of those Czech bars."

"What about the voice?" Sarah asked. "Anything you can tell us on that?"

Greg started the tape again, and they listened to the soft voice suggest that the television people might want to go to the parking garage at Prestonwood Mall. No matter how many times she'd listened to it, Sarah was still surprised to feel a chill every time she heard the well-modulated voice. It was more suited to delivering ad-lines for radio than directions to a murder scene.

"I'm going to have to do a lot of guessing on this, too," Greg said after the taped voice faded into silence. "The only thing I know for sure is that it is definitely a male. And I don't think he was making a great effort to disguise his normal speaking voice.

There were no discrepancies in letter sounds that you would normally find with someone trying to do that."

"What kind of discrepancies do you mean?" Angel asked.

"When you're just talking, there's a consistency in how you pronounce your words. For instance, all As would sound the same. When people try to change their voice, they lose that consistency. You wouldn't notice just listening, but we've got a machine that can show you if you're interested."

"I don't think so," Angel said. "We can take your word for it."

"Really appreciate your help." Sarah took the cassette Greg held out to her.

"No problem." He grinned. "The city will get my bill."

The women started to leave, and Greg called out, "Hey, is that guy the doer?"

Sarah turned back. "You know better than to ask me that."

"Damn!"

Stepping out of the air-conditioned building was like walking into a smelting chamber and the heat took Sarah's breath away. "God, it's got to be a hundred and ten degrees out here."

"Actually, it's only hundred and five," Angel said.

"Big fucking difference."

"Now what do we do?" Angel asked as they walked across the parking lot where the blazing sun created a hazy mirage on the concrete.

"Get this car running, blast out the air-conditioning, then go get something to eat." Sarah opened the car door. "How does fast food grab you?"

"Just so it's not a hamburger." Angel held her door open so some of the interior heat could escape. "I'd rather clog my arteries with something I enjoy."

"Mexican?" Sarah slid into her seat and rumbled the engine to life. Then she glanced at Angel, who nodded.

Sarah pointed the car east where the Dallas skyline rose above the flat horizon, stretching into the sky with fingers of steel, concrete, and glass. A couple of miles down I-35 she spotted a strip-mall boasting a Taco Bell sign and pulled off the highway.

After easing into a parking spot partially shaded by a tree, Sarah cut the engine, and the women hurried into the cool interior of the restaurant. Sarah was relieved to find it only sparsely populated with customers. A slightly sour aroma, unique to Mexican cooking, permeated the air, and she marveled at how something that smelled so bad could taste so good. Thank God sour cream and guacamole rested easier on the palate than the nose.

"How's your mother doing?" Sarah asked when they were settled in a booth, an array of tacos and burritos spread on the table between them.

"Still holding her own." Angel set her taco down and gazed out the large plate-glass window.

Sarah took a long, welcome swallow of her iced tea, noting the quiet, pensive mood that had claimed her partner. Now she understood where those periods of disconnectedness had come from off and on all day, and she admired Angel's ability to keep on working with this personal fear lurking in the background.

Angel gave herself a little shake and turned away from the window, picking up her taco again. "I suppose it's too much to hope that we'll find the place where the killer made that call."

"Don't be such a pessimist," Sarah said, wiping a smear of salsa from her chin. "It could happen."

"You want to start after we finish here?"

Sarah shook her head. "Better to wait until closer to the actual time it happened. It's our best chance of picking up the sounds again." She paused to take the last bite of her taco and licked guacamole from her fingers. "A run by the hospital might be more productive this afternoon."

Watching her partner struggle for control, Sarah wondered if she should have ignored her impulse. She knew it was easier to appear strong if nobody touched you.

The moment struck Sarah as painfully intimate, and she wondered if they'd reached a turning point. Three whole days had passed without an eruption of hostilities. Did she dare believe they were starting to build a foundation that could support a partnership?

# Chapter Fifteen

Sarah regretted the decision to come to the hospital with Angel the minute they stepped through the door. She recoiled from the faint but unmistakable hospital smell that no amount of filtering could cleanse, each distinct odor triggering a painful memory.

The sting of the disinfectant soap they'd given her to wash John's blood off her hands. The nausea of her mother's rotting flesh as death had turned itself inside out, a death that had been immune to the latest medical treatment or a child's prayer. And the bite of stale urine that had marked the last loss of dignity for a senile old woman who hadn't done such a terrible job at trying to care for a motherless child.

"You don't have to come up," Angel said.

The words pulled Sarah out of her dark thoughts, and she realized she'd been lagging behind. "It's okay."

Angel stopped at the elevator, pushed the up button, then gave Sarah a long look. "I should have thought . . ." she faltered. "This has to be hard for you."

"I'm fine." Sarah stepped quickly into the elevator that whispered open in front of them, hoping to step as easily away from the sear of white-hot pain inflicted on her by remembering. Angel pushed the button for the third floor, and they rode up in silence.

An air of somberness permeated the ICU waiting room, as if the ghosts of all the tragedies it had seen through the years still lingered. The colorful pictures and comfortable furniture strained to make the room something better, but the effort failed. Sarah's pain was mirrored in the faces of the few people clustered in small anxious groups around the room.

Angel went directly to two men sitting on the edges of chairs bracketing a corner. Empty coffee cups and old magazines graced the table between them. The younger man smiled at Angel, and when he stood to wrap Angel in his arms, the action confirmed Sarah's assumption that he was the brother.

Sarah hung back, uncertain under the careful scrutiny leveled at her by the other man. It wasn't a look of open hostility. That she might have been able to deal with. But it was so closed, so guarded that she had no idea what thoughts it concealed.

Angel turned to the older man. "Daddy, this is my partner, Sarah Kingsly."

Sarah took two quick steps forward and offered her hand. The man's response hesitated, and Sarah only had a moment to debate whether it was because he was unaccustomed to shaking hands with women or if there was another reason. Then Angel introduced her brother.

LaVon's grasp was more confident, but his eyes held some of the same guardedness of the older man. Under the polite greeting, Sarah recognized that she was considered an unwelcome intrusion. Too bad. They might all feel better about being here if they could at least be friendly. But she wasn't about to stay where she knew she wasn't wanted.

Touching Angel's shoulder, Sarah drew her to one side. "I'm going downstairs."

"You don't have to leave."

Sarah glanced at the impassive faces of the men. "I'll be in the lobby."

Feeling like she couldn't just walk out without some gesture of compassion, Sarah turned to Angel's father. "I hope your wife continues to improve."

"Thank you." His voice was so soft, Sarah wondered if she'd misinterpreted his reserve after all. Perhaps it was just the anguish of the circumstance that held him so aloof. But that still didn't change her mind about leaving. No matter whose pain it was, she didn't want to be in the same room with it. Angel watched Sarah until she was out of the room, then turned to Gilbert. "She was nice enough to bring me here. The least you could have done was be civil."

"Come on, Baby. Chill out." LaVon moved to put his arm around her, but Angel stepped out of his attempt.

"I am not going to chill out. You two treated her like the devil incarnate."

"It's real hard to be sociable under the circumstances," Gilbert said.

"That's not what's going on and you know it." Angel waited for one of them to deny the truth, but they kept quiet.

"Whether you like it or not," she continued. "I have to work with that woman. And one of these days my life could depend on her. She'd be a hell of a lot more willing if she got even a hint of support from you."

"She's white. You ain't ever gonna be able to count on her." Her father delivered the line in an emotionless voice, but it still took Angel's breath away.

To his credit, LaVon turned away as if embarrassed, but her father merely sat there with that same damned unreadable expression that had so frustrated her since childhood.

Angel clenched her jaw in an effort not to scream. Why did he always make these pronouncements as if they were gospel, then leave her spinning in the aftermath? She wanted to challenge him, ask him how he could be so certain, but his stony reserve and her own doubts always pulled her up short.

Swallowing her anger and her pride, Angel turned and walked

out of the room. She'd come to visit her mother, not to argue with her father.

Chad drove back to the station, a deep sense of satisfaction keeping him company. Like most people, the rent-a-cop had mistaken Chad's easy-going manner for weakness. The poor fool had thought he could stand firm on his lie and the cop would buy it.

But this cop don't buy bullshit, Chad thought, remembering the flash of alarm on the other man's face at the boom of Chad's hand slamming down on the table. His hand still hurt, but the pain was worth it. The little creep had crumbled like a sand castle in the tide, admitting that he hadn't made the midnight sweep of the downstairs.

The head of mall security wasn't going to be too thrilled to find out his guys weren't doing their jobs. But of greater importance was the question of who might have known security was lax and been able to take advantage of it?

Another car pulled into the lot behind Chad and slipped into an empty space nearby. Chad smiled when he saw Angel and Sarah step out.

Despite the way Angel treated him, he always felt like smiling when he was around her. His brother would probably have a lot to say about that, about letting some she-ra diss him. But Chad didn't buy into his brother's attitudes or his jive.

Still smiling, he slid out of his seat and strode briskly toward the women.

Only Sarah returned his smile and he hung back with her while Angel entered the building. "What's the deal?" Chad asked when he was sure Angel was far enough ahead not to overhear.

"We just came from the hospital."

"Bad?"

"No change."

"Damn." Chad's sympathy was equally divided between Angel and himself. He hated to see the anguish she was going through. But he also hated the obstacle it presented. He could hardly ask her out when she had such a legitimate reason to turn him down.

"Are you up for another night-time prowl of the city?" Sarah asked Chad when they were all settled in a conference room with cold drinks. He looked at Angel with a wide grin.

"We're not playing undercover roles," Angel said. "And you get to ride in the back this time."

"That's cool," Chad said. "I'm not afraid to let a woman go first."

Sarah ignored the electric charge between the other two detectives and filled Chad in on what they'd learned from Greg. Then they listened as Chad recounted his experience with the security guard.

"That means that somebody could have been in that downstairs hall for several hours," Sarah said, picking up a pencil from the table and making a note to add to the case file.

"That's what I was thinking." Chad paused to take a long swallow of his soda. "We should probably find out how widespread this dereliction of duty was."

"I'll get Grotelli to send a couple of uniformed officers to check out the other rent-a-cops," Sarah said.

"But ultimately, what has that got to do with the murders?"

Sarah gave her partner a long look. "What do you mean?"

"Okay. The accessibility angle might give us some room to maneuver with Halsley. Someone who had a beef with him and knew about the lax security came in and waited for an opportunity. But it doesn't connect with Durham. He *was* security."

"You saying we should just drop this whole angle?" Chad asked.

"Of course not. I just don't think, in the long run, it's going to lead us to the solution."

"I don't know what's going to give us the answer." Sarah tapped the eraser end of her pencil against her cheek. "Wish we had that stuff back from Quantico."

"Me, too," Angel said. "And it would be great if they could give us name, rank, and social security number along with the profile."

"But just think," Chad said. "If they could do that, we wouldn't have any job security."

Sarah threw her pencil at him, but Chad dodged it easily.

*As the beam of light from the television screen probed the darkness of the room, he waited eagerly for the beginning of the ten o'clock news. In a few minutes that pretty, young reporter would give his message to the whole city, and people would have to take notice.*

*Expecting the same undercurrent of tightly suppressed excitement that had marked the opening of the broadcast the other night, his eagerness dimmed when the leadoff story centered on the fighting in Bosnia. But he doused the flicker of anger that made his stomach tighten. There was still plenty of time for his story. He just had to be patient.*

*Anger bolted him out of the chair when the anchor said to stay tuned for the weather right after this commercial break.*

*They weren't going to do his story?*

*What the fuck is this? He tuned out the TV and paced the dim room. Didn't they care? Didn't anyone care? He paused to wipe large beads of perspiration off his face with the back of his hand.*

*Taking a deep breath to still the wild, erratic thump of his heart, he forced his mind to think. Was everybody fuckin' blind? Didn't they see the whole world was upside down? The criminals got away with everything. Only the innocent paid.*

*A spear of raw pain set his feet in motion again. It couldn't keep on like this. It couldn't. But what was he supposed to do now?*

*The answer came to him with ringing clarity. He was going to have to leave another message. One that couldn't be missed.*

*Then he thought of the "deed" and a wave of revulsion swept over him, settling with a chokehold on his throat.*

*He paced, the war between need and reluctance thundering in his chest.*

*Killing was supposed to be easier after the first time. But it wasn't. To feel the current of life slipping through his fingers had left him with trembling knees and a heavy, sick feeling deep inside. Only the absolute necessity of what he was doing had given him the courage to even consider the next one.*

*That's when he'd decided to call it the "deed." Maybe then it wouldn't make him want to puke his guts out. But it had been worse. He could still feel the fight. The man grabbing and clutching and wrenching in desperation. Holding the jerking body in that perverse dance of death had been obscene, and remembering brought new spasms of revulsion.*

*But he was just going to have to get over that, wasn't he? He couldn't abandon the mission now.*

Sarah was relieved to see the evening news devoid of any comment about the case. Even if Price was a prick, he was an effective prick. He must have pulled some heavy-duty strings to get this media reprieve, and Sarah just hoped it would last for a while.

The timer blared from the kitchen, signaling that her frozen pizza was done. Sarah pulled herself out of the recliner and went into the kitchen, Cat padding along behind her.

"Don't get your hopes up too far," she told him as she pulled the pizza from the oven, filling the room with the tantalizing aroma of Italian spices and Pepperoni. "I'm hungry enough to eat it all."

He continued to watch her with hopeful eyes, and she laughed as she slid the pie onto a plate where the bubbling cheese could cool. Opening the refrigerator, she grabbed a beer.

After cutting the pizza, she put everything on the table and suddenly felt an unexpected wash of desolation. A pizza for one looked so . . . lonely.

Normally, she enjoyed her solitude. It was a pleasant break from the hustle of work, and she could stay up half the night watching movies with no one to object. But lately she'd begun to feel an emptiness that wasn't only because of John's death. And it didn't speak well of her state of mind that she talked to a cat every night.

Impulsively, she dug through her junk drawer where she'd thrown the business card after making that first call. Then she dialed the home number penned on the back. Paul answered on the third ring, and Sarah was suddenly afraid to open her mouth for fear the wrong thing would slip out.

"Hello?" he said again.

"Hi. It's Sarah." She paused, not sure where to go next with this conversation. Or lack thereof. Finally, her mind latched onto something rendered harmless by being so inane. "Just had a break and thought I'd call."

"Weren't you supposed to be off today?"

It impressed Sarah that he remembered that little detail from their conversation last night, but then, details were his business. "Things change pretty routinely in my line of work."

"Anything you can talk about?"

"Not really. Regulations."

"You have time to get together. Have a drink?"

Sarah pulled some of the cheese off the pizza and gave it to Cat. "I don't think so. I have to go back to work at eight."

"It's only six now," Paul said. "Have you eaten yet?"

Sarah pushed the pizza aside. "No."

"Well, my frozen dinner looks awfully lonely on this big table.

Care to join me?"

She smiled at the coincidence of images and realized that she did very much want to join him.

As if mistaking her silence for deliberation, Paul offered a stronger incentive. "I'll throw the fake chicken out and make us something real."

"Give me your address."

Sarah followed Paul's directions to one of the nicer apartment complexes on Preston Road in North Dallas. Her estimation of his success rose as she pulled through the security gate after entering the numbers he'd given her. It was no minor monthly fee that allowed one to live in the lap of such luxury.

After pulling into a visitor's spot near Paul's apartment, Sarah went to the door and rang the bell with a trembling finger. Now that she was here, she was having more than one second thought. It had been a silly whim to dash over here like a teenager experiencing her first crush.

The trembling increased when Paul opened the door and stood there, his deep tan contrasted by white shorts and a white polo shirt. His bare toes, digging into the plush pile of the small rug just inside the door, had the same impact on her had he been completely nude.

Hoping he'd mistake her blush for sunburn, she raised her eyes, and he surprised her by brushing her cheek with a soft kiss. "Come on in," he said. "I know you're pressed for time, so I have everything ready to cook."

He led her through a spacious living area with a parquet floor accented by a large Oriental rug. Japanese screens with cascading flowers in vivid primary colors stood behind the plush white sofa that could have been molded out of marshmallows. A round, glass-topped table supported by a black metal pedestal stood between the sofa and two matching chairs. Throw pillows picked up the colors of the screens, otherwise the room was stark and white.

An archway opened to another room, which Sarah guessed most people would have used for formal dining. Instead of a table, a stunning baby Grand dominated the center of the room, a myriad of light from the chandelier sparkling across the ebony lacquer.

"Do you play?" Sarah nodded toward the piano.

Paul stopped to give a self-deprecating shrug. "Some."

"Mozart I bet. Right?"

"No. My tastes run more to B. B. King."

"Oh." Sarah smiled. "I wouldn't have guessed."

"Just another way to break stereotype."

His casual remark triggered her detective's instinct, and she studied his face for a moment to see what, if anything, was hidden beneath the words. Either he was very good, or there was nothing.

Turning away from her gaze, he motioned for her to follow him into the kitchen.

Stepping into this room was like opening another page in a decorating magazine. The dominant color, again, was white, broken with the accents of brass cabinet pulls, copper cooking utensils on a rack by the stove, and stainless steel canisters sharing space with glass jars on the leathery texture of the counters. The room was big enough to comfortably accommodate a family of six.

"Kind of a waste for just one person," Paul remarked, and Sarah wondered if something in her expression had revealed her thoughts. She also wondered if living here alone had been part of his original plan. The place just had the look and feel of a feminine touch. Not that she could have ever pulled this kind of decorating off, but she really didn't think he had, either. Men were more in tune to function than form, and it was the rare one that broke out of the mold.

"Make yourself comfortable." Paul motioned to barstools snuggled against the broad expanse of counter where small piles of chopped mushrooms, onions, and green pepper stood in miniature mountains on a cutting board. "Do you want a drink? I've got some wine."

"Coffee? Don't want to fall asleep on the job tonight." Sarah pulled one of the stools out and sat down while Paul brought her a heavy ceramic mug. Then she watched as he whisked eggs and poured them into a large sauté skillet.

Taking the cutting board, Paul sprinkled the vegetables into the egg mixture and topped it all liberally with cheese. The egg mixture sizzled. Then, at just the right moment, he flipped the top half over, the vegetables and cheese now blanketed with a golden brown crust.

"That was quite a story in the *Herald* this morning." Paul expertly cut the omelet and slid each half onto its own plate. "Do you feel like the monster you were purported to be?"

She laughed at the ease of his exaggeration. "Don't tell me you're one of the last holdouts who still believes what he reads in the paper."

"Is that your way of saying you can't talk about it?"

"No. That's not off limits." Sarah accepted the plate, letting the spicy aroma that rode the steam remind her of how nice it was to eat something that didn't come out of a cardboard box. "Just not sure I want to talk about it."

Paul pulled out the stool next to her and sat down. "It must be a bitch to work under a microscope like that."

She acknowledged his perception with a smile and dipped her fork into the enticing offering. "Mmmm. This is good," she said, still chewing the first bite.

"I do try to live up to my promises."

The memory of what his body had promised last night made her wonder if the deeper meaning she attached to his words belonged only to her. Feeling the warmth of a flush crawl up her neck, she risked a sidelong glance at him. Delight danced across his face and settled with a satisfied sparkle in his eyes.

Deciding to steer clear of something that made her feel like a teenager again, Sarah asked Paul how he'd acquired his culinary skills.

"My mother found a clever way to satisfy my need for money when I was in high school that didn't entail sacrificing my grades with a part-time job. She's always valued education above all, even when times were lean."

Sarah nodded to show her interest but didn't interrupt with another question.

"So she taught me to cook, then went out and got a job. She paid me to take care of my brothers and sister after school and have dinner ready when she came home."

"Interesting," Sarah said. "But I wouldn't have pegged you as the domestic type."

"It did have its drawbacks. But it also had one huge advantage."

"What's that?"

"I didn't have to come home from a fast-food job smelling like a French fry."

The laughter turned poignant when Sarah realized she envied Paul his normal-sounding childhood. Hers had been anything but, and she knew that lack had been a prime motivator for her Sundays with John's family. God how she missed them. Yet she still couldn't screw up the courage to call Jeanette. She had called Paul instead.

The realization that her impulse may not have been what she'd first thought it was unnerved her. She was second-guessing herself all over the place, and it had to stop.

A quick look at her watch told her it was time to go. "My job has a bad habit of interfering," she said after he declined her offer to help clean up.

"Maybe we'll have to do something about that." He drew her into a deep good-bye kiss that left her wishing she didn't have to leave.

It wasn't until Sarah was back in her car that she really had time to think about his parting statement. Was it just another teasing, throwaway line designed to fan the fire of mutual desire? Or was he one of those control freaks? Should she worry about how much of his profession influenced his life?

He was accustomed to nice, tidy, predictable columns of figures and balance sheets that stayed where they belonged and did what they were told.

There wasn't much about her that could be considered tidy or predictable. Although she did consider herself nice on occasion.

Then Sarah burst out laughing and the woman in the Corvette next to her at the light gave her a curious glance. Sarah couldn't believe she was wasting her time even thinking about it. It wasn't like they were on the brink of planning their future together and she had to worry about that kind of compatibility. They were hardly past the point of extreme lust, and there was no guarantee they would even do anything about that.

# CHAPTER SIXTEEN

On Monday morning, Sarah stopped by the station before it was time to go to the Review Board. She reasoned that she was just checking up on some of the details of the investigation, but the tight knot that had tied itself around her stomach told her otherwise. She needed the assurance of the people here to use as armor against the coming attack.

It was bad enough that their progress toward solving the cases could be measured like the movement of a glacier. Last night had been a total bust, despite her earlier optimism that they would locate the place the doer had called from. But having to appear before the Board this morning was a final indignity. She couldn't even take comfort in the fact that it excused her from the meeting with McGregor, leaving Angel and Chad to be smothered by the lava of his wrath.

Angel glanced up when Sarah paused by her desk. "My, my, my. Don't you look fit to meet royalty."

Sarah laughed, easing one foot out of the strain of high heels. "I guess I should do this more often to really carry the ruse off, huh?"

Angel noticed that Sarah's eyes weren't laughing. The gray depths carried a cloud of anxiety. "Listen," Angel said. "For what it's worth. I don't think you're getting a fair shake."

"Thanks."

Angel nodded, then diverted her attention to some notes she'd been reviewing. The next question surprised her.

"So you don't buy the racial angle?"

"I didn't say that." Angel slowly swung her eyes back to Sarah. "I just don't think any cop should have to answer to a review board."

"I'm surprised. I thought . . ." Sarah faltered over the words.

"What?" Angel asked. "That I'd support the board because I'm black?"

"It's just . . ." Sarah picked at the edge of a paper on the desk. "Well, black voices have called the loudest for it."

"I don't run with any crowd. It doesn't matter who's sounding the trumpet."

Sarah continued to fidget, and Angel wondered if she was ever going to respond. Finally, Sarah lifted her eyes to meet Angel's gaze. "So what *do* you think?"

"I don't know. My own personal jury's still out."

Sarah nodded, then slipped her foot back into her shoe. "I'd better go."

"Good luck." Saying the words, Angel realized she really did mean them. The trouble with microscopes was that a lot of good cops got caught on the slide.

Lowering herself to the single chair placed in the middle of the room, Sarah resisted an urge to tug at her suit coat. She swallowed her nervousness and commanded her hands to stay quiet in her lap while she tried not to melt under the harsh scrutiny of the thirteen pairs of eyes. Despite McGregor's warning, she hadn't expected the almost palpable hostility or the overwhelming sense of aloneness.

The chair, positioned without benefit of a table to provide cover for restless fingers, only added to her feeling of desolation. Helplessness hovered like a hawk ready to swoop down and pluck her resolve.

"Detective Kingsly." The smooth, well-modulated voice of

Larry Holcomb broke the silence. "We appreciate your co-operation in responding to our summons."

*Right. Like I had a choice.*

"We have just a few points to clarify. Then you will be free to go." Holcomb consulted a yellow legal pad on the table. "First, let me say that we have reviewed all the reports. Yours, and those from the Special Investigative Unit. What is imperative at this juncture is to have your verbal account of the incident."

"Everything's in the report," Sarah said.

Holcomb put the legal pad down and looked at her. "Yes. But it would be advantageous for us to be apprised of any details that may have inadvertently been omitted from your paperwork."

"Nothing was left out."

"I see." Holcomb glanced at some of the other board members as if garnering silent support, then turned back to her. "Is there perhaps some mitigating circumstance that makes you reluctant to share this information with us?"

His convoluted choice of words prompted a laugh Sarah had to fight to control. *How can a prick like this be in charge of a panel overseeing police conduct when he doesn't have the first clue what it means to be a cop?*

Turning the laugh into a cough, Sarah met Holcomb's gaze. "May I have a drink?"

"Certainly. Certainly."

Sarah watched Holcomb seek assistance from the rest of the group with a sweep of his eyes. He was rewarded by a woman at the end of the table who poured water in the glass set in front of her, then rose to take it to Sarah.

The woman offered a tentative smile along with the drink, and Sarah accepted both with a nod of thanks. Then she drank deep and long before looking back at Holcomb. "Perhaps instead of wasting a lot of time with what you all have already read, our time would be better served if we just address any questions that may have surfaced."

"We're capable of deciding what is the most beneficial use of our resources."

Silence followed Holcomb's sharp retort, and Sarah waited it out.

Finally, the woman who'd given her the drink spoke up, "Very well, Detective. The main question I have in mind is whether you had any option other than shooting that boy?"

Sarah sighed. "Don't you think I would have used an option if there was one?"

"Is it a departmental mandate to answer all questions with a question?" Holcomb asked.

"No need to get into personalities here, Larry," the black woman sitting next to Holcomb said. "Let's move on to something else, Detective."

"Fine." Sarah took another sip of water, the cool liquid soothing the dryness in her throat, then set the glass down on the floor next to the leg of the chair.

"Have you ever used the pejorative term, 'Nigger'?"

"Not that I can recall."

"Oh, really?" The woman pulled a paper out of the stack in front of her. "We have a statement from one of your fellow officers that—"

"Jesus H. Christ!" Sarah exploded out of the chair, sending it, and the glass of water, crashing across the floor. "The implication you're making is absurd. I didn't shoot that kid because he was black. I shot him because he was standing there with a fucking gun in his hand."

"There is no need—"

Sarah cut Holcomb off with a sweep of her hand. "What there's no need for, counselor, is a continuation of this farce. We're here to establish whether this was a racially motivated action. Well, I can tell you, unequivocally, that the answer is no.

So why don't we all adjourn to more important matters."

Letting the force of her anger drive her, Sarah strode toward the door, ignoring the swell of protest from the assembly that followed her down the hall. Just before pushing the heavy doors of City Hall open, she paused and took a deep breath to slow the rapid thumping of her heart. Then she squared her shoulders and stepped out. A swarm of reporters swooped up the steps, their questions beating restless wings of urgency all around her.

"How do you feel about the shooting now, Detective Kingsly?"

"The same as I did before." Sarah elbowed her way through the crowd.

"What about your new partnership? Is that just a departmental effort to smooth things over?"

Sarah shot the question-bearer a cold look. "Only if you say so."

Clearing the tangle of print reporters, Sarah faced the gauntlet of mini-cams at the bottom of the steps. She tried to hurry by, but Bianca waved her cameraman over and ran toward her. "Did the Review Board give you any indication of how they would rule?"

"No comment."

"Come on, Detective." Bianca scurried after Sarah. "You've got to give me something."

Sarah whirled and glared at the reporter. "All right. How about this? Everyone is so concerned about that poor boy who died. What about my partner? Who's crying for him? Who thinks it's a rotten shame that a fine police officer had to die? Put that in your fucking six o'clock report."

A flurry of movement caught her eye, and Angel turned from the coffee she was pouring to see Chad poke his head into the break room. "Where's Sarah?"

"I don't know." Angel set the pot back on the burner. "McGregor came by and got her a little while ago. They didn't tell me where they were going."

"Then I guess we get to do this one by ourselves."

"This one what?"

"Ditch your coffee and come on. I'll tell you on the way."

Angel took a hasty swallow, which she regretted as the hot liquid scalded her mouth and throat. "Damn!" She put the cup down and followed Chad who was already out the door.

"Our man at Danny's finally picked up a break for us," he explained, leading Angel through a maze of desks toward the area that housed the interrogation rooms for Vice. "He got wind of a big powwow and tipped Humphries. The narcs raided the joint and picked up a few interesting people in the net, along with some hefty amounts of money."

"No dope?" Hurrying to keep up with Chad's long strides, Angel skirted a trashcan that was overflowing with the paper remains of too many fast-food meals.

"Not a grain. And that'll make it tougher for their case." Chad paused outside the door of one of the rooms. "But I figured while we've got them here, we might push a little on the murders."

"Okay." Angel offered him a smile. "Since you strive to be nicer than I am, you get to be good cop."

"It'll be a pleasure." Chad pushed the door open.

With the exception of the one-way mirror, the interrogation room was a twin of the one in the Homicide department, including replicas of the wooden table and the battered chairs. One of the chairs held an Asian man Angel guessed to be in his early twenties.

"What have you got?" Angel asked the sandy-haired narcotics officer who rose and wiped a hand across his face as they entered.

The officer handed her a piece of paper. "Name and his attorney's phone number is about all he'd give us. But he did clarify he's Korean. Didn't want to be confused with any of the other gooks out there."

Angel froze him with a cold look. "Is that your idea of racial sensitivity?"

"Sorry." The man at least had the good sense to flush. "I didn't mean anything by it. It's been a hell of a night that should have ended hours ago."

It was a weak excuse, but Angel accepted it. Being gritty-eyed and bone-weary did tend to dull one's sensibilities. She gave the officer a slight nod. Then he turned and shuffled out the door, pausing briefly to acknowledge Chad. Angel focused her attention on the suspect.

Displaying none of the swagger of the home-boys or the macho-driven belligerence of the Hispanics, the Korean was wrapped in a rigid control not unlike what Angel had seen at martial arts tournaments. But even without the outward signs of contempt or bravado, Angel recognized the dare of his posture. *Prove something if you think you can.*

She gave a slight bow and greeted him in Korean. If the deference had an impact on him, he didn't let it show.

"Mr. Smith?" Angel switched to English and glanced from the paper the officer had given her back to the unblinking eyes of the young man.

"I am second generation," he replied with only an occasional hesitation revealing that he had probably learned most of his English from someone who was more comfortable with another language. "My father took the new name so people would not forget we are Americans."

"And what would your father think of the business you do?"

"It pleases the father to see the son succeed."

"So your old man is part of it?"

"My father is not so far advanced to be one of the ancients. But it is as you say. He works at the market we own."

"That's not the business I'm talking about, and you know it."

"It is the only business we do."

"I don't think so," Angel said, a low growl in her voice. "I think you're a dirty, lying piece of shit who'd rather sell a nickel bag than pick up an honest nickel off the street."

With every word, Angel pushed on the table until it forced Smith's chair back on two legs. As he teetered precariously, the first crack of fear opened in his eyes.

Taking his cue, Chad rushed forward and grabbed Angel by the arm. "Maybe you'd better go out and settle yourself down."

"I don't want to settle down." Angel tore her arm out of Chad's grasp. "I want to nail this asshole." She gave the table a final shove, sending the chair and the Korean sprawling.

"That does it." Chad's anger was so convincing Angel couldn't tell if it was the real thing or they were still playing their game. "Go get some coffee. I'll finish here."

Angel watched for just a moment as Chad helped Smith to his feet. Then she turned and left, slamming the door for effect. She walked around the corner where Humphries worried a toothpick from one side of his mouth to the other.

"Hell of a performance," he said, motioning to the interrogation room visible from his side of the one-way mirror.

Angel went over to get a vantage point next to the man who towered over her without making her feel diminished. "You going to be able to hold him on the drug thing?"

"I don't know." Humphries pulled the well-chewed toothpick out of his mouth and replaced it with a fresh one. "DA says the case is too flimsy."

They listened for a few minutes while Chad patiently explained to Smith that everyone wanted to help him come out of this the best way he could. And to do that, they needed his cooperation. Watching the silence enfold the Korean again, Angel realized they'd made the switch too soon. The guy wasn't going to respond to Chad's kindness or his charm.

She turned away from the window as another person joined them. "This is Ryan O'Donnell," Humphries said, turning off the speaker from the interrogation room. "He's our in at Danny's."

Ryan could have played Mel Gibson playing Martin Riggs in *Lethal Weapon,* and Angel accepted his handshake with a wry grin. "Angel Johnson."

"What's going down?" Ryan motioned toward the scene on the other side of the glass.

"We're handling those Mall Murders—"

"Lucky you." Ryan cocked an irreverent eyebrow at her. "All that high profile shit. Does wonders for the career path."

Angel laughed, and even Humphries chuckled as he turned to leave. "I've got to go meet the DA," he said.

Giving a nod of acknowledgment, Angel turned back to Ryan. "Anyway," she continued, "we're trying to see if the homicides could be part of the Asian inroads into the drug business."

"Do you really believe that?"

"No."

"That's good. Cause I think you're dead wrong." Ryan threaded his fingers through the tangle of curls brushing the neckband of his Rolling Stones T-shirt, then shrugged in an "aw shucks" gesture. "That is, if you want my opinion."

"Certainly," Angel said, warming to his directness and charm.

"A gang warfare theory just won't fit. They want to take over new territory," he nodded at the Korean, "an Uzi clears a faster path. Sure, there are some gangs that do weird shit. I heard of one in Detroit that does all kinds of fun things with wire and electricity. But that's discipline. Stuff to keep the troops in line.

Scare the piss out of them so they don't think of taking an Adios."

While his commentary only confirmed what Angel had been thinking, it was good to hear someone else spell it out. "Does your opinion extend beyond what we shouldn't be looking at?"

Ryan tore his eyes from the window and gave her a sharp look as if measuring her hostility level. Apparently satisfied that it wasn't in a red zone, he continued. "First off, the doer's got to be someone who's singularly obsessed."

"But the victims have nothing in common."

"Sure they do." A little bit of Mel Gibson slipped back with his smile. "You just haven't found it yet."

"And where do your psychic powers tell us we should be looking?"

"Hell, if I was psychic, I'd just conjure up the bad guy and hand him to you."

Angel smiled. "I don't think psychics conjure."

"See? I don't know shit."

Using that as an exit line, Ryan tipped an invisible hat and sauntered out, but some of his words lingered in the silence. *Someone singularly obsessed. One reason. One point to make.*

Watching the pantomime of interaction between Chad and the Korean, Angel became more convinced that Ryan was right. Of course knowing that was a far cry from tracking down the singularly obsessed person. Maybe she'd call Sanchez and see if the missive from Quantico came today.

"I'm supposed to reprimand you for your language," McGregor said, handing Sarah a steaming barbecue sandwich.

"Just what was it they objected to? My grammar or my word usage?"

"Don't be flip." McGregor fished in his pocket for the money to pay the vendor.

"It's pretty hard not to be." Sarah grabbed a couple of napkins. "I walked out and their biggest concern is that I said 'fuck' in mixed company?"

She led the way to the only park bench in the shade. "And why couldn't we have gone to some place with air-conditioning for lunch."

"Thought barbecue would taste better."

"Now who's being flip?"

McGregor took a bite, and Sarah could feel his eyes studying her. "You got yourself into some deep shit here, you know."

"Yeah. But I'm only sorry for the trouble it caused you." She absently watched a teenager on in-line skates negotiate quick turns around the concrete planters near the Bank One entrance. Currently, he was the only other inhabitant of the plaza, the blistering heat keeping most of downtown inside, so she supposed it didn't matter how fast the kid skated.

"They're filing all kinds of complaints against you. It could go beyond a departmental write-up."

Sarah had trouble swallowing her bite of food. "Could they force a firing?"

"They're not supposed to have that kind of power." McGregor paused to wipe ineffectually at a dollop of sauce on his tie. "But if they stir enough shit, the Commissioner might capitulate before he drowns in it."

"Is that why you invited me to this exciting lunch spot? To warn me?" Sarah washed the last of her sandwich down with a big swallow of her cold drink, then held the cup against her forehead, where she swore it sizzled.

"I'll fight it as hard as I can, but . . ." McGregor shrugged the rest of his sentence away, and Sarah felt the tightness in her throat again. *Damn. It wasn't supposed to happen this way.*

She watched the skater again for a moment until the sound of McGregor's voice called her attention. "Hey, you could always solve those murders. Nobody'd fire a hero."

His effort touched her, and the tiniest trace of a smile flitted at the corner of her mouth. "Appreciate the encouragement. But it's going to take a goddam miracle."

"Then go to church and pray." McGregor matched her smile. "And go to confession while you're at it. Last time I heard, taking the Lord's name in vain was still a sin."

# CHAPTER SEVENTEEN

Angel supported the plastic cup so her mother could grasp the straw and take a sip of water. Even that simple action felt like a miracle. The older woman was far from well, but she was also now further from death. Her skin no longer hung in flaccid folds, and the ashen pallor that had dusted her deep chocolate-colored skin was gone.

"Are you sure you don't want any more lunch?" Angel asked.

"I couldn't." Martha let her trembling hand flutter back to the bed.

Angel put the water on the tray next to the half-finished broth. "I guess I can't blame you. This isn't really eating."

A soft chuckle rewarded her efforts and she smiled at her mother, glad that fate had not robbed her of this relationship too soon. Whenever things were really bad in her life, she had always found comfort and wisdom with this woman, and perhaps it was that need, as much as concern, that had brought her to the hospital today.

The case seemed hopelessly mired, every possible lead taking them nowhere. There were quite a few pieces missing from this puzzle they were trying to put together, and their inability to find them frustrated Angel. Still no luck in nailing the location the killer had called from, and Jimmy's alibi had held up. Not that she figured it wouldn't. The longer this went on, the more she was convinced that drugs had nothing to do with it. But whatever the common denominator was, it was beating the hell out of her and everyone else.

"Where'd you go off to, Honey?"

The sound of her mother's voice startled Angel. "What?"

"You done left me for a little while."

"I'm sorry. I was just wishing I could've pulled some simple homicide for my first case."

"That've been too easy." Martha smiled. "No way to show off all those powerful brains."

"Thank you, Mama. I need a good cheerleader."

Martha closed her eyes for a moment, and Angel wondered if her mother was drifting into sleep. Maybe it would be best to go and let her rest. She was just reaching to turn off the TV when her mother spoke again. "Your Daddy said Sarah brought you to the hospital the other day."

Angel turned back to see her mother's eyes flutter open, and the old woman smiled. "I tol' you she was a nice person."

"Better not let Daddy hear you say that. He'll think you're a traitor."

"He knows I don't always agree with him. And that's okay."

Angel glanced out the window to break eye contact. So why wasn't it okay for her not to agree with him? They'd resurrected the argument and the anger the day Sarah walked out on the Review Board. Nothing Angel had said could shake him from his conviction that the only issue was race.

Angel wanted to ask her mother how she could get past this impasse with her father, but this was not the time to be a needy child. Arranging her face into a neutral expression, she faced her mother again. "What did the doctor have to say today?"

"He's happy I'm doing good. And he wants me up walking soon."

"But you've only been out of ICU a couple of days. What does he expect?"

"Now, Honey, don't you start getting all . . ."

An urgent voice overrode her mother's, drawing Angel's attention to the TV where the face of Bianca Gomaz filled the screen. Maintaining a somber and most serious expression, the reporter continued the special segment with a breathless delivery. "In the dark pre-dawn hours when most of us had nothing urgent to pull us from the comfort of our beds, one poor soul was struggling with the need to kill again."

"What the—"

"Shh!" Angel pushed the button to increase the volume on the TV, and Bianca's voice continued with even more dramatic undertones, pulling Angel deeper into the current of dread.

"According to an exclusive statement we received this morning, the person responsible for the grisly Mall Murders doesn't like what he's had to do. And he doesn't like the possibility that he might have to do it again. But, in his own words, he doesn't see that he has much choice. Not as long as innocent people are harmed by thousands of addicts who will do anything to get their dope. The man said he's given the police long enough to do the job, and they failed."

"Oh, God!" Angel pushed the button until the TV flickered out of light to darkness. What else could possibly go wrong?

"Got me a mind to tell that woman to hush. She don't know what she's talking about."

Angel pulled up her best effort at a smile. "If I thought it would do any good, I'd dial her number for you."

"Somebody needs to tell her."

Noticing a fresh sheen of perspiration on her mother's face, Angel stroked the woman's arm, careful to avoid the bruising from the IVs. "You just forget about it, Mama. It'll be okay." She waited for an answering nod, then grabbed her purse. "I'd better get back to the station."

Her mother nodded and Angel gave her a kiss. "You mind the doctors, now."

"I always do."

In the hallway Angel didn't have to pretend anymore. This latest broadcast had the potential for disaster, and she shuddered at the thought of who could get caught in the aftermath. The bigger the spotlight, the greater the risk for anyone associated with the case, and this one was downright blinding.

"The killer is making us look like circus clowns." Chief Helen Dorsett plopped her ungainly body into her swivel chair and sighed.

McGregor shifted uncomfortably from one foot to the other in front of her desk.

"Sit down," Helen said. "I'm not going to throttle you. Although I would, by God, love to get my hands on a certain reporter."

Easing his weight onto the edge of the chair, McGregor suppressed a smile. 'Twas neither the time nor the place for humor.

"So what's the hold-up on this investigation?" Helen tucked a wisp of graying hair into her trademark upsweep. "And don't piss and moan about how hard this is. I didn't get here by winning a popularity contest."

This time McGregor didn't stop the smile. He'd trailed behind Helen's career by only a few years and could cite chapter and verse of every award and special recognition that had carried her from foot patrol to Chief of Detectives.

"What are you smiling about?" Helen asked.

"Just remembering."

"Well, we'll go have a beer sometime and pull out the scrapbooks. In the meantime, I've got to have something soothing to say to the Mayor and the Commissioner."

"Maybe we should invite them to spend a day with us. Let 'em see we're not wasting valuable tax-payer money."

"That's not the point, and you know it."

McGregor sighed and leaned back in the chair, easing a thumb through the waistband of his pants. Damn enchiladas he'd had for lunch were visiting his gall bladder. "Well, if I can be so trite, we are doing everything we can."

"What about the Fibbies?"

"Expect to hear from Sanchez later today. But he already warned us that Quantico wouldn't get much from the notes or the tape. Too brief. Both of them. They need more from the killer to do a good profile."

"So I guess there's one good thing about today's broadcast."

"Yeah. I've already got someone picking up the latest offering."

Helen drummed short, stubby fingers on the top of her desk. "Tell me about Detective Kingsly."

The vagueness of the comment caught McGregor up short. Tell her *what* about Sarah?

Helen's probing gaze finally pulled a response from him. "She's a damn fine cop."

"I'm acquainted with her file, Lieutenant. I just want your take on recent events."

Nerves beat against the walls of his stomach like trapped butterflies. He thought the whole Review Board issue had been put to rest last week. Had something else come up that he wasn't aware of? "Why don't you help me out here, Chief. I don't know where you're going with this."

"Okay." Helen sat forward, propped her elbows on the desk and rested her chin on her clasped hands. "The suggestion has come up again to take her off the case."

"Why?"

"Even after your riveting rhetoric following the Review Board fiasco, there were some who still weren't convinced she wouldn't go rogue."

"Oh, come on! Those white-shirts really believe she's impeding the investigation because she's walked off the edge?"

"It is an explanation."

"Bullshit!" McGregor wished he had a drink to calm the tremble in his hand and his stomach. "It's a wild-assed grab at something to take the heat."

"So you wouldn't consider giving someone else the lead on this?"

"Is that an order?"

"Not yet."

Thoughtfully tapping a finger on his lower lip, McGregor considered the implications of her words. He felt like he was caught in the middle of a squeeze play. "Maybe we should have that little trip down memory lane real soon. Just in case you've forgotten what it's like."

"The memories are vivid, Lieutenant."

McGregor could tell by her tight lips and the red creeping up her neck that she was fighting to contain her anger, and he mentally kicked his lapse in judgment. How could he have forgotten? When she'd accidentally shot a kid during a domestic disturbance call that had gone way out of control, he was the only one who hadn't bet that she wouldn't come back to work.

"Listen," McGregor waved his hand in a vague gesture of apology. "Other than her little stunt last week, there's been nothing to indicate Sarah is in any kind of trouble. The investigation is crawling because there isn't anything to run with."

"They said it was my call." Helen offered him a wry grin. "But it's like a mother saying to her kid, 'pick your own curfew.' You know damn well what your mother expects."

"Maybe Mom's wrong this time."

"Are you willing to stake your shield on that?"

"If I have to."

"Just be sure what you're betting on, Tom. Someone might call you on it."

Sarah pulled her hand away from the receiver when she saw Sanchez threading his way through the bustle of late-afternoon activity in the squad room. His lean, angular face gave nothing away. She'd been hoping for a smile.

"The report's kind of thin." Sanchez plopped a folder on her desk. "But I warned you."

"Let me see if the Lieutenant's free," Sarah said, reaching for the phone again. "I'm sure he'd like to get this first hand."

After McGregor told her he was available, she nodded to Angel who followed them into the Lieutenant's office. McGregor, shirt rumpled and tie askew, looked like he'd been rode hard and put up wet. Sarah felt a twinge of sympathy. He stood up and offered his hand to Sanchez who said, "I already told Detective Kingsly—"

"You can call me Sarah."

Sanchez flashed her a smile, then turned back to McGregor. "Anyway, we didn't get much."

A frown of disappointment furrowed itself in McGregor's forehead as he sat back down, motioning the agent to take the chair in front of his desk. "Give us what you got."

Angel and Sarah pulled up the extra chairs from against the wall and positioned them next to Sanchez.

"The obvious things you've probably already latched onto," Sanchez said, folding his long frame into the chair, crossing his legs and resting one hand casually on his knee. "Both of the notes carry a tone of vengeance. Revenge, or some kind of vindication. Could easily fit the profile of a real psychotic. Someone who thinks he's God's avenger sent here to rid the world of evil."

"But he's not?" Sarah asked.

Sanchez shook his head. "The group that analyzed the tape didn't think so. They thought he sounded too hesitant. Not confident enough. Even as whacko as their motives and actions are to us, psychos know exactly what they are doing and why. And they see nothing wrong with it. In their minds, their actions are justifiable."

"Any first-year psych student could figure that out," Angel said.

"That's probably true," Sanchez said. "But remember, I started this session with a disclaimer."

Sarah's estimation of Sanchez went up a few notches—quite a few notches—and she gave Angel a warning glance. They didn't need to alienate the Fibbies. No matter how the relationship was portrayed for dramatic effect in fiction, most departments worked smoothly with the Agency, and this guy could help them a lot.

"We've got another tape for your team to take a run at," Sarah said, setting the cassette on McGregor's desk. "But could you give us a quick impression first?"

"Sure." Sanchez patted his shirt pocket and pulled out a cinnamon stick that he stuck in the corner of his mouth.

Sarah gave him an inquisitive glance and he smiled. "My pacifier since I quit smoking."

McGregor grabbed the cassette and stuck it in a small tape player, then they all listened attentively as the soft voice began, *"You've got to help me."*

Even though she'd already heard it once, Sarah still felt the anguish in the voice tug at a chord of sympathy she didn't think she should have.

*"Help you how?"* a male voice asked.

*"I don't want to do it again. They're making me do it."*

*"Who? Who's making you?"*

*"The police."*

171

"Well, at least Ms. Gomaz was accurate in her reporting," McGregor said with a slight shake of his head.

Sarah smiled as the other taped voice prompted, *"Why do you say that?"*

*"They're doing it all wrong. They're going after those that sell drugs. Not the ones who are robbing and killing to get drugs."*

*"Is that what you've been trying to say with your messages?"*

*"Yes."* The caller paused and the harsh sound of his breathing could be heard. *"I didn't want to do it, God knows. I tried not to. But . . . Someone's got to listen. You tell that reporter lady to say it again. I can't keep . . ."*

The voice faded into a heavy silence and McGregor pushed the OFF button on the machine.

"That doesn't sound like the usual nut case," Sarah said.

"You're right." Sanchez took the cinnamon stick from his mouth and a sweet odor drifted pleasantly in the room. "Some of this will be just me guessing. He doesn't appear delusional in the true psychotic sense. He's not hearing voices or receiving some mystical mandate. His focus is on real people and a real problem that actually frustrates many of us."

"You saying you don't think he's psychologically sick?" Angel asked.

"Oh, yes I do. Anybody who'd kill the way he has and feel justified is sick. He's just not sick in the same way as a Ted Bundy or a Son of Sam."

"He's not having a good time?" McGregor offered.

"Exactly," Sanchez nodded at the Lieutenant, then turned back to Angel. "Most psychotic serialists find some perverse pleasure in the act as well as everything that surrounds it. The thrill of the hunt. The excitement of notoriety. The satisfaction of fulfilling a destiny of sorts." He shrugged. "This guy's not getting any of it."

"What's your take on motive?" Sarah asked.

"I'll still go with the initial assessment. He's got some kind of cause. And it's got to be pretty significant for him to be this singularly obsessed."

"That's interesting," Angel said. "Another detective said the same thing. He even used those same words."

"Pretty good sidewalk psychology, I'd say." Sanchez put the cinnamon stick back in his mouth.

"Is he going to do it again?" McGregor asked.

"Maybe. Depends on how driven he is. And whether that drive is strong enough to push him past his reluctance." Sanchez shrugged. "You've got to consider that the fact he called again indicates he hasn't accomplished his goal."

McGregor sighed and popped the cassette out of the machine.

"If you want, I could send that on to the team in Virginia," Sanchez said. "But I don't think they'll be able to give you any more than I have."

"We're digging for any scrap we can find here," Sarah said. "It couldn't hurt."

"Sure." Sanchez stood and pocketed the tape. Then he shook hands all around and left.

"How many days since the last one?" McGregor asked, after the door closed.

"Six," Sarah answered.

"And what was the interval between the first and second?"

"Four or five days, depending on whether Halsley was killed before or after midnight," Angel said.

"I don't think timing is a factor," Sarah said. "Our perp doesn't come across as a killing-junkie needing his next fix on a regular basis. Actually," she paused to reconsider what she was about to say. It had started with that little twinge of sympathy. Now she was about to label him as just a poor slob who would only kill again if he had to? The fact that he'd already offed two people automatically disqualified him from the "poor slob" category.

"Are you just going to leave us in suspense?" McGregor asked.

"No." Sarah rubbed at the slow throb that had started in her temple. "I was just going to say that he's only going to kill as a last resort."

"You think if we arrest a few dope-heads and parade them on TV, it'll make him happy? He won't kill again?"

"There's more at issue here, Lieutenant," Angel said. "If he's trying to help us get rid of all the dopers, why doesn't he just take a gun to a street corner in South Oak Cliff and open fire? Why did he pick these two guys? And why did he do them at a mall?"

"If I knew the answers to those questions, I'd nail your killer for you."

Sarah laughed at his attempt at humor, but there was nothing she would like better than to turn this whole case over to someone else. Let them get an ulcer over it.

Watching McGregor toss back a generous half of his latest drink, Sarah wondered if it was just the strain of the case. Not that she was such an informed judge of his drinking habits. They hadn't socialized much in the last couple of years. But she hadn't felt personally insulted.

After his wife left him, McGregor had wrapped himself in a blanket of anger and grief and withdrawn from everyone. In fact, his invitation for tonight had been a big surprise, except for the fact that they all needed a drink after the events of the day.

"I hope the silence means your incredible deductive powers are sorting out the case for us," McGregor said.

"Actually, I was just wondering if we're destined to turn into stereotypical cops. You know, the ones who screw up their lives and end up drinking themselves to death."

"Is your life screwed?"

Despite the amount of alcohol he'd consumed, McGregor's gaze was steady, and it made Sarah wonder. "Have you been playing with the politicians again?" she asked.

He laughed. "What makes you think that?"

"Oh, I don't know." Sarah gave a dramatic shrug. "Maybe the broadly defined question. Or the subtle undercurrent of anxiety."

"You found me out." McGregor lost his smile in another swallow of his drink, then plunked the glass back on the table. "I had a visit with Chief Dorsett."

"There you go again."

"What?"

"Visit. You didn't have a visit. You had a meeting. You talked. But you didn't spend an hour in companionable conversation." Sarah reached across the table and nudged his arm. "Come on, Lieu, you're a regular guy. Talk to me like one."

"There's some . . . Dorsett asked if you were on the edge—"

"The edge? The edge of what?"

"Of going rogue."

"What an absurd . . ." Sarah sat back, wondering at the combined stupidity of people in high places. But at least now she knew why she'd been the only one invited to this drink fest. "Is it still because of my poor manners at the Review Board?"

"Partially." McGregor danced the bottom of his glass on the cocktail napkin. "And just for the record, the question doesn't originate with her. It comes from higher up. The white-shirts are all pissing in their pants over this case—"

"—and they're wondering if it isn't getting solved because I'm too busy going off the deep end," Sarah finished.

"Something like that."

"What did you tell her?"

"That you're okay." McGregor raised his eyes to her. "And now I need to ask if you really are."

Sarah shook her head at the absurdity of it. Okay? Was it okay to be angry every time she looked up and saw Angel instead of John? Was it okay to break out into a cold sweat every time she passed a dark alley? Had it been okay to pull her weapon on Angel's source?

If McGregor had formed any judgments during the silence, Sarah could see no sign of them when she met his eyes again. "I guess it depends on your definition," she said. "How 'okay' can anyone be after all that's happened? But has it impaired my ability? I don't think so. Unless there's some lapse I'm not aware of that you can point out for me."

"I don't like to have to wonder about this any more than you do. So I won't." McGregor paused to signal the waitress for another round. "But don't let me down, Kingsly."

Sarah nodded, fiddling with the swizzle stick to cover the trembling in her hands.

# CHAPTER EIGHTEEN

After her morning run, Sarah treated herself to an extra-long shower. Then, instead of throwing on the first thing she put a hand to, she dressed leisurely, actually coordinating an outfit of black slacks and a jacket the color of a fine burgundy wine.

To hell with the time clock. As much overtime as she was raking in, she could afford to go in a little late. She even cooked herself a real breakfast of scrambled eggs and ham that she shared with Cat. When they were finished, he purred contentedly in her lap.

The quiet was conducive to uninterrupted thinking and Sarah considered various angles of the case. What connected the victims other than drugs? They both worked at malls. But there was no evidence that they'd ever worked at the same mall at the same time.

Treated independently, either man could have been killed for a variety of reasons. A love triangle. A dispute with a family member. Someone they'd pissed off at work. But that reasoning didn't work when the two murders became one case.

Sarah worked her fingers in slow circles on Cat's neck, remembering something John had told her when she was a rookie, "Don't develop theories, then force the facts to fit. Let the facts talk to you."

Okay. The most significant fact was how the victims were killed. Garroting was unusual in this era of extreme firepower. So why? Not because the perp couldn't get a gun. Anybody could get a gun. But guns make a lot of noise. So the guy's not experienced enough to know about silencers?

Filing that thought in her mental notebook, she considered the intimacy of the MO. It suggested that the victims knew the perp and weren't afraid of him. So how could the killer know both guys if they didn't know each other? Or did they know each other and the connection hadn't been found yet? If they weren't connected by work, they had to be connected outside of work.

So how? Friends? Neither man appeared to have many, and no one admitted to knowing the other guy. Of course they wouldn't if the socializing had been done over a fine line of white powder.

Maybe it was time to talk to some of those friends again.

Nestling Cat comfortably in the crook of her arm, Sarah rose and carried her dishes to the sink. After rinsing her plate one-handed, she stopped and looked at the kitten. "This is stupid you know." He responded by nipping her playfully on the arm, then he licked the spot with his sandpaper tongue. "I'm turning into one of those silly old—"

The peal of the telephone saved her from having to finish the comment. She put the cat down and picked up the receiver, "Hello?"

The sound of Paul's voice reminded her that it wasn't too late to avoid the label she'd almost given herself.

"I'm glad you called. I was afraid I'd become too unsavory for you to associate with."

"What do you mean?"

"Some of your high-profile clients might have objected to my rude and unladylike behavior toward some of Dallas's finest."

"Were you rude and unladylike?"

"Very."

The music of Paul's laughter rumbled lightly in her ear.

"Actually. I've been pretty busy. But even so, my personal life is totally separate from my professional one."

Sarah found his words reassuring.

"I called the station and they said you weren't in yet. Took a chance that you were still at home. I'd like to see you again."

Those words were *very* reassuring.

"Me, too."

"Any chance of that happening soon?"

"I don't know. Unless you've been off on some deserted island, you've got to know the pressure is really on us."

"Yeah. I was just hoping."

"Can I call you if a window of opportunity comes up?"

Paul laughed. "That's an interesting way of putting it. But sure. I told you my personal and professional lives don't mix. I can be spontaneous."

Clicking the receiver back on its base, Sarah felt buoyed by the contact. She'd needed to hear a friendly voice as much as she'd needed the substantial breakfast.

She rinsed the rest of the dishes and put them in the dishwasher. The racks were only sparsely filled, but she decided she'd better run the machine anyway. It wasn't a good sign that she couldn't remember how long some of the dishes had been in there.

"You're late," McGregor said when Sarah walked into the squad room a half hour later.

"So fire me."

"Don't tempt me."

His sour attitude pulled her up short. Had something else happened since last night? It couldn't have. She'd listened to KRMD on the way in, and the airways had been blessedly bereft of news about the case or the department.

"You okay, Lieu?"

"I'm fine. Would've appreciated a phone call, that's all."

179

Watching him stride away, a disquieting thought hit her. He wasn't normally a hardass about hours and reporting in. Was it just a matter of the pressure getting to him? Or was he feeling the effects of last night too much?

That question raised a prickle of apprehension. Just a few months ago the Commissioner had issued a get-tough policy on drinking. Licensed to enforce that policy, officers from Internal Affairs were busy re-creating *The Untouchables,* and a couple of detectives had already been offered a choice of early retirement or outright firing. McGregor couldn't afford the risk of someone deciding to look under his rock.

"What's with the Lieutenant?" Angel asked.

Sarah turned, startled. She hadn't heard anyone approach. "I don't know. If I said PMS, would you laugh this time?"

"Probably not." Angel gave her a wry smile. "As a joke it's just not very funny."

The brief exchange wore comfortably, like a favorite pair of jeans. Yet it surprised Sarah as much as Angel's periodic bursts of antagonism. Understanding this woman was beginning to be as difficult as solving the case.

"Did I miss something important at the briefing this morning?" Sarah asked.

Angel shook her head, tugging at the lapel of her green serge jacket. "It was a very short meeting. To sum it all up, McGregor basically said to carry on."

"Then I guess that's what we'd better do, huh?"

Sarah walked over to her desk, then turned to Angel who had followed. "Somehow, someway these two guys had to cross paths." She handed over the Halsley file. "You go back through this and talk to everyone you can get a hold of. The boss. The landlord. Rita. See if any of them knew Durham or might have heard Halsley mention him. I'll work with Durham's file and see if anything tracks back to Halsley."

Reading the file didn't take long. Durham's landlord hadn't said much more than that the guy paid his rent on time and none of the other tenants had ever complained about him. Patrol officers had talked to the tenants, most of whom didn't know Durham. The guy who lived next to Durham said he seemed to take his job seriously. Wore the uniform like he thought he was the chief of police. But he never saw any drug dealers coming or going from the apartment.

The boss had been a dry well of information, too. Even in a second interview, he'd stuck to his original statement that he didn't know Durham had done drugs. *Must have started after being hired.* Sarah checked the start date. Seven years ago. That was longer than most rent-a-cops stayed with one job. And he had passed several random drug tests during that time. So, either he wasn't a user, or he stayed off the stuff long enough to pass the drug tests.

Interesting. Sarah dropped the folder on her desk and cupped her chin in her hand. Casual drug users were less apt to seek solitude for their fix than addicts. Causal often meant recreational, and recreational meant someone to recreate with. Rita had indicated that Mel liked to have a good time. And Durham liked to have a good time. So it's possible they could have had a good time together.

Maybe they should talk to Durham's girlfriend again. See if she could remember a little more about his social life.

Francie Stark lived in an apartment complex on Spring Valley Road on the edge of the Dallas/Richardson border. The apartments used to be decent, modestly priced havens for newly marrieds or young singles eager to test the waters of independence. Now they were a crumbling relic of that time when young people could look forward with a certainty that life would only get better.

Seeing places like this always reminded Angel she had a lot to be thankful for. She didn't have to agree with her father to appreciate his dedication and hard work that had provided her with security. Without it, she wasn't sure if she would have done any better with her life than those who lived on a legacy of entitlements. It was awfully hard to aspire to anything better if you perceived your life as hopeless.

A woman, whose world-weary expression added depth to the parenthesis of wrinkles around her mouth, opened the door to their knock. She gave Angel a puzzled look, then nodded in recognition of Sarah. "Oh. It's you. What do you want?"

"Just a few follow-up questions, Ms. Stark."

"Be quick about it. Only got a few hours to sleep before the boys come home."

"Can we come in?" Angel asked.

Despite the look that told Angel she'd rather not, the woman opened the door wider and let the detectives step in. She led them into a small living room that held a dingy blue sofa with a matching chair, two bean-bag chairs pushed against the wall and a couple of small tables. What the room lacked in decor, it made up for in cleanliness.

Two eight-by-tens in standing frames held what were obviously school pictures of the boys Francie had referred to. Almost identical in looks, they shared their mother's mousy brown hair and pale blue eyes, but their smiles were more natural and endearing. Angel motioned to the picture. "Where are your boys?"

"Summer program at the Rec Center. Don't know what I'd do without it. Can't work all night, then stay up all day looking after them."

"It appears you're doing a fine job," Angel said, and the woman softened visibly. "We were hoping you might have thought of something that could help us with the investigation."

"I'm sorry, Detective. I haven't."

Angel pulled out her notebook even though she didn't have anything written there. She consulted the blank page, then looked at Francie. "In your initial statement, you said you never knew Walter to use drugs. Is that right?"

"Yes."

"So you and he never . . . ?" Angel purposely let the question fade.

"No. Listen." A momentary panic flickered in the woman's eyes. "I was messed up a few years ago. Almost lost my kids. But I got into a program. Haven't touched the stuff since. Don't even want to be around it."

"But Walter *did* do drugs."

"No."

"That wasn't a question. It was a statement of fact. We have the proof."

Francie slowly sank to the edge of the sofa, shaking her head. "I thought he was a decent man. Not the best. But good enough. And the boys needed a strong, authority figure."

Sarah walked over and sat down next to Francie. "You told me before that the two of you were seeing each other exclusively."

"Yes."

"And you never went to a party or anything where there were drugs?"

Francie shook her head.

"Were you together every night he had off?"

Francie shook her head again. "A lot of our dates were daytime. Here. When the boys were at school."

Angel recognized the pain that crossed the woman's face. It was the pain of discovering the deceit in someone you thought you could trust. She was glad that Sarah had taken over the interview.

"How often did you see each other?" Sarah asked.

"Once a week. But we didn't always go out. Most of the time he'd come here. I'd cook dinner. The boys liked that. It was almost like being a family again."

"But he had two nights off."

"He kept the other for himself. Called it his boy's night out."

"Any idea what he did?"

"Got together with friends."

"Did you know any of them?"

Francie shook her head, pleating the cotton fabric of her shift with fingers reddened from years of hard work.

"Did he ever mention any names?"

Again, Francie shook her head, then looked up at Sarah. "But one guy called here a few times. During the day when Walter . . ." She paused to wave away her embarrassment. "I heard Walter making plans to meet him. Called him Freddie."

"Anybody else ever call here?"

"No."

"And you're sure Walter never mentioned knowing Mel Halsley?"

"No, Ma'am. He never did."

Angel answered Sarah's questioning look with a shrug. There didn't seem to be any point in prolonging this.

"We appreciate your help," Sarah said, rising from the sofa. "We shouldn't have to bother you again."

Francie walked them to the door, and Angel hung back a moment to shake hands. It was a gesture the woman seemed unaccustomed to, but Angel was pleased to see the slight stiffening of her back. It was like she needed something to help her feel respectable again.

Sarah was surprised to see Chad at the station when they got back. "Hey, what happened to your day off?"

184

"Just couldn't stay away." The look he gave Angel spoke volumes, and Sarah covered her face to hide a smile.

"Actually," he amended, returning his gaze to Sarah. "It's too damn hot to go to the batting cages and I was bored stiff rambling around my apartment."

"You need a hobby."

Whatever response Chad was about to make was cut short by the urgent peal of Sarah's phone. She reached out to answer it, her contributions to the conversation confined to a few uh-huhs and yesses. Then she replaced the receiver with a smile. "Sanchez is on his way over. He pushed to get a twenty-four-hour turnaround on that second tape analysis."

When Sanchez arrived, they elected to use McGregor's office for their conference. The Lieutenant was upstairs meeting with the brass, and Sarah didn't envy him that. What she did envy was his office and title. Sitting down in his chair, she wondered how soon she could realistically even hope to have an office of her own. Plenty of women made sergeant nowadays. But the ranks of women as lieutenants or captains were pretty slim. Still, it didn't hurt to dream.

Today, Sanchez wore a tousled look along with what appeared to be the same suit he had on the other day. Sarah wondered what J. Edgar would have had to say about one of his men looking less than pristine.

Sanchez took the chair opposite Sarah, and Angel sat down next to him. Chad remained standing, leaning one shoulder against the wall.

"There's not much to add to the original analysis." Sanchez took a piece of paper out of his breast pocket and pushed it across the desk to Sarah. "They faxed me the results about an hour ago. They revised their initial estimate that the guy is in his late thirties or early forties. He could be at least ten years older."

"Isn't that a bit unusual?" Sarah asked.

"Yeah. But not unheard of. Especially in cases where the guy moves around a lot and his need to kill only crops up sporadically."

"But you said before that our doer wasn't the typical serial killer," Angel interjected. "So how do we know if he even killed in the past?"

"You don't." Sanchez leaned back and swept both Angel and Chad in his glance. "I'm just relating the facts."

"What else?" Sarah asked.

"He's probably going to do it again."

"Even though he said he didn't want to?"

"Yeah. The team in Quantico read him as consumed with this need. They convinced me."

A silence followed that pronouncement, and Sarah noted the uneasy glance that passed between Angel and Chad.

"But I did run across something else that might help you." Sanchez drew another piece of paper out of his pocket. "I spent a little time digging around in our data-bank and came across an interesting case."

"What is it?" Sarah glanced longingly at the paper Sanchez held.

"An unsolved in the LA area. Some of the elements of your case are similar."

"Like what?" Chad asked.

"The victims were garroted for one." Sanchez said.

"Pretty significant considering the rarity of that particular MO," Angel offered.

"Yeah. But there were no notes."

"Damn."

"Don't discount it yet," Sanchez said. "The victims have a lot in common with your guys. Somewhat shady backgrounds. Less than stellar jobs. And casual drug use. Could be the guy started to make his statement out there. Then moved here and decided to be more didactic."

"How many victims?" Sarah asked.

"Three in a six week span." Sanchez glanced down the page of information then stuck his finger by a name and handed the paper to Sarah. "Here's the detective who was handling it. Fletcher. LAPD. Pretty decent guy according to our agent out there. He'd probably be thrilled with an opportunity to close his case."

"We appreciate the extra effort you put into this." Sarah stood and offered her hand to Sanchez. "Maybe someday we can return the favor."

Sanchez nodded.

# CHAPTER NINETEEN

The noise could be heard a half a block away from the Municipal Building, but it wasn't until she got nearer that Sarah could put sight to sound. An unruly mob of protesters faced a cordon of officers in full riot gear, and the officers didn't seem to think much of the crowd's right to demonstrate.

Placards waved in the air, calling for justice for blacks and the termination of the kid-killing cop. At the front of the crowd, Sarah recognized the familiar face of the Reverend Billie Norton. She also recognized Bianca Gomaz leading the pack of reporters.

Frustration and anger hung as heavily in the air as the heat and humidity, and Sarah brought her steps to a halt. They'd kill her if she tried to get through to the front door. She glanced back over her shoulder to see if the way was clear to the side entrance, then changed her mind. *Fuck 'em. I'm not going to let them intimidate me. That's what they want.*

Squaring her shoulders and keeping her eyes straight ahead, she marched toward the front steps, ignoring the fierce pounding of her heart and the stench of her fear that mingled with the sour smell that emanated from the crowd.

A few people jostled her as she passed through, elbows digging painfully into her sides, but others moved aside to give her room. *They don't even know who I am.* She found that a pathetic indicator of how far some people were removed from what they were protesting. They just came and shouted because someone told them it was the thing to do.

The piercing look the good Reverend gave her left no doubt that he knew who she was. Norton opened his mouth to say something, but a stir of movement from behind robbed him of the opportunity.

As the crowd parted, Sarah caught a glimpse of Bianca and her cameraman, thrusting their way forward. Bianca gripped a microphone, taping her voice-over. "In a dramatic moment here on the steps of the Municipal Building, Detective Sarah Kingsly faces off with the Reverend Billie Norton. Norton leads a crowd of close to a hundred people protesting the decision by the Police Commissioner to table the recommendation of the Dallas Review Board to sanction Detective Kingsly for the June 24th shooting of a fourteen-year-old black youth."

Bianca thrust the microphone over the Reverend's shoulder. "Detective. You must be pleased with the support from administration."

"I haven't been pleased about anything since this started."

"Does that include the unfortunate act of ending a young boy's life?"

Sarah fought a wave of guilt, forcing herself not to see that boy sprawled in the alley, his life-blood seeping into the concrete. She stared into Norton's rheumy brown eyes, willing him to understand. "I took no pleasure in that act. I did what I had to do."

A swell of verbal protest rumbled through the crowd and angry faces leaned close to Sarah. "That's a lie!" A fist sunk itself in her stomach and Sarah gasped for breath, stumbling on the concrete steps. Before she went down, one of the uniformed officers grabbed her and pulled her to the other side of their line. She scrabbled up the last few steps to the building and slipped inside, closing the door on the hysteria.

Knees weak and heart racing, Sarah staggered to the wall and leaned against it, fighting to catch her breath. She hadn't been surprised at the Review Board's decision calling for disciplinary action. The members had their minds made up about this before deliberations ever started. She wasn't even surprised by the Commissioner's reaction.

Any fool could see it would be a disaster to pull her off the current investigation. What surprised her was the depth of feeling people who didn't even know her could have. If hate had a face, it would look like the Reverend Billie Norton.

Finally regaining some control, Sarah made her way to the elevators and rode to the third floor. Inside the squad room a tension crackled, and Sarah noticed an unprecedented interest in paperwork by most of her fellow officers when she walked in. *What the hell?*

She cornered Burtweiler with an imploring gaze and asked, "What did I do?"

Burtweiler looked away.

Sarah addressed the room at large. "Come on, guys. It's not my fault."

Simms stepped forward, then took a deep breath and looked her in the eye. "Maybe if you hadn't let your mouth run away with you, the Board would have been more understanding in their decision."

"Bullshit!"

"Yeah? Tell that to the next guy who gets his ass nailed to their wall."

Clinging to the last shred of her composure, Sarah whirled and stomped to her desk.

*He took a deep, welcome swallow of cold beer and wiped his mouth with the back of his hand. When this was over, he was going to have to do something about how much he was drinking. But not now.*

*Right now, he needed all the courage he could find, bottled or otherwise.*

*The theme music for the five-o'clock newscast drew his attention to the TV. The face of that pretty little reporter filled the screen. He shouldn't have called her again. It was stupid to think she would understand. No one understood.*

*A picture of the confrontation outside the Municipal Building replaced the headshot. He leaned forward with interest. A mob was protesting about something. And there, leading the pack, was the righteous Reverend Billie Norton.*

*He reached out to push the* OFF *button, but drew his hand back when he saw* that *detective stop before the good Reverend. It took some balls to walk through the crowd.*

*He listened to the reporter's first question, and the detective's answer struck a responsive chord. He mentally replayed the words, "Nothing about this has pleased me . . ."*

*"She knows," he murmured, losing the gist of the reporter's next question in his thoughts. But he didn't miss the detective's response, "I took no pleasure in that act. I did what I had to do."*

*That's it exactly! It's like she looked into his heart and saw the words written there. She understands.*

*Jumping up, he bumped the little table and the beer bottle started to teeter. The fact that he could grab it before it fell was like an omen.*

*What the detective said. That was like an omen, too. She did what she had to do. Maybe she puked her guts out afterward like he did. But she did it. And he had no doubt she'd do it again if she had to.*

*Could he do any less?*

Sarah listened to the slow, steady rhythm of Paul's breathing, the scent of their spent passion still floating in the air. What on earth had she done?

A high, full moon laced through the slats of his vertical blinds, creating a jagged, zebra effect across the rumpled sheets and up the adjoining wall. She felt splintered like the moonlight, the two parts of her not quite fitting together.

She didn't have to ask herself why she had come here. Standing in the middle of the squad room this morning, she had never felt so alone in her life. If she'd have been more brazen, she would have called Paul right then.

But she'd suffered through a frustrating day of trying to make contact with the Fletcher guy in LA. When they finally connected, her hopes of really having something evaporated.

The LA victims had all been done with electrical wire. The bodies had been transported and then dumped in remote areas along the interstate.

Too many differences to try to squeeze them into a matched set. Fletcher had been nice enough, his gravelly voice etching a mental picture of the seasoned veteran with twenty years to his credit, a few too many beers under his belt, and the perpetual cigarette hanging off his lip. But nice wasn't enough to make something work, and they both knew it by the time they ended the conversation.

Fletcher had faxed her pages of the case file, and she had honored the courtesy by spending some time going over them. She'd even given copies to Chad and Angel. But the bottom line was, there was no bottom line. It was zero, zilch, nada.

It had been that association with numbers that made her think of Paul and reach automatically for the phone. The logical side of her warned against accepting his offer of another home-cooked meal. She shouldn't go to his place feeling this needy. But sometimes logic was over-rated. Paul seemed to have sensed Sarah's need the minute he opened the door, and they'd never made it to the kitchen.

Feeling the pull of another basic human need, she disengaged her legs from the tangle of sheets and eased off the bed, trying not to disturb Paul. She didn't know what she'd say to him if he woke up. I'm so glad you had condoms in your nightstand?

A sliver of the moonlight guided her past the trail of their discarded clothing and into the bathroom, illuminating it enough that she refrained from turning on the light. She did her business quickly, rinsed her hands in the porcelain sink, and dried them on a soft towel. Then she padded quietly back into the bedroom.

What should she do now? Leave?

A soft rumble in her stomach reminded her she still hadn't eaten.

"I guess I wasn't a very gracious host."

Sarah glanced at Paul who had raised himself on one elbow. The state of her undress became uncomfortable and she grabbed for her T-shirt on the floor.

"Don't do that. Please?"

She held the shirt in front of her, torn between her unease and his gentle persuasion.

"You really are quite beautiful you know. You were made for moonlight."

Sarah realized that if she'd read that line in a book she would have laughed out loud, but coming from him it felt so right. Nobody had ever reverenced her body the way he had.

Paul patted the bed. "Come back. Just for a minute. Then I promise I'll feed you."

She walked over to the bed and put one knee on the mattress. He trailed his fingers up the inside of her thigh, then across her stomach. "I knew you'd be delicious."

Whether it was the touch of his hand or his words, Sarah felt a stirring of desire deep inside and a rush of warmth peaked her nipples. Without consciously deciding to, she lowered herself to his inviting embrace.

He kissed her long and deep, his tongue thrusting and seeking while his hands caressed the length of her back, leaving a tingling trail of heat where they touched. Then he pulled out of the kiss, dancing his tongue lightly across her lips and down her cheek into the softness of her neck. When he finally reached his ultimate destination, Sarah gasped as he teased first one nipple, then the other.

Nothing he could cook could ever be this satisfying.

As if reading her mind, Paul leaned back with a soft chuckle. "You like?"

"Yes. I definitely like."

Sarah ran her fingers across the broad expanse of his chest, idly wondering what he did to stay in shape. Muscles like this did not come from pushing a pencil.

The tempo of Paul's breathing increased and Sarah felt an answering throb of renewed desire that swallowed her moment of curiosity. Slowly, she retraced the route her hands had taken across his body earlier, taking time to savor the still new discoveries.

Paul, likewise, seemed to want to prolong the ecstasy, not hurrying his renewed explorations. It was as if they were silently reaffirming what had gone before. Time suspended itself as tidal waves of passion swept over her, powered by his expert touch. Her body screamed for fulfillment, and when he finally entered her, the satisfaction radiated to the very depths of her soul. His deep thrusts lifted her off the bed, and she rode the rhythm of his beat, which began slowly and built to a shuddering crescendo.

As the final note faded into stillness, he lowered himself until his body stretched gently across hers. Their combined heat enveloped her in a cocoon that felt protective and comforting.

"Are you ready for me to fix you something to eat yet?" he asked.

"Well, I still feel a little stuffed right now."

His laughter rang pleasantly against her ear. "If I stay here much longer I'm going to want to do things I don't have the strength for." He brushed her cheek with a feather-light kiss, then eased away.

While Paul was in the bathroom, Sarah sorted through the scramble of clothes until she found her bra, panties, jeans and T-shirt. When he emerged, the moon slid out from under a cloud and bathed him in white, highlighting the lean power of chiseled muscles. His penis stirred, lifting away from the cradle of pubic hair. "Seems to have a mind of his own," he said, touching himself unselfconsciously.

Sarah resisted the impulse to toss her clothes and cross the distance between them. Man does not live on food alone. Nor does woman. "I've heard a good pinch can be very effective."

He grabbed his clothes and dressed quickly. "I think I'll go cook."

Paul was breaking strands of pasta into boiling water when Sarah came into the kitchen a few minutes later. The sweet aroma of basil rode the exhaust of his microwave.

"Smells good," Sarah said, peeking through the glass door to see what was heating.

"Luckily for us I keep a bowl of sauce in the freezer for just such a contingency."

"Does the opportunity present itself very often?"

"No."

The abruptness of his answer surprised her, the slight unease fanned by his equally abrupt turn away from her. "Did I say something wrong?"

"No." Paul stirred the steaming pasta for a moment, then tapped the spoon against the side of the pot and laid it on the stove. He turned to face her again. "I just thought tonight we should concentrate on the now. Not get snarled in the past."

"I see." A little bit more of the glow dimmed, and Sarah had her first serious regret. She had been right in her initial assessment. Their sex had been glorious. But had they held out against instant gratification, the intensity of their passion could have created other avenues of intimacy. Now that the edge had been dulled, would they have the same incentive?

Not wanting to force a stand neither of them was ready to take, Sarah opted for the safety of their light banter. "Then feed me, Seymour. I'm starved."

Later, Sarah pleaded the necessity of taking care of Cat and the late hour to gently refuse his offer that she stay. But after she was snuggled in her bed with a contented Cat purring softly in the bend of her waist, she acknowledged the disappointment created by Paul's emotional aloofness.

It was exciting to be considered beautiful and desirable, but it was more than her body or ego that needed satisfying. And what was it about Paul that kept him so distant? Letting her professionalism take over, she tried to deduce what had caused him to parry her playful attempts to draw him out during dinner.

The avoidance had been masked in fun, but it couldn't have been mistaken for anything else.

Was he hiding something? A painful past love affair? Or something more serious? He could be some kind of criminal, just toying with her.

The absurdity of that made her laugh out loud.

# CHAPTER TWENTY

The first thing Sarah noticed when they got to the second floor of the Galaxy Mall was the high-pitched keening of a hysterical feminine voice. Drawing closer to the woman who was thin enough to be on the brink of anorexia, Sarah could begin to make out words. "I didn't notice at first . . . just wondered where he was . . . doesn't leave usually . . . then the window . . . God! The window!"

Sarah looked at the patrol officer who'd drawn the short stick on this one, and he nodded toward the display window where fashions that would never fit in Sarah's budget were artfully displayed. The flowing lines of soft fabric were rudely interrupted by the incongruity of a corpse propped up in the corner. It was ignored by the mannequin next to it who had people to see and business to attend to in her Liz Claiborne power suit.

"Double goddam," Angel breathed beside her.

Stepping closer to the window, Sarah noted that the dead man's burgundy silk shirt fit within the fashion requirements of the display. What didn't fit was the notebook paper pinned to his chest. Today's message, EVIL WILL BE PUNISHED, was written in the now-familiar scrawl.

Damn! The last shred of hope that this one would be different seeped out of her. What in the hell were they up against?

Sarah turned back to the patrol officer who was gamely trying to control the hysterical woman. "Take her over there and have her sit down." Sarah pointed to a nearby bench that was pretending to be in a park by associating with two potted trees. "Then have someone get her something to drink. But stay with her until we're ready to take her statement."

"Yes, Ma'am."

The officer started to move away and Angel called after him. "Call for more backup, too. We're going to need crowd control in a big way."

Sarah followed her partner's gaze to the first wave of early shoppers rolling toward them. *Holy shit. Hadn't anyone locked the doors?*

Catching the attention of the rent-a-cop who was nervously eyeing the approaching horde, Sarah asked, "Anybody else here from security?"

The guy shook his head.

"Then you're it. Come on."

Sarah positioned the rent-a-cop and the other uniformed officer next to her with their arms out. Then she faced the crowd holding her shield so it was clearly visible. "Stop!"

The sharp command halted the advancing tide as effectively as if the people had run into a rope stretched across the walkway. So far, so good, Sarah thought. Now what the hell was she going to do with them?

"We're sorry about the inconvenience folks . . ." Sarah turned with surprise as Angel delivered the spiel, sounding like a representative from the mall's public relations department.

A familiar figure pushed to the front of the crowd and Sarah stepped forward to intercept the reporter. "That's far enough."

"This is a public place. That gives me full access." Bianca shot the detective a defiant look.

"Not today," Sarah called out over the rising swell of noise from the crowd. "This is a crime scene. Nobody comes past this point until we're finished."

Angel stepped forward and Bianca hesitated for a moment

before resurrecting her bravado. "The people have a right to know."

Only the presence of "the people," as Bianca so magnanimously referred to them, kept Sarah from saying what she wanted to. She was relieved to see four uniformed officers shouldering their way to the front of the crowd.

Right behind the new officers was a stocky man in a suit and tie who quickly took in the scene, then looked at Sarah. "I'm Dave Woodard, the manager. What can I do to help?"

"Can you take care of these people?"

"Sure." He gave her a quick smile then turned to the crowd. "There'll only be a slight delay here, folks. If you'll come with me, I'll try to make it up to you."

The crowd responded to Woodard's offer for refreshments, moving like lemmings toward the food court.

Bianca and her cameraman didn't join the exodus, so Sarah directed the patrol officers to hold their position. No way was the reporter going to encroach on the crime scene. Then Sarah walked back toward the store window, noting with satisfaction that Walt had arrived to make a preliminary medical exam. Good. Then they could get the body the hell out of there.

At the other end of the walkway she saw an officer diverting another group of people who'd been drawn to the excitement. She recognized a tall man in brown and touched Angel's shoulder. "Isn't that your friend?"

Angel followed Sarah's pointing finger. "Yeah. He must be here making deliveries. I'll go talk to him."

After Angel moved away, Sarah walked over to the woman who'd discovered the body.

The woman, who gave her name as Rhoda McAffries, had lost the fine edge of hysteria, and Sarah motioned to the young officer that he could leave them alone. Then she sat down and pulled her notebook out. "Can you give me the victim's full name?"

"John Baxter. He's worked for me for five years."

"Did he always come in early?"

"No. Not always. Sometimes. When we had something pressing like . . ."

Sarah recognized the signs of increasing agitation as Rhoda plucked at the folds of her skirt with almost spastic motions, but before the onslaught could be averted, the woman rushed on. "If only I'd listened to him. He wouldn't have had to come back. I shouldn't have made him come back. Especially not today."

"Why today?"

Rhoda took a ragged breath. "He's always been terribly superstitious. Didn't want to go anywhere on the thirteenth. Afraid something would happen. And look. He was right. Bad luck caught up with him."

Fresh tears rolled out of her eyes, pulling streaks of mascara across the make-up she'd probably spent an hour applying this morning.

Sarah gave the woman a few minutes to get control, wishing it was something as simple as bad luck that had caught up with John Baxter.

When she thought Rhoda was ready, Sarah asked the next question. "Why was he here early today?"

"That's why I feel so responsible. I told him he had to come back and redo the window. It wasn't right."

"Redo? As in?"

"The design. He's . . . was . . . a very clever window dresser."

Sarah glanced over her shoulder at the window, finally understanding what the woman was talking about. Then she turned back. "Is that all he did for you?"

"Oh, no." Rhoda shook her mass of red curls as if shocked

that Sarah could even think that. "He was my top sales clerk."

"Isn't that a bit unusual? A man in a woman's boutique?"

"Perhaps. It's more common for men to be in design than sales. But certain, uh, men have such an innate understanding of femininity. And of course, you can't overlook the charm. My customers blossomed under his attention and so did their charge accounts."

The last few words were said with such regret, Sarah had to wonder if it was for the person of John or the potential dent in revenue his demise would trigger. But the tears streaking down the woman's cheeks looked sincere enough.

"When you referred to 'certain men' did you mean that John was gay?"

Rhoda nodded, so Sarah followed with the next logical question. "Did he have a lover?"

"He's been with Cliff for almost ten years. But I think he'd be insulted to be thought of as only a lover. They were life-mates. Had a ceremony and everything."

"I see." Sarah turned to a fresh page in her notebook. "We'll need Baxter's address."

"I'll get it for you as soon as . . ." Rhoda's words faded into renewed tears as she looked over in time to see John's body being removed from the window.

"Right. I'll get back to you later." Sarah stood and went to meet Angel who was coming back from talking to her friend.

"Anything?" Sarah asked.

"No. He said he got here about eight and started with the deliveries. Didn't see anything out of the ordinary."

Sarah checked her watch to confirm the time. Almost eleven. "Does it always take three hours to drop his stuff off?"

"I didn't ask. It didn't seem pertinent."

"Anybody near a crime scene is pertinent."

Sarah intended her comment as an observation, not a judgment, and was surprised when Angel bristled.

"Okay. On that token we should grill the rent-a-cop and the manager. They were here, too."

"Of course we'll—"

"No. I don't mean the routine questions. I mean the third degree. Probe into every little detail and scrutinize it."

"Get a grip, Angel. I was just suggesting—"

"Strange you didn't suggest anything about the white guys."

"What the hell do you want from me? Do I have to paint my face black to prove something?"

A faint chuckle broke into the hostilities, and Sarah whirled to see Roberts at her side. "Now that would be a sight worth seeing," he said.

Sarah froze him with a glare. "What is it?"

"The forensic team's about finished."

Sarah lost her anger in hope. "Please tell me you found something good?"

"I'd like to help you out, Detective." Roberts's smile was slightly suggestive. "But about the only break we're going to get on this one is that there won't be ten thousand prints to sort through. But to make up for it, we've got twenty thousand fiber samples."

"You're kidding, right?"

"Yeah. It's only about five thousand."

Sarah turned her attention back to Angel who still wore a tight, angry expression. She wished they could settle this matter now, but in her current state of mind it could create another murder scene. Better leave it alone.

"Go tell the manager we're almost done," Sarah directed. "He can re-open this section of the mall in the next hour."

Angel nodded curtly and strode away. Sarah pulled her mind reluctantly away from her personal problem and went to get Baxter's address from the storeowner.

"There won't be anybody there," Rhoda said, after passing on the needed information. "Cliff has been out of town. He's not due back until tonight. Poor thing. He'll be so—"

"Do you know where he is?" Sarah quickly inserted the question hoping to steer the woman away from another eruption of grief.

"He's visiting his parents. In Houston, I think."

"You wouldn't have a number or address, by chance?"

"No. But it should be there in the apartment somewhere. The last name is Roland."

During the short ride to the address provided by Rhoda, Angel sat quietly in the passenger seat, so Sarah let her be. She recognized that this problem between them wasn't just theirs. Generations of prejudice and mistrust had created it, and each of them brought something to the table. She glanced at Angel. *What is it going to be, girl? Are we going to be enemies forever?*

At the apartment complex, they rousted the manager, a sixty-ish man with a military haircut and a green T-shirt, who obligingly opened the door to apartment 252.

The interior was a stunning contrast to the blandness of the rest of the complex. Bold, impressionistic paintings adorned cream-colored walls, and a wide variety of pots and vases sat on glass-topped tables like museum displays. A deep green sofa in some kind of soft cloth was situated in front of a large window draped, literally, in a paisley print over lace sheers.

"The fashion industry must pay well," Angel observed, and Sarah welcomed the break in the uncomfortable silence.

"His boss indicated he was pretty damn good at it." Sarah looked around the living room, then to Angel. "I'll take this. You check the rest."

Angel nodded, then turned right into a short hallway and entered the master bedroom. It, too, revealed a penchant for neatness and a sparse, but effective, turn of decorating.

Making a methodical search of the closets and sifting through the contents of dresser drawers brought a prickle of unease to Angel's arms. The final indignity of death rendered privacy obsolete. She'd read that somewhere in one of her textbooks, but it had remained a vague concept until she'd gone to her first murder scene. It was of little consolation that the victims were never there to watch her probe into the most secret places of their former lives.

One of the secrets Angel didn't want to probe today was what went on in the king-sized bed. Like many people, she maintained a neutral attitude about homosexuality by not thinking about the physical part of it. But neutrality was hard to hang on to when the bed kept trying to claim her attention by the sheer brilliance of the scarlet satin comforter.

After discovering a few pictures and an address book in the drawers in the night tables, Angel went to see if Sarah had had any luck.

Having found the pristine living room devoid of anything personal, Sarah had taken a quick look through a small second bedroom that doubled as a home office and a guestroom.

A short filing cabinet was stuffed with manila folders labeled to designate medical records, insurance, and a variety of other categories of daily living. There was even a file for entertainment and Sarah wondered at the compulsiveness that led some people to constrict their lives to such order. Hers was tossed in a shoebox on the top shelf of her closet.

A narrow galley kitchen opened to an eating area where a small table nestled with two chairs. Sarah scanned the room with a practiced eye, registering the scrupulously clean counters and the shining stainless steel sink.

At the end of a tier of cabinets, a message board hung over a telephone stand holding the required instrument. The words,

"Cliff's parents" were written on the board in block letters with a telephone number following.

Wishing that all necessary information could be acquired that easily, Sarah pointed to the message when Angel walked into the room.

"How convenient," Angel said.

"Just what I was thinking." Sarah shifted the strap of her shoulder holster, which was setting uncomfortably on her collarbone. "You want to do the honors, or should I?"

"Go ahead." Angel crossed her arms and leaned against the edge of the opposite counter.

Sarah pulled out her cell phone and dialed the number. After a moment, she asked for Cliff Roland and had to wait again until he came to the phone.

"Mr. Roland. This is Detective Kingsly in Dallas. I'm sorry to have to call you . . ."

Listening to her partner's direct, yet gentle statement of facts, followed by a string of soothing words, Angel found herself rethinking her earlier attitude. Maybe the woman wasn't such a hard-ass after all.

"I'm glad I don't have to do that very often," Sarah said after she put the receiver back on the phone.

Angel wanted to say something conciliatory, maybe take a first step, but her mind was mute.

"What did you find?" The question broke into Angel's thoughts.

"Some pictures and an address book." She held them out. "If nothing else it will help us in tracking down known acquaintances."

Sarah shook her head at the thought of all that legwork. It would probably add up to nothing. The possibility of the killer being on the list of friends was about as remote as the most distant star in the universe.

"What about the lover?" Angel asked. "Is he going to co-operate with us?"

"Yeah. He said he could come to the station in the morning. His parents are going to drive back with him this afternoon."

"You think he could be involved in the killing?"

"Are you serious?" Sarah took the lead back through the apartment to the front door.

"Partially."

Sarah paused and looked back. "Why?"

"Nothing specific." Angel shrugged. "It's just that gays aren't known as fine, upstanding citizens."

"Oh, come on."

"Sorry. Shouldn't have made such a blanket statement. I guess I just worked Oak Lawn too long."

"Okay. Some of them aren't upstanding citizens. But you seem to forget. Roland was in Houston."

"So he hired it done."

"And what about our other two victims? He just off them to confuse the investigation?"

Angel shrugged again.

Sarah thoughtfully chewed a knuckle. "You don't like gays, do you?"

"That has nothing to do with it."

"I'll take your word for that if you'll take mine about shooting that boy."

Angel didn't respond. She pushed past Sarah with a hard set to her jaw.

# Chapter Twenty-One

Sarah didn't look forward to the meeting with McGregor. They had precious little to report this morning, and their favorite reporter had really put the screws to them in yesterday's evening news. Even without access to the actual paper left at the latest murder scene, Bianca had managed to get the killer's message across. Sarah could imagine the jangle of frantic telephone calls from the top of the pyramid down. McGregor may have already gotten his.

Balancing her mug of coffee, Sarah pushed the door to McGregor's office open, noting that Angel and Chad were already there. Maybe they thought punctuality would count for something.

"Glad you could make it, Detective." McGregor leaned back in his chair, the swivel creaking in protest.

Sarah glanced at the institutional clock on the wall above the overflowing file cabinets to reassure herself she wasn't late. Trading a sympathetic smile with Chad, Sarah sat down.

"I've already filled the Lieutenant in on our search of the victim's residence," Angel said. "Told him we found no signs of drug use."

"But that doesn't mean he didn't," Chad offered. "Most people don't leave their stuff just lying around."

"We can lean on the lover a little bit when he comes in," Sarah said. "See what we can squeeze out of him."

McGregor nodded. "Any chance this could have been a copycat?"

Angel shook her head. "All the preliminary stuff says no. Cause of death. The message. It all looks the same."

"But putting the body in the window like that," McGregor said. "Any indication he'd moved the other two bodies at all?"

"No," Sarah answered. "And if the analysis from the Fibbies was right, he probably didn't want to touch the bodies after the fact. So maybe he killed him there in the window."

"Or maybe he put the body there to make his point," Angel said. "And you have to admit it was a dramatic statement."

A silence followed Angel's comment, underscored by the soft *thump, thump, thump* of McGregor beating a rhythmic tattoo on a stack of papers with a pencil.

"The more important question is how the killer knew that Baxter was going to be there," Sarah said. "It's a pretty big co-incidence that he just happened to stumble on Baxter doing some unscheduled work."

Another silence settled on the room, then Chad leaned forward. "Maybe the killer picks his victims in advance then stalks them."

"To the mall?" Angel shook her head. "That doesn't sound plausible."

"But it wouldn't hurt to review all the witness statements," McGregor said. "See if anyone turns up that shouldn't have been there."

The shrill ring of the phone interrupted McGregor, and he grabbed the receiver with a beefy hand. Sarah watched his face draw into tight lines as he responded to the caller in brief monosyllables. Then McGregor slammed the receiver back, almost pushing the phone off the edge of the desk.

"That was Price," McGregor said in response to Sarah's questioning look. "The Commissioner scheduled a press conference at five this afternoon."

"Damn," Angel said.

"Yeah. Fucking damn." McGregor pushed his chair away from the desk. "I'm going to end up with footprints all over my back."

"Do you want us there?" Chad asked.

"No. It'll hardly look like we're doing everything we can if you have time to meet with the press."

After leaving McGregor's office, the detectives split up the case load. Angel went to interview Rhoda again. Chad went to hound Roberts into pushing through the forensic testing. And Sarah drew the short straw. She spent the next couple of hours reviewing the paperwork and talking to the uniformed officers who'd been on the scene.

Her stomach burning from too much coffee, Sarah read the report from the security guard one more time. He'd stated that nobody who wasn't supposed to could have been in the building. But how could he guarantee that? Employees with keys could gain access any time through the back entrances. If they left those doors unlocked, anyone else could come in. Plus, the main doors were open early for mall-walkers.

Picking up her pen, Sarah made a note to talk to the security guard again. See how often they patrolled in those early hours. A shadow crossing the page distracted her, and she looked up to see Gladys, a petite woman in her fifties who was fondly dubbed "the keeper of the gate."

"There's a very fine-looking young man to see you," Gladys said, and Sarah smiled at the glint of mischief in the older woman's eyes.

"Very mysterious," Gladys continued. "He wouldn't give his name, but I'm sure he's okay. He just looks so . . . sad and forlorn."

Intrigued, Sarah got up and followed the woman to the only

entrance to Crimes Against Persons. Security required that the door be locked at all times. People seeking entrance had to state their case to Gladys, whose desk sat just opposite the glass window. As staunch as any guard at the Denver Mint, the woman was very careful about the people she buzzed through.

She was also a very good judge of gorgeous, Sarah thought, surveying the striking young man with dark curly hair and a distinct Mediterranean cast to his complexion. "Detective Kingsly?" he asked.

"Yes."

"I'm Cliff Roland."

Now Sarah understood what had triggered Gladys's assessment. When she stepped closer she could see that his eyes were swollen with the ravages of grief and the strain of coping with it had carved deep lines around his mouth.

"Come on in," Sarah said. "I'll see if I can find us a place to talk privately."

Both interrogation rooms were in use, and Sarah was contemplating the wisdom of talking to Roland at her desk, when McGregor came out of the coffee room. He gave Roland a once-over, then turned questioning eyes to Sarah.

"This is Baxter's partner. I'm looking for a place to talk to him."

"Use my office." McGregor leaned closer to Sarah. "And get the guy some coffee or something. He looks like shit warmed over."

"Better be careful, Lieu," Sarah whispered back. "Word might get around that you really are a good guy."

McGregor made a sound deep in his chest that came out like a cross between a growl and a rumble, then turned away. Sarah motioned Roland toward the office.

"I know this is difficult for you," Sarah said once they were settled. "I'll try to make it as brief as possible."

Roland toyed with the Styrofoam cup of coffee, avoiding Sarah's eyes. "I just don't understand how anybody could do that to . . ."

Sarah waited a moment while he reined in his emotions. Then he glanced up at her, the plea as strong in his eyes as in his voice. "Do you have any leads?"

"Not yet. We were hoping you could help with that."

"Everybody liked John."

"Obviously somebody didn't."

A visible tremor passed through Roland's body, and Sarah softened her approach. "We need to know about John's drug use."

"That hardly matters now."

"So he *did* use drugs?"

Roland shifted in his chair and glanced away. Sarah touched his arm. "A drug bust isn't high on our priority list right now."

Taking a hasty swallow of coffee, Roland remained silent, so Sarah tried a different tact. "Did you and John talk about the other homicides in the malls?"

"Oh my God. You mean he was . . ." Roland choked on the words, then regained his composure. "I told him to be careful. And you know what he said?" Roland shook his head. "He said he didn't have anything to worry about. The pervert only went after low-life assholes. God! He thought his money made him immune."

"Did you fight about that?"

"No."

"What did you fight about?"

Roland shot her an angry glance. "We didn't fight."

"Come on. Every relationship has disagreements."

"So you just naturally assume I got pissed and killed him."

"It's worth a thought."

"No wonder you cops get such bad press."

Sarah tried to stop her angry outburst. She'd even been trying real hard to be sympathetic to this guy, but that fried it. "You'll have your own share of bad press if you don't start being straight with me. We could get real interested in your drug habits and make sure your arrest makes the front page of the Metro section."

He shot her a defiant look. "Should I call my lawyer?"

"Only if you think you have to."

Sarah waited the ensuing silence out, and finally Roland gave a little shrug.

"Okay. Tell me about the drugs."

Roland complied, revealing a story of recreational drug use in a series of faltering statements. The final one cost him the most effort. "A couple of times we got in a little deep to the dealer. Had to do some business for him to take care of it."

"What kind of business?"

Roland didn't answer and Sarah sighed. This guy wasn't going to incriminate himself, and she didn't want to lose him again. "Did this dealer ever threaten you or John?"

Roland shook his head.

"Not even when you owed him the money?"

Roland shook his head again. "It didn't happen that often. I guess he valued us as customers."

Yeah, Sarah thought. The fucking mega-mart of narcotics. "You've got to give us his name."

He didn't want to. Sarah could see that in the wild look that flashed through his eyes, but eventually wisdom won out.

"Lester."

Sarah stood up and cleared a corner of McGregor's desk, then handed a legal pad and a pen to Roland. "Give me a detailed accounting of your time for the past forty-eight hours. Including names and phone numbers of anyone who can verify that. I'll be right back."

Grabbing Roland's empty cup, Sarah stepped out of the office and ran into Angel on the way to the coffee room.

"Baxter's lover come in yet?" Angel asked.

"Yeah. I've got him in Lieu's office."

"Does he look possible?"

"I don't think so. But we got another dealer to check out. Hold on to Chad when he comes back. We might as well start tonight."

As Sarah turned to walk back, Angel called out, "Great. Another cardboard supper."

The comment was so close to something John might have said, Sarah had to fight an urge to turn around to see if he was standing there. These moments always caught her off guard, and when they had first come, she would always give in to the impulse to look, making her experience the pain of grief all over again.

Not today. With a firm resolve, she shook off the sentiment and walked the last few steps to the office. It had been a whole week since she'd thought about John, and she didn't know whether to feel good about that or not.

Angel stared at her partner's retreating back, wondering what had prompted the slight hesitation in Sarah's steps. Or had she just imagined it? She felt like their partnership was under a huge microscope, and sometimes she found herself looking through the lens without even realizing it. Maybe this was one of those moments.

Grabbing a cup of coffee, Angel headed back to her desk to write up her report of the interview with Rhoda. After adding the report to the others in the crime folder, Angel put her handwritten notes in her own personal file. Then she saw Chad stepping down into the homicide area, head thrust forward as if in a hurry to get somewhere important.

"Hope you don't have any big plans for tonight," Angel called out to him.

Chad paused and flashed her a crooked smile. "Is that a proposition?"

A tingle of response surprised her, and she turned away before her face could betray her. "We're pulling some more overtime."

"How soon?"

"I don't know." Angel faced him again. "Sarah's finishing up with Baxter's lover."

"What do you say we grab a bite while we're waiting?"

After leaving a message for Sarah, Angel and Chad walked the few blocks to Bek's, fighting a stream of pedestrians hurrying to parking garages to start the nightly crawl home to the suburbs.

Angel carried her salad and chicken sandwich to the counter abutting the front windows and hoisted herself on one of the stools. Chad pulled another stool next to her and the spicy aroma of his chili dog made her mouth water.

"You one of those health conscious people?" Chad asked, motioning to her salad.

"It doesn't hurt to give your body a vitamin or two every now and then."

They ate in a comfortable silence for a while, then Angel turned to Chad. "Any luck with Roberts?"

"Not much." Chad mopped traces of chili from his mouth with his napkin. "He's anxious to get the scrapings from the autopsy to see if anything matches the first two, but Walt couldn't get to it until tonight."

"Guess we're not the only ones raking in the overtime on this."

Chad took the last bite of his sandwich, then wiped his face again. "How's your mother doing?"

"Better. Might get to come home in a few days."

"What a relief, huh?"

"Yes it is." Angel gave him a thoughtful look. "I appreciate you asking."

"I care."

The words softened the intense scrutiny of his eyes, and for a moment Angel couldn't breathe. It was getting harder to pretend the signals weren't there, and sooner or later she was going to have to acknowledge them. But he was such a contradiction.

Sometimes she looked at him and saw Darien with that "king of the hood" swagger that had marked his transition from the fringes of the bad guys into the real thing.

She had been foolish to think the love of a good woman would derail his train of self-destruction. Part of the ache of losing him had been the pain of lost love. The rest had come from the pain of self-deception. She'd vowed never to love like that again. Perhaps never to love at all.

Now there was Chad, inviting her with brief glimpses of strength and security beneath a playful façade. And she was scared to death to look into those velvet eyes too long, lest she see more.

Wadding up the paper her sandwich had been wrapped in, Angel stuffed it in her empty drink cup and slid off the stool. "We'd better get back."

She heard Chad sigh, a light and lonely sound, then the rustle of paper as he gathered his things to follow her.

# Chapter Twenty-Two

After putting through a request to Grotelli to have someone from patrol check out Roland's story, Sarah grabbed her jacket and went downstairs to see what the vending machines might offer for supper. Stepping out of the elevator, she winced from the glare of mini-cam lights and wondered if this was another bright idea from Price. Then she laughed at her inadvertent pun. Most of Price's ideas weren't that good.

On the other hand, setting the press conference against the backdrop of the throng of people waiting for their moment in court was an interesting touch. John Q. Public could see with his or her own eyes how serious the system was about offenders. Even if most of those offenders were there for a parking ticket.

Commissioner Hanson, resplendent in his three-piece hand-tailored suit, wore his smile as comfortably as his clothes, and his full head of white hair shimmered in the light. He didn't even sweat. In contrast, McGregor looked like he'd spent the last week in his clothes and was trying to mop beads of perspiration from his face as discreetly as possible.

Sarah glanced at her watch. Almost six. No wonder the poor guy looked beat up. Shielding her face so she wouldn't be recognized, she joined a small group of people and skirted around the reporters to reach the hallway on the other side. Hearing her name, she paused, thinking someone was trying to get her attention, but then she realized it had been part of a question thrown out by one of the reporters. She took a few steps back and heard Hanson respond in his smooth, well-rehearsed style, "I'm sure she's doing an adequate job, wouldn't you say so, Lieutenant?"

Even from a distance, Sarah read McGregor's body language well enough to recognize the barely suppressed anger and frustration. She wondered if the Commissioner was fool enough to think the Lieutenant's smile was real. "Detective Kingsly is more than adequately coordinating a vast and most difficult investigation," McGregor said, the smile staying firmly in place. "The whole team is doing an outstanding job."

"Why have certain facts been withheld from the press?" a strident, male voice called out.

Sarah watched McGregor's jaw clench and unclench. She was really afraid that this time he was going to lose it, but somehow he held himself in control. His answer was even diplomatic. Instead of calling the reporter a stupid moron for even asking the question, he said, "Because to reveal certain details would jeopardize our case."

Holding up his hands against the assault of more questions, McGregor deferred to Hanson and stepped away from the half-circle of microphones.

Sarah could tell the Commissioner wasn't happy about the Lieutenant walking off, but she knew he'd be even more unhappy if McGregor stayed and exploded. The stiffness of his back as he strode toward the elevators told Sarah he was close to ignition.

Sarah turned back down the hallway, a myriad of emotions fighting for dominance. McGregor's solid endorsement of her still played through her mind, but dismay that her ability continued to be questioned dulled the pleasure. And how long could his staunch defenses hold against the flood of doubts that seemed to be gaining momentum. If they didn't solve this case soon, a lot of people were going to drown.

Settling for a Snickers bar and a diet cola, Sarah started back toward the elevators, then paused when she saw Chad and Angel push through the front door. By the rather dejected expression on Chad's face, Sarah guessed he hadn't had much luck in furthering his cause. Nobody was having much luck lately.

"We going to play dress-up again?" Chad asked after Sarah told him what they needed to do.

"No. We'll do this one straight."

"Okay. Let me make a couple of calls and see if any of my buddies know anything about this Lester."

Sarah noted that Angel watched Chad stride away with particular interest, and she wondered about the apparent wall her partner had built in regard to this man. The curiosity took voice, "What is it with you and Chad?"

Angel shifted her gaze to meet Sarah's eyes. "I don't recall asking your opinion."

The words assaulted her, and Sarah took a half-step back. "Pardon me for being interested in your life."

"Sorry." Angel shrugged and broke eye contact. "Just don't want to talk about it. Okay?"

"Whatever."

A sense of unease hung heavy in the air between them, rigid and unyielding, until Angel shifted her weight from one foot to the other. "Guess I could go get us a car."

"Yeah. Pick us up out front."

Sarah made a quick trip to the restroom, giving herself a quick sermonette while she washed her hands. Don't worry about McGregor having his balls in a wringer. Don't try to figure Angel out. And don't take any of this shit personally. "Yeah, right," she told her reflection in the mirror. "It's about as personal as it can get."

After going back to wait for Chad to return, Sarah ate the

candy bar and tried to convince her stomach it had received a three-course dinner. Then she saw him approaching.

"Where's Angel?" he asked.

"Went to get us a car." Sarah started toward the front doors. "Did you have any luck?"

Chad hurried to keep pace. "Yeah. Lester has a favorite place to play pool. And the bartender there is someone I dealt with a while back. I could probably convince him to cooperate."

Heat shimmered on the line of cars filling the street and Sarah welcomed the breath of cool air when she opened the door of the car idling at the curb. She slid in next to Angel, and Chad got in back.

Angel nosed the car out until a driver in a blue Lexus had to let her join the stream of traffic inching along the downtown streets. Chad gave Angel directions as needed. Otherwise silence reigned in the car.

Finally, Angel pulled into a small parking area beside the pool hall, and Chad turned to Sarah. "How do you want to do this?"

"You take the lead. Get the bartender to finger Lester if he's here."

Stepping through the door, Sarah was assailed by the sour smell of stale beer and too many unwashed bodies. Layers of smoke drifted slowly on meager air currents created by two ceiling fans vainly trying to live up to their billing. A sad, country song wailed out of the jukebox, competing with a sportscaster calling the first game of a Ranger's double-header from the television above the bar.

A short, slight man behind the bar looked like he wanted to crawl into some corner and pull his skin after him as Chad approached. "Hey, Frankie, how're you doing?" Chad leaned one elbow on the bar, and a guy two stools down picked up his drink and took it to the other end of the bar.

Frankie moved a nervous gaze from Chad to the women, back to Chad again. "Nothin' that interests you."

"Glad to hear that, Frankie. 'Cause I'd hate to have to bust you again. You're down for two already, and the next pitch is a game breaker. You get my drift?"

"You got no call to hassle me," Frankie said, running a nervous hand through his sparse blonde hair. "I've been straight for five years now."

"I'm not hassling you, Frankie. I just want one teensy little favor. Then I'm outta your face."

"What kind of favor?"

"We're looking for Lester."

Frankie didn't answer, but he shot a quick look at a pool table in the far corner where a small crowd was gathered to watch two men compete.

"Which one is he?" Chad prodded.

Frankie sighed. "The white guy, shooting."

"Thank you, Frankie. You won't regret this."

Before moving away from the bar, Sarah noted that Frankie didn't look like he believed Chad.

Lester was tall and thin with a wise-guy outfit including a silk jacket and a neck full of gold chains. His opponent was a wiry black guy with dreadlocks and a pained expression. Lester called, then sank the eight ball in the side pocket as the detectives approached the table.

A heightened sense of tension settled on the group watching the game, three junior wise-guys who moved to stand behind Lester. After sliding a bill across the rail, the black guy joined them.

"We need to talk to you, Lester," Sarah said.

He pocketed the money without acknowledging her, and Sarah felt the heat of hostility radiate from the group. Some of the eyes told her they were willing to risk a confrontation to teach the cops who was king of this turf. But was Lester?

He reached under the table and brought up a small leather case. He set it on the table and snapped the clasps to reveal a plush, red velvet lining ready to nestle the pieces of his cue stick. Then he started to break the stick down, still not saying anything.

"We're not here to make any trouble for you," Angel said. "We just need some information."

Lester gave her a look, then resumed wiping the finely polished wood with a soft cloth. The cool, methodical way he worked convinced Sarah that bullying or intimidation wouldn't work. And if they threatened to take him in, he'd say, "So what? My lawyer will have me out before you can take a piss. Then we'll file a harassment charge."

Sarah took a cue stick off the wall and hefted it. "You ever been beaten by a woman, Lester?"

Her question stirred a ripple of laughter from Lester's fan club, and he shot her a cold look.

"Afraid to try?"

The dare was met by a nervous gasp from the small black guy who looked quickly to Lester for some signal. He held up a detaining hand and continued to look at Sarah. "Why should I bother?"

"You wouldn't want people to think you backed down from a woman, would you?"

It felt like an eternity before Lester made a move. Sarah could sense Chad and Angel tensing with her as she withstood the icy intensity of Lester's pale blue eyes.

Finally, Lester gave a barely perceptible sign, and the defenders stepped back from the table. Still maintaining eye contact with her, he slowly tightened the stick. Then he closed the case and pulled it off the table. "Name your game."

"Whatever you were playing before is fine."

"Eight ball."

"That the one with solids and stripes? You shoot one and I shoot the other?"

Lester smiled. "Right."

Chad and Angel moved against the wall, and Sarah was glad to see that they positioned themselves to watch the fan club. That should negate any impulse to interfere.

Lester racked the balls, clacking them smartly together. Then he lined them up on the spot, stepped back and motioned to Sarah. "You break."

"Go ahead. I'm not very good at that."

A snort of laughter from one of the watchers followed her remark. Lester stepped up and placed the cue ball. With careful ritual, he chalked the end of his stick, powdered his hands, then bent over the stick. His shot sent the cue ball rocketing into the triangle, which exploded with a loud crack, spinning the balls wildly across the table. The two ball clunked down the side pocket, and Lester smiled. He sank two more solids before missing a banked shot by the merest breath.

Sarah made an easy sink on the thirteen hanging on the lip of the corner pocket, then missed on her next try. She went to stand by Chad and Angel as Lester sank two more balls in quick succession.

"What the hell are you doing?" Angel asked in a soft whisper. "Why'd you challenge him if you can't play?"

"It was the only thing I could think of to keep him here."

"Oh, great."

"It'd be worse if I beat him. He'd probably kill us."

Sarah intended the little joke to reassure herself as much as Angel. She didn't have a clue how to work this to her advantage, but the way he was clearing the table, she'd better figure out something fast.

Hoping for some last minute inspiration, Sarah stepped back

to the table when Lester missed another shot. She sank one and thought maybe she could at least delay the inevitable by stretching the game out a bit. But then she scratched on her next shot.

Smiling, Lester retrieved the cue ball. He set it up for an easy tap on the seven in a side pocket, leaving the white ball right where he wanted it for access to the three on the other side and the eight waiting for him in the corner. He didn't prolong the agony. When he was finished, he looked up with a smile. "No. I've never lost to a woman."

"Now that I've helped you save face, how about answering a couple of questions?"

Lester eyed her carefully.

"You got some nerve, lady."

"Yeah. Makes up for how badly I play pool."

Sarah watched the expression on Lester's face soften around his eyes as his fans laughed appreciatively. Then he gave a slight nod. "Five minutes."

"Did you have a beef with John Baxter?"

"Who?"

"Don't try to snow me, here. We know you did business."

Lester began an instant replay of packing his stick. Sarah leaned one hip against the rail and waited.

Finally, he looked at her. "Do I get a visit from a narc later?"

"No."

He studied her for a moment, then was apparently satisfied that she wasn't lying. "I wouldn't off a good customer."

"What about somebody else taking your customers out?"

"We got rules."

"Yeah. But some of the new guys on the block seem to have misplaced the rule book."

"I ain't had any trouble like that."

"What about Baxter? He ever go to another store? Then piss somebody off by coming back to you?"

"No." Lester settled the sections of his stick in their appropriate places in the case.

"How can you be so sure?"

"He was a valued customer."

"So I heard."

Lester closed the case and snapped the clasps. "Your five minutes are up."

Walking back to the car a few minutes later, Chad nudged Sarah. "Pretty good show in there."

"For all the good it did."

Angel laughed. "There for a while I thought you'd lost your mind."

Sarah opened the passenger door. "Me, too."

Sliding into the back seat and slamming the door, Chad asked, "Now what, Boss?"

"I don't know." Sarah leaned against the headrest with a sigh. "It just keeps getting weirder and weirder."

Angel started the engine and adjusted the air-conditioning to high. "You'd think after all this we would have turned up at least one good lead."

"Maybe we're looking at the wrong side of this."

Chad hunched forward and looked at Sarah. "What do you mean?"

"Going after the people on the business end." Sarah turned so both Chad and Angel were in her line of vision. "Think about it. This guy's trying to make a statement, right?" She paused for their nods of assent. "So what's he saying by offing users?"

"That he doesn't like drugs?" Angel suggested.

"But if it was just his own personal war against drugs there's lots of damage he could do to upset the business," Sarah said. "He could start territorial disputes. Disrupt sales. All kinds of things. So why isn't he?"

"Because his cause isn't general. It's personal," Chad said.

"Someone singularly obsessed," Angel mused.

Sarah gave her a puzzled look. "What?"

Angel turned to face her. "It's what Ryan said. And Sanchez. That the killer is singularly obsessed."

"Yeah. Someone who was victimized by drugs." Chad tapped the back of the seat for emphasis. "Had a friend or relative who OD'd. Or was shot in a turf war."

"But if he wants revenge, why kill these guys?" Angel asked. "If I was pissed because someone I loved died in some drug thing, I'd go after the dealers."

"That makes sense," Chad agreed. "Why kill three insignificant little users?"

"That, my friends, may be the big question," Sarah said.

"And where do we start looking for the answer?" Angel asked.

"Records of drug-related deaths."

"And you expect to randomly pull our killer from about forty thousand files?" Angel asked.

"No. I don't expect anything," Sarah said. "But I'd rather be doing something other than hopelessly spinning our wheels."

"We aren't going to do it tonight are we?" Angel asked.

"No. First thing in the morning. And we'll start with the unsolved cases. That'll narrow the field."

# CHAPTER TWENTY-THREE

It took almost six hours and what seemed like hundreds of cups of coffee, but Sarah finally came across something that reeked of possibility. A fourteen-year-old boy had been shot in one of the run-down residential areas off Harry Hines near Love Field two years ago.

According to initial statements by family, the kid, Elisha Hammel, was one of the rare breed who can grow up in the middle of shit and not get tainted. He didn't do drugs or run with a gang.

He'd been taken out execution style, and no one could figure motive until the possibility of mistaken identity came up. When leaned on a little, one neighborhood thug finally allowed that Elisha looked a lot like a drug dealer who'd been having some trouble in the area. A contract hit that went bad?

Unfortunately, it happened, even to kids.

The case had never been solved, and the angry father had hounded the investigating officers unmercifully in the first year. Recent notations in the file documented his continuing interest.

A routine check of Elisha Hammel Senior had shown that he wasn't averse to violence if necessary. He'd had several arrests for assault in his younger years. The other thing Sarah liked about him was his job. He made deliveries for UPS. If he still worked there, that gave him a lot of freedom and possible access to the malls.

A quick call verified that Hammel was still happily employed.

Sarah picked up the folder and walked over to where Angel was buried in a stack of files a foot high. "What do you think of this one?" Sarah dropped the report on top of the one Angel was reading.

After scanning a few pages, Angel looked up at her. "It's definitely better than anything I've come up with."

"I'll see if McGregor's free."

It took only a few minutes for McGregor to get excited about the possibility of Elisha Hammel Senior being the doer. "We need to handle this very carefully," he cautioned.

"We know that, Lieu," Sarah said. "We're not going to go charging around and scare him off."

"Okay. Let's see what we can get before we confront him. Talk to his boss. Do a neighborhood thing. But play it real low-key. Tell 'em you're doing a routine background check or something like that."

"What about talking to his family?" Angel asked.

"Only if we have to," McGregor said. "They'd be more likely to tip him. Let's see what we get from our other efforts first."

"Should we wait for Chad?" Sarah asked.

"Where is he?"

"Out checking on a possibility he turned up a couple of hours ago," Angel said.

McGregor shook his head. "No telling when he'll get back. We've got to move on this now."

Back at her desk, Sarah called UPS again and made an appointment to meet the route supervisor at four-thirty that afternoon. She pushed to try to get the meeting sooner, but he couldn't get free any earlier. Then she and Angel headed out to Hammel's neighborhood.

The nearer they got to the airport, the sharper the air pollution became, and Sarah pushed the button to recycle the inside air. How could people stand to live out here with the constant scream of jets and the acrid bite of their exhaust clogging the atmosphere?

Turning down the street, Sarah realized the absurdity of her question. The people who lived here didn't have many options. For most of them, this was probably the last stop before the projects or something worse. A sense of despair and hopelessness was reflected in the old frame houses, held together in some cases by pieces of tin clinging gamely to decaying wood.

Little had been done to improve the aesthetic appeal of the area. Junk landscaped most of the yards, and the only attempt at beautifying the neighborhood Sarah could see was a red Geranium peeking out of the top of an old coffee can. It was on the front porch of the house next to Hammel's.

Seeing the flower reminded Sarah of Miss Millie, who'd lived down the road when Sarah was a child. Millie always planted a part of her garden in flowers. The neighbors, Sarah's mother included, considered the woman's efforts a stupid waste of good ground. "The old fool'll starve come winter," her mother had often said, " 'cause she didn't have the good sense to plant enough beans."

Millie had believed the flowers were important. She had told a curious child that when people don't make the effort to create a little beauty in their lives, then they've sunk about as low as they can go. When the last wildflower had died in her own yard, Sarah had finally figured out what the old woman had meant.

Shaking her head to get rid of the distracting thoughts, Sarah pulled the car to a stop a few houses down from Hammel's address.

"We're not likely to get much from these neighbors," Angel observed, opening her door and getting out.

"Don't be such a pessimist." Sarah slammed her door closed. "You want to start across the street?"

"Sure."

Sarah looked back toward the house next to Hammel's, drawn by the brave little flower and a curiosity about who had planted it.

Walking up to the front of the house, which was holding up fairly well despite the peeling paint and broken porch railing, Sarah reviewed the story they had decided on while driving over. They were updating the records on the old homicide, making sure they had the latest information in case they got a break in the case. Sarah had figured the neighbors would respond better to a shared tragedy than an ambiguous "background check" on Hammel.

The woman who answered the knock could have been anywhere from fifty to seventy. Age was not defined on her skin, the color of deep, rich chocolate, and only a hint of grey dusted the neatly combed hair. The maturity radiated from eyes as dark as coal. In the steady gaze, Sarah could sense the pride and dignity that held the woman above the cesspool of life in the neighborhood.

Wearing a threadbare, yet clean and pressed housedress, the woman stood as tall as her five-foot-two frame allowed, and she didn't flinch when Sarah showed her shield.

"How may I help you, Detective?"

"How long have you lived here, Ms . . . ?"

"Mrs. Mavis Hogan." The woman smiled briefly as if amused by the feminist term Sarah had used. "Used to be Mrs. Fred Hogan. But a woman's not supposed to use her husband's name when he passes on." This time her smile was a little wistful. "But that's not what you asked is it? I've been here coming on to fifty years."

"So you know Mr. Hammel next door?"

"Oh, yes. The poor man. To lose his son like that. What a—"

Sensing that the woman could waste a lot of valuable time rambling, Sarah cut her off with an explanation for why she was there and an apology for any perceived rudeness.

Mavis said she didn't consider it rude and invited Sarah in. The door opened directly into a living room cluttered with pictures and mementos that obviously covered many years and several generations. Despite the lack of air-conditioning, the room was comfortable. Sunlight was held at bay by drawn curtains, and a small oscillating fan stirred the air that smelled pleasantly of freshly baked bread.

Sarah politely refused the offer of a cool drink. She didn't want the woman distracted with something to do. She did, however, accept the offer to sit on the old sofa, covered in a floral design rendered indistinct over years of use.

"Have you found the horrible person what killed that boy?" Mavis asked, taking a seat in a small wooden chair with padded seat and back opposite Sarah.

"No." Sarah opened her notebook. "But we haven't stopped looking either."

"That's good." The woman folded her hands primly in her lap. "People who do things like that ought not to get away with it."

"We're trying real hard to make sure that doesn't happen," Sarah said. "That's why we're keeping the case active."

That reassurance seemed to please Mavis, and she nodded for Sarah to go on.

"Were you home the night it happened?"

"Yes. And I'll never forget it." She shook her head as if trying to erase the mental picture. "You'd think remembering the killing would dull in time. Like all the others that happened in the neighborhood. But Elisha was different." She paused again, dark eyes filling with moisture. "He shouldn't have died like that."

"Was it unusual for him to be out that late?"

"Oh, no. He worked every day after supper. Cleaning up for

Mr. Potter who owned that grocery on the next street. Mr. Hammel had the boy do his homework right after school. Then he could play for an hour before supper. They ate together most days. Then Elisha would go to Potter's."

"What about Elisha's mother?"

Sarah realized it was going to take a while to get past the questions that were covering old ground. All this had been in the case file, but she figured the time invested would be well spent if it established rapport before she started probing into more current history.

Mrs. Hogan's statement about Elisha's mother dying a couple of years before he had didn't contradict the earlier information, and Sarah followed with another question. "What about the neighbor's attempts to help the police?"

"Some folks got together a few times. Wanted to help Elisha Senior. But we were looking out for us, too. Didn't want nothing like that to happen around here again."

"Does the group still meet?"

"No." A trace of disappointment underscored the word. "I suppose it would've been different if we could've done something. Maybe caught the terrible person who shot poor Elisha. But nothing happened and folks stopped coming."

"What about recently?" Sarah asked. "Have there been any attempts to pull a neighborhood group together again?"

"No."

It was the first one-word answer that Mavis had given, and Sarah didn't miss the edge of wariness that crept into the woman's gaze. Apparently, a very smart woman resided under the façade of a lonely widow with too few audiences.

"Mr. Hammel certainly has been through a difficult time." Sarah closed her notebook, hoping a less-formal approach would put the woman back at ease. "But sometimes, time heals the pain and people get on with their lives."

"I suppose that's true."

Sarah forced her expression to remain benign, while Mavis studied her. The effort was rewarded when the woman relaxed slightly, then started to speak again. "I can talk about Fred's passing now easier than before."

"Is it the same for Mr. Hammel?"

Mavis shook her head. " 'Course I don't see much of him anymore."

"His job keep him pretty busy?"

"No. That's not it. Most evenings I see his car there. So I know he's home. He just don't come out like he used to."

"He's been keeping to himself," Sarah prompted.

"But even when I see him, he don't say much. It's like he wants to keep himself . . . remote."

There was a distinct questioning tone at the end of the comment, and Sarah wondered at the incongruity of such a formal word thrown into the middle of down home, country easy-speak. Then she realized that the woman's entire manner of expressing herself had been a contradiction. It was like she had been falling in and out of character like some ill-prepared actress.

Was she just smoking her?

Mentally chewing on the question, Sarah considered the posture and open gaze of the other woman and decided maybe not. Maybe she was just caught in some limbo between the kind of person one expected to find in a place like this and the person she was striving to be.

"Perhaps Mr. Hammel is just having a harder time with his grief," Sarah suggested. "The death of a child can be devastating."

"That's true." Mavis paused as if applying some kind of measuring stick to the validity of Sarah's comment. "But there are other things. He's been drinking more. I've seen bottles in his trash can. And he's been coming and going at odd hours.

"It's not that I'm spying, mind you. Just some nights I don't sleep so good, so I get up and watch a little TV. I hear his car pulling in at all different times."

Sarah felt a stir of excitement that she hoped she effectively masked. "Does this happen a lot?"

"I don't know. I don't wake up in the night that often."

Sarah realized she'd gone as far as she could without threatening the woman's loyalty, so she decided to stop for now. They could always push for more details later, after they found out if they had enough to warrant the push.

Outside, Sarah didn't see Angel so she walked back to the car to wait. She was trying not to bank too much on Mrs. Hogan's statement of Hammel's "strange behavior," but it would be interesting if they turned up anything else to add some substance to suspicion.

The heat took her breath away, so Sarah got in the car and turned on the air-conditioning, waiting impatiently for the initial blast of hot air to cool. The beep of her cellular phone, startled her, and she pulled it out of her inside jacket pocket. "Kingsly here."

"I want to have a briefing this afternoon," McGregor said without preamble. "What time can you and Angel make it back?"

"Not till late, Lieu. We're scheduled with the boss at four-thirty. That'll put us back at the station by six at the earliest."

"Okay. I'll hang on to Chad when he gets back."

"Order us in some pizza or something, huh?" The words were out of her mouth before Sarah realized she was talking to a dead line.

McGregor didn't comment on their tardiness when Angel and Sarah walked in close to six forty-five. Both he and Chad looked at them expectantly, and Sarah was glad they had something encouraging to report. She pulled up a chair and sat down. "Things are starting to point pretty strongly at Hammel."

McGregor leaned back with the beginnings of a satisfied smile. "Tell me what you got."

Quickly, Sarah gave the high points of her interview with Mavis Hogan. Angel added verification from the two neighbors she had found who were willing to talk.

"Even though that's not a total bomb-out like mine was," Chad said, "it's still pretty thin."

"But it gets better," Sarah said. "According to Hammel's work schedule, he was off the date of the last murder."

She paused to give them time to assimilate that information.

"So he could have been there at the mall." McGregor rubbed his chin thoughtfully.

"He has a familiarity, too," Angel said. "One day a week he makes deliveries from a local distributor to bookstores in the malls."

"No shit?" McGregor let the smile blossom.

"No shit," Sarah answered. "And, the boss also told us that Hammel's performance on the job has been slipping. A couple of weeks ago when he had to talk to Hammel about some mistakes, the guy blew up at him. The boss said if it wasn't for feeling sorry for him, he'd have canned him. But he's a little worried about Hammel. As he put it, 'the guy acts like he doesn't give a damn.' "

"If I can play devil's advocate here for just a moment," Chad said. "The behavior can be explained by the grief the guy's going through."

"Except," Angel countered, "it didn't start right after the son died. Hammel took about a month off, then came back and worked just fine until a few weeks ago."

"It all sounds pretty good sitting here talking about it," Chad said, "but what about evidence?"

Angel shrugged and turned to McGregor. "What do you think? Do we have enough to ask for a search warrant?"

"I'll call Chief Dorsett and see."

Sarah tried not to fidget while McGregor was on the phone. Likewise, she tried not to second-guess his pitch. Either it would work or it wouldn't. No sense in getting in a lather about it.

The relief in the room was tangible when McGregor hung up and faced them with a grin. "She thinks she can get Judge Richmond to sign," McGregor said. "Part of his re-election campaign is based on 'victim's rights over criminal rights.' He's willing to accept almost anything as probable cause. We'll stipulate we're looking for a piano, the tool used to cut the wire, and black cloth gloves to match the fibers from victim number two."

"Can we get it tonight?" Sarah asked.

"She's pretty sure. It'll take a while to go through channels, but she'll get back to me within an hour."

# CHAPTER TWENTY-FOUR

Daylight was holding its last stand against the invasion of night as the detectives returned to Hammel's neighborhood.

This time Sarah parked right in front of Hammel's house. After killing the engine, she sat in the gathering silence and contemplated the flower on Mrs. Hogan's porch. The color was indistinct now, muted in the dying sunlight like an old black-and-white photograph.

Angel nudged Sarah and pointed to the rusting hulk of a Camaro, vintage early '70s, sitting in the driveway. "Hammel must be home," Angel said. "That's his car."

"Good." Chad opened the passenger door and stepped out. "Then we can serve the warrant, nice and legal."

Walking toward the front door, Sarah glanced at a side-window of Mrs. Hogan's house and thought she saw the flutter of a curtain. Was the old woman looking out? If so, she'd probably realize the earlier visit wasn't as innocent as Sarah had made it out to be. Sarah knew she shouldn't feel bad about that. It was her job. But a little part of her didn't like having to deceive people. Especially nice, decent people like Mavis Hogan who could now tell all her family and friends what tricks the police play.

"You with us here, boss lady?" Chad asked as they stepped up on the splintering wood of the porch.

"Yeah." Sarah turned and contemplated the new storm door, which contrasted sharply with the disrepair of the rest of the house. There was no doorbell, so she reached out and rapped sharply against the aluminum, her knock ringing hollowly. When the inside door opened a crack, she called out, "Police, Mr. Hammel. Open up."

The inside door gaped wider, but the shadowy figure made no move to open the other one. Sarah held up her shield long enough for him to read the numbers if he wanted to, then she substituted it for the legal document. "We'd like to do this nice and simple, Mr. Hammel. We've got a search warrant, so we're coming in one way or another."

Sarah saw Hammel transfer his gaze from the paper to the other detectives flanking her. Then he suddenly bolted into the dim interior.

"Cover the back," Sarah yelled.

Angel jumped off the porch and ran around a dying Rose of Sharon bush.

Sarah drew her weapon and clenched it with both hands, then stepped through when Chad opened the door. He covered her back as she paused a moment to let her eyes adjust.

A quick scan of the room revealed an extreme state of disorder, but no sign of life. Then she heard the sounds of movement from a room in back she assumed was a kitchen. Skirting along the wall, Sarah approached a doorway, then took a quick look. Hammel was heading toward escape through a back door.

As Sarah stepped around the corner, the back door burst open with a resounding thud and Angel charged in. The sudden intrusion seemed to startle Hammel for a second. Then he lunged at Angel.

"Freeze," Sarah shouted, but the command didn't stop him.

In the split second that Sarah debated the wisdom of using deadly force, Angel whirled and landed a kick high on Hammel's chest that sent him reeling backwards.

Sarah closed the distance quickly and put the barrel of her

weapon against the back of his head. "Don't move."

If Hammel was considering any more defiance, the urge apparently gave way to good sense. He stood still while Angel came around and cuffed him.

Sarah holstered her gun then turned to Chad. "Bring him out here and watch him. We'll look around."

An open bottle of bourbon on a living room table explained, at least in part, Hammel's bravado. Sarah couldn't wait to find out what else had driven him to make that desperate move. Did he have a specific reason to be afraid of a search warrant? Or had he just run on general principle?

The similarity between this house and the one next door ended with general layout. The clutter here represented months of neglect. Carelessly tossed papers, pieces of junk mail, and rumpled clothes joined an assortment of dirty dishes on every flat surface in the room, and the sickening aroma of something rotten wafted in the closed air. Whatever pride Hammel may have had before had apparently died with his son.

A quick look around dimmed Sarah's hope and her enthusiasm. There was no piano in sight. Since it wasn't as easy to hide as a gun, she could see the first big hole in their theory widening.

"I'll check out the other rooms," Angel said, and Sarah nodded reluctantly. That left her to dig through the filth in here. One small consolation was the possibility that the other rooms wouldn't be much better.

Sarah could feel Hammel's eyes following her as she sifted through the debris on the torn sofa. "You have no right to be touching my clothes," he said.

"If you'll read the document I gave you," Sarah said without stopping her search, "you'll see exactly what we have the right to do."

A sudden movement caught her attention and she looked up

quickly. Chad caught the lunging Hammel by the upper arm and slammed him back against the wall. "You don't want to push your luck with me," Chad said. "I won't be as gentle as the lady was."

Confident that Chad had the other man under control, Sarah moved to the large round table in front of the sofa and started methodically diminishing the jumbled piles of junk. Under an unopened sweepstakes entry packet—the announcement that Hammel could be the next millionaire blurred with smears of dried catsup—she saw the finger of a black glove sticking out. Retrieving the glove, Sarah held it up to Hammel. "Yours?"

He glared. "What of it? It's just a glove."

"Maybe not," Sarah said, and slipped it into a plastic evidence bag, tagging it.

Angel stepped back into the living room and Sarah turned to look at her. "Anything?"

Angel shook her head. "But there is a garage out back."

"Attached?"

"No."

"Damn." Sarah knew she could interpret the word "premises" in the section of the warrant designating where they could search as including the garage. But she'd seen more than one case thrown out when a judge decided a separate building on the property didn't qualify.

"Just a minute," Chad said, walking into the kitchen. Keeping a careful eye on Hammel, Sarah heard the sound of the back door opening, then Chad's footsteps thumping on the tile as he returned. He was smiling. "For a garage to be attached, it just has to be touching the house in some way, right?"

Sarah nodded.

"Then come and see."

Sarah motioned to Angel to stay with Hammel, then followed Chad out through the back. He pointed to a large rectangle of corrugated plastic tacked on one edge of the roof of the house. The other end was secured under the eaves of the garage. "This could satisfy the letter of the law, don't you think?"

"Yeah, I do."

The side door of the garage was warped, and Sarah had to give it a kick to get it open. When she stepped over the threshold, she realized the inside of the small building hadn't seen a car since the ice-age.

In the dim light she could see junk, boxes and bins of it stacked clear to the ceiling in precarious towers. What may have once been a workbench was likewise spilling over with a jumble of dusty cardboard boxes and rusting tools. "Check around there," Sarah said, pointing to the bench. "See if you can find any pliers or wire cutters."

Chad moved some boxes and made his way toward the workbench. Led by the beam of her flashlight, Sarah found some space between two cardboard pillars and followed the narrow passage toward the back wall. Cobwebs brushed her cheeks, and she checked carefully for any eight-legged creatures that might be home.

She played the light over the rusted frames of bicycles without wheels, a lawnmower that looked like it had put down roots, and an old swivel rocker. Some creatures, hopefully mice and not rats, had nested in the seat, pulling tufts of stuffing out of the gaping hole.

Repressing a shudder, Sarah probed the darkness in the far corner. There, almost hidden by another tower of cardboard, was the top end of a large piece of furniture. "Chad. Come here and help me," she called.

A variety of thumps and clumps measured Chad's progress through the maze to the back wall. Together, they hoisted boxes, pushed bicycle parts aside, and finally revealed an old upright piano.

Covered with grime and triumph, Sarah smiled.

"Little big for an evidence bag," Chad observed, wiping his face where the dust had mingled with sweat.

Sarah laughed. "That's all right. I love it anyway."

Then she turned and wove her way back toward the door. "You have any luck with the tools?"

Chad shook his head.

"Then look in his car. Maybe he never put them back in the garage."

Before opening the heavy wooden door at the back of the house, Sarah pulled out her cell phone and called Roberts to arrange for a forensic team. Then she called McGregor and told him they were bringing Hammel in.

Leaning against the edge of the sink in the restroom, Sarah surveyed the damages in the large rectangle of mirror. Water and a paper towel hardly worked like a shower, but they were effective against the top layer of dirt. Luckily, the debris had combed out of her hair and the slight musty odor wouldn't be noticeable from a distance. Her clothes had suffered the worst damage, and brushing at them only rearranged the dirt. Giving it up as a fruitless endeavor, she was glad she'd worn a jacket that was already overdue for a trip to the cleaners.

About twenty minutes ago they'd stashed Hammel in one of the interrogation rooms where he was hopefully contemplating his past sins and how much the police might know about them. It was a cheap psychological trick, but sometimes it worked.

Angel came out of one of the stalls and stepped to the sink. She held her silence like a shield, and Sarah wondered why her partner seemed so unwilling to share in the emotional rush of having a suspect. She tried a light touch to break through the reserve. "Why so glum? According to SOP, we're supposed to be elated at finally having a break in the case."

Angel shrugged.

Sarah studied her partner's reflection in the mirror, then frowned. "You got a problem?"

The rush of running water filled the silence as Angel finished the ritual of hand washing. Sarah didn't know if her partner was symbolically absolving herself of something or just stalling. Finally Angel turned off the faucet and spoke. "I just wish it didn't have to be another black man."

"That didn't seem to matter when you were kicking the shit out of him."

"I was doing the job. That doesn't mean I always have to agree with it."

Sarah frowned. "What the hell does that mean?"

"It'll be so much easier to get an indictment and a guilty verdict on someone like him."

"And where was that concern before we went out there? You thought he was a dandy suspect then."

Angel broke eye contact and grabbed a couple of paper towels out of the dispenser. "I haven't changed my mind. I just wish it wasn't so hard for someone like him. He doesn't have a chance against the system."

"What are you saying? That we shouldn't arrest anyone who can't buy their way out of a guilty verdict?"

"That's not what I mean, and you know it."

"No, I don't." Sarah blew out a breath in exasperation. "I don't know what the fuck you're driving at."

Angel lifted her chin and glared.

Thrusting her hands deep in her pockets to avoid acting on the urge to smack the defiance off Angel's face, a sudden realization slammed into Sarah like a lead ball. She controlled the force of her words with an effort. "Do you really think I'll treat Hammel any differently than a white suspect?"

"I suppose that's a question you need to answer first."

"Jesus H. Christ!" Sarah whirled and kicked the trash can, sending it clattering across the tile floor. Anger pulled her with the strength of a runaway horse, and Sarah desperately clawed at the reins to bring it under control. Then she turned and faced Angel again. "Why does everything have to come down to color?"

"Because that's the difference. Black and white." Angel took a step closer and pulled up her sleeve to hold her arm next to Sarah's. "There's a whole history written on this, and you'll act on that history whether you realize it or not."

"And what about you, huh? What history are you acting on? Or is it only us white folks who have to answer for what we do?"

The slap caught her off guard and Angel was out the door before Sarah even registered the stinging on her cheek. She reached up and touched the spot, feeling the radiating heat.

*How dare she?* Sarah pounded the towel dispenser. *Well fuck her. Fuck all of them that think that way.*

Looking for more victims for her rage, Sarah turned on the trash can again, chasing it along the wall with relentless kicks that sent tremors up her legs.

A uniformed officer poked her head in, then quickly backed out.

Finally, Sarah stopped. She stood for a moment, panting and nursing her aching muscles. Damn she felt good! She'd have to pay for the damages, but that was okay. It was worth every penny.

She turned back to the sink and repaired the most recent damages to her body, still fighting with her emotions. *I am not, by God, a racist, and that little chick had better accept that pretty goddam soon.*

Heading back to the interrogation area, Sarah stopped at the break room. She acknowledged Chad, who was munching on a bag of corn chips. Pouring a cup of coffee, she was surprised to see her hand still shaking.

"You okay?" McGregor asked, coming up behind her and reaching for the coffeepot when she set it back on the burner.

Sarah nodded, keeping her eyes and hands occupied with her coffee.

"Where's Angel?" McGregor asked.

The question was answered when Angel walked into the room a moment later, an air of tension trailing her like heavy perfume. Sarah could see a hard expression on the woman's face, then caught the questioning glance McGregor gave her. She took a sudden interest in the tattered Wanted poster on the wall.

The crinkle of cellophane as Chad finished his chips echoed loudly in the room. Sarah wondered how long this verbal hold-out could last and was relieved when McGregor asked Angel about her mother. The answer was polite, yet clipped, and he shot Sarah another look.

McGregor slurped the rest of his coffee, then set his mug down and faced Sarah. "You ready to do this?"

She nodded, slid her cup onto the table and walked into the hall.

Outside the box, McGregor put a hand on Angel's arm. "Chad'll go in with Sarah."

Sarah could feel the other woman stiffen, but didn't want to risk a look at her, or McGregor. Better to pretend ignorance.

"Since you wounded his pride, he might be a little hostile," McGregor offered as explanation.

Now Sarah risked the glance, and she knew he was covering. The pretense that nothing was wrong between her and Angel had been blown to hell.

Turning quickly, Sarah nodded to Chad who followed her into the interrogation room. Hammel sat in one of the battered chairs with his elbows propped on the table. Sarah looked for any sign that the half-hour wait had unnerved him in any way, but he appeared more belligerent than frightened.

"Why'd you drag me down here?" he asked. "I didn't do nothing."

Sarah almost laughed. What did she expect? Nobody who was brought in here ever did anything. She approached the table. "We have some questions regarding a new investigation."

"What investigation?"

Sarah was glad to see the quick flick of his eyes, first on her, then Chad, who leaned a shoulder against the closed door. People usually weren't nervous unless they had something to be nervous about. "Before we get into that," she said, injecting a note of casualness into her voice. "I want to make sure your rights are completely covered here. So, just for the record, I want to Mirandize you."

Sarah motioned to Chad, who made a big show out of pulling a card from his inside pocket and reading the familiar warning. Sarah watched Hammel as the words echoed softly in the room. His expression changed from surprise to anger to caution in about three heartbeats. "Are you arresting me?"

"No. But you are a suspect. And if we make some progress here today, maybe we can clear this up before it has to go any further."

Hammel regarded her cautiously but didn't say anything.

"How well did you know Mel Halsley?" Sarah asked.

Hammel sat mute.

"Walter Durham?"

No answer.

"John Baxter?"

That name triggered a frantic look from Sarah, to Chad, back to Sarah again. "You think I did those Mall guys?"

Sarah let the question hang there, and Hammel pushed his chair back and stood up. "That's bullshit! I didn't have nothing

245

to do with that."

"Sit down!"

After a moment of calculation, Hammel finally obeyed the command. Sarah took a few minutes to lay out the factors that pointed to him. When she got to the part about motive, he looked like he wanted to come flying out of the chair again. "How would offing those dudes avenge my boy?"

"I don't know. You tell me."

Hammel drummed his fingers on the table as if the idea was too ridiculous to even consider, so Sarah decided to take another approach. "Why'd you run from us before?"

He shrugged.

Sarah leaned into his face. "People with nothing to hide don't run."

"I was scared."

"You were scared?" Sarah looked to Chad as if including him in her surprise, then turned back to Hammel. "How come you were scared if you didn't do anything?"

Hammel sat mute while beads of perspiration followed the trails of wrinkles down his face.

Sarah walked around his chair, forcing him to turn to keep her in view. "We know you have a history of violence."

His look said, "So what?"

"When the officers talked to you after your son was killed, you denied having a record. Why'd you lie to them?"

"Didn't want to give them reason to decide I did my own kid."

"Why did you think that would have happened?"

"Oh, man. Get real. It's what all you white cops think of us."

"Us? What 'us,' Mr. Hammel? Men over fifty. Delivery people. Or just men in general?"

"You know what I mean."

"I'm afraid I don't."

"Niggers. We're nothing but worthless niggers killing each other all over the place."

The implication was so close to what Angel had said, it stunned Sarah. Up until this moment she'd thought the words and the attitude were carefully cultivated to ensure certain gains. That people espoused them for their power to stir debate, but she'd never considered that so many people actually believed the propaganda.

"And what do black cops think of you, Mr. Hammel?" Chad stepped forward with his question, and Sarah gave him a nod.

"You're only black on the outside," Hammel said with a sneer.

"What brought you to that stunning conclusion?"

"Cause you play by all the honky rules. You and all the others who done forgot where they came from."

Chad sighed. Sounded like the same litany he kept hearing from his brother. It was always the same old shit. That the only reason Chad had made it was because he had sold out.

From past experience, Chad knew there was no use in debating the issue with Hammel. He was no more ready to hear about education and hard work than his brother ever was.

"Tell me, Mr. Hammel, did the police ever accuse you of killing your son?" Chad asked.

"Not outright. But they asked me where I was when it happened."

"That's routine. We'd ask the Mayor the same question if his son was killed."

Hammel's air of belligerence dissipated just a bit, yet Chad knew that this small piece of ground they'd found to agree on didn't mark the end of the war. They still had a lot of battles to drag him through.

"According to the case file, you were pretty angry that the police didn't catch whoever shot your son," Chad said.

Hammel gave him a look that asked, "Wouldn't you be?"

"What did you do with that anger?"

The other man looked at him like he didn't get the question. Chad pulled out the chair across from him and sat down, adopting a manner of just being two friends chatting. "It's a funny thing about anger," he said. "You either have to work it out of your system. You know, do something a little physical. Or it sits there deep inside, rotting and fermenting. Then one day it blows sky-high. And man, we can do some crazy things."

"I didn't do nothing."

"You never once thought of avenging your son?"

Hammel eyed him cautiously.

"Come on," Chad prompted. "If it'd been my kid, I sure as hell would've thought about it."

"And you'd nail my black ass if I say I wanted to get the scum who did that?"

"People aren't convicted for wanting to kill someone. They're convicted for doing it." Chad thought that was a good point to let Hammel ponder for a bit. He nodded to Sarah, then stood and glanced back at Hammel. "We've got to take a little break here. You want us to bring you anything? Coffee? A soft drink?"

Hammel wiped thick fingers across his deeply lined face. "Coffee."

Chad closed and locked the door behind them, and Sarah turned to McGregor, who was rubbing his chin. "Think he's going to crack?" he asked.

"I don't know. It could go either way."

"Then let Chad have him for a while," McGregor said. "Maybe Hammel can't wait to tell his new best friend everything."

Sarah smiled. If only it could be that easy.

# CHAPTER TWENTY-FIVE

Sarah dragged her unwilling body back to the station at nine-thirty the next morning. Taking turns, they'd worked Hammel until almost eleven last night, coming up with little beyond a weak attempt at alibis for the times of the murders. The miracle she'd been hoping for—that he might actually confess and end this nightmare for everyone—hadn't happened.

Continuing the nice-guy approach, McGregor had opted not to hold Hammel for the resistance and attempt to flee. "They're pretty weak charges anyway, and it might be more interesting to keep him under surveillance," had been his reasoning. He'd even gotten Roberts to commit to a forensic report ASAP. That left the responsibility of checking alibis to the detectives. Angel and Chad were already out doing their share.

Sarah felt a tingle of anticipation as she considered the possibility that they could have this guy wrapped up by tonight. Having the doer signed, sealed, and delivered to the DA would give her time to think about something else for more than a minute at a time.

She knew McGregor was right. Her life was out of control and she needed to do something about it. But it was hard to figure out what to do in the middle of all this. She'd even considered making an appointment with Doc Murray and found that a scary thought. So her immediate solution was not to think at all. Not about Paul. Not about McGregor's drinking.

And not about what the hell she was going to do about her partner.

Grabbing her notebook, Sarah left the station to go check Hammel's alibi for the morning of Baxter's murder. The official TOD had come in at between seven-thirty and eight that morning, and Sarah was still amazed that no one in the mall had seen anything. Not that the malls teemed at that hour in the morning, but people were there. Deliveries were made. Mall-walkers shed their pounds and increased their heart rate. Store employees came in early to set up for the day. On the other hand, it would be easy for a man in a UPS uniform to hang around and not generate any suspicion.

Sarah checked her notebook for the address of the diner on Mockingbird where Hammel had said he'd been eating breakfast on the morning Baxter had been killed. Hammel swore he'd been there at eight and a waitress, Lucy, could verify that. If she did, they could erase Hammel's name from their short list of suspects. No way could he have made it from the mall to this area in under thirty minutes. Not on a weekday when traffic snarled on all streets leading into the city.

Only a few stragglers remained of the breakfast crowd, and Sarah took a seat at the counter, the smell of bacon tempting her. A young waitress with her long blonde hair pulled back in a clip brought a cup and a coffeepot over and inquired with a raised eyebrow.

Sarah nodded and the girl poured.

"Are you Lucy?" Sarah asked.

"No. That's her over there." The girl indicated a middle-aged woman with dark brown hair serving stacks of pancakes to two construction workers in a corner booth.

"Thanks."

"No problem." The girl flashed perfect teeth in a wide smile. Sarah didn't consider herself unattractive, but in the presence of women like this, she felt downright dowdy.

Sarah sipped her coffee and waited until Lucy came back behind the counter. "Lucy?"

The woman turned, meeting Sarah's gaze with soft brown eyes.

"Detective Kingsly." Sarah pushed the lapel of her denim jacket to one side to reveal the shield pinned to her white shirt. "Need to ask you a few questions."

Lucy glanced at her tables of customers as if concerned how an interruption of service might affect her tips.

"It won't take long," Sarah said.

"Okay." Lucy wiped her well-worked hands on the small square of red material that served as an apron and stepped closer.

"Do you know an Elisha Hammel?"

The question elicited a puzzled frown from Lucy, so Sarah described him. "Oh, that guy," Lucy said. "He's one of the regulars. But we don't usually know names."

"Were you working this past Tuesday morning?"

"Yeah."

"Was Hammel here?"

"Tuesday?" Lucy pursed her lips and thought for a moment. "Yeah. He was right there." She pointed to the end of the counter. "That's his favorite seat."

"Do you remember what time?"

"I don't know if I can be exact . . ."

Lucy let the sentence fade into deliberation, and Sarah noted that if this ever came to trial, the woman would be an excellent witness. Juries liked precise, well thought out answers. It gave testimony an added depth of credibility.

The deliberation over, Lucy returned her gaze to Sarah. "It was about nine o'clock."

"Not any earlier?"

"A few minutes maybe. But not much."

"How can you be so sure?"

"On Tuesday the manager was sick. He called and asked me to sign for deliveries. I'm sort of the assistant around here," she offered by way of explanation. "Anyway. The produce guy came about quarter to nine. Hammel wasn't here before I went in the back. When I finished, there he was."

"And this was at nine? When you came out front again?"

"Yeah. Give or take a few."

The adrenaline started to pump as Sarah wrote Lucy's address and phone number down. The woman would be more than happy to talk to her again if necessary. And it would be necessary. Sarah was certain of that. This may be the first hole in Hammel's story, but it gaped wide. And if he lied about this, what else was he lying about?

Leaving money on the counter for her coffee and a generous tip, Sarah thanked Lucy and stood up. Then she pushed her way through the door, eager to get back to the station to see what else might have turned up.

A few minutes after Sarah returned to the squad room, Chad walked in with a satisfied smile. "Tell me you've got something good," Sarah said when he paused by her desk.

"I got something good." Chad pulled up a chair and sat down. "Remember Hammel said he was visiting his father the night Durham was killed?"

Sarah nodded.

"He said they had a couple of beers. Watched TV. He stayed until eleven."

"But he wasn't there?" Sarah asked hopefully.

"He was there, but the old man can't swear to the exact time. He drinks a bit and sometimes falls asleep." Chad rummaged in his pocket and pulled out a notebook. "The father states he's not sure when Hammel left. 'He was there until just before the news. But then I sorta dozed off. When I woke up around midnight, he was gone.' " Chad snapped his notebook closed and looked at Sarah. "I'm beginning to like the way this one's fitting."

"Me, too. But let's not let enthusiasm get in the way of our work. We still have a case to build."

"Hey, we're entitled to a few minutes of gloating. The opportunities are so few and far between."

Sarah returned his smile. "You're right. We'll take five right now."

Chad stood up, started to walk away, then turned back. "If you've got a couple of minutes, could I talk to you?"

"What is it?"

"Uh, not here." Chad glanced around at the detectives seated at desks throughout the room. "Could we go downstairs and get a soda?"

"Sure." Sarah grabbed some change out of a box she kept in her desk drawer and followed Chad out.

They went down to the vending area on the first floor, and Sarah bought a cold drink, while Chad opted for a candy bar. Sarah popped the tab on the can, releasing the air pressure with a hiss, then took a refreshing swallow of the cool drink. Her curiosity about what Chad wanted to talk about was piqued as she watched him drag out the routine of unwrapping the candy, taking a bite, and chewing for what seemed to be forever. The little alcove housing the vending machines was empty, so there was nothing causing the delay except his own reluctance.

"We can't stay down here forever," Sarah said, gently prodding him.

"I know. This is just a little awkward." Chad took another bite, then looked at her rather sheepishly. "It's about Angel."

Sarah was pretty sure what was coming, but she played dumb anyway. She enjoyed making him squirm. She knew she shouldn't. He was a nice guy and it wasn't entirely his fault that he'd been struck with an almost terminal case of adolescent hormones. Mother Nature had a cruel sense of humor.

"I just wondered if you could help me figure out what's going on with her," Chad finally said.

The temptation to continue the clueless charade tugged at her, but Sarah decided that would be too sadistic. "What do I look like?" she asked. "President of the Lonely Hearts Club?"

Chad laughed. "I just thought you might be able to fill me in."

"Sorry, pal. I don't know her any better than you do."

Chad appeared genuinely surprised at that. "But I thought you were supposed to relate to each other. You know, all that woman-to-woman stuff the magazines keep saying you're so good at."

"It doesn't always work." Sarah shrugged, trying to give the impression it was no big deal. But after yesterday, she had no idea how it was going to work out with her and Angel, personally or professionally.

And the surprising thing was that a couple of weeks ago it wouldn't have mattered. She could have easily chunked the partnership and not thought much of it. But something had become increasingly clear as they'd worked together. They were a good team. Not the same as with John, but still good. When that happens, you don't want to throw it away. But Angel may have taken that choice away from her.

"So, no words of wisdom for the heartsick boy?" Chad asked.

Sarah shook her head. "Can't help you."

Angel didn't get back to the station until a few minutes before the scheduled briefing with McGregor. Sarah was relieved to see there was no open animosity. The matter had to be settled between them, but not here and certainly not with an audience.

As soon as Angel started giving the results of her day's activities, Sarah's concern for personal matters faded. Angel drove the first chink in their case by revealing that Hammel's alibi for the Halsley murder was pretty tight.

"It took me a while to track the woman down," Angel said. "She wasn't at her apartment and her roommate wasn't home. Finally got the manager to give me the other woman's name and a work number. When I called, she said she had no idea where Arleen was. She's usually home sleeping during the day. Then after a bit she remembers that Arleen had to pick up her car today. She gave me the name of the garage and that's where I found Arleen.

"She didn't want to talk to me at first. Said Elisha was a good guy, and she wasn't going to help the cops pin something on him. So I worried her some with the idea that we could pin something on her for solicitation. She got a little huffy, saying their relationship no longer involved money. I told her that didn't matter. We'd just make sure Vice kept an extra special eye on her. Suddenly she was the poster girl for cooperation.

"But the bad news is that she corroborated his story about that night."

"She's probably lying," Chad said.

"Could be." Angel shrugged. "But unless we can prove the lie, her statement stands."

"That still won't kill the case," Sarah said. "And since the other alibis fell apart, this one won't stand so strong in front of a jury. Especially considering the witness is a hooker."

"But only if we've got some other evidence to throw at them," McGregor said. "I called Roberts earlier, and he said he had some of the forensic stuff for us. He's bringing it over personally in about," he paused to check his watch, "fifteen minutes."

In the pause, Sarah glanced at Angel who kept her face averted. Chad stood up and announced he was going to see if anyone left anything good to eat in the break room.

"Sounds like a good idea," Sarah said. "I'll go with you."

"Bring me back some coffee," McGregor pushed his mug toward her.

"Is the word 'please' anywhere in your vocabulary?" Sarah made sure he saw her smile so there would be no misunderstanding. Then she turned to Angel. "What about you?"

The question forced a direct look, and Sarah searched carefully for some sign of where her partner stood. The look was impassive and the offer was declined.

*Fine.* Sarah grabbed McGregor's cup and strode out the door. *She doesn't want to even make an attempt. I don't care.*

Roberts had arrived by the time Sarah and Chad returned with mugs of coffee to wash down the donuts they'd found.

Sarah handed McGregor his coffee, then set hers on the corner of his desk and plopped wearily in the chair. Ignoring Angel, Sarah turned her attention to Roberts.

"Like I started to tell the Lieutenant before you walked in," Roberts said. "I've got a mixed bag here." He tapped a folder on his lap. "You want to hear all the details?"

"Just give us the gist of it."

"Okay." Roberts made a minor adjustment to his bow tie. "On the plus side, we got a match on the glove. The fibers from Durham's fingernails definitely matches it, or one like it."

"One like it?" Sarah asked.

"Yeah. Had one of my guys contact the manufacturer. It's a pretty common work glove. They roll them out of production like tortillas. Thousands can come from the same fabric and dye lot. And they ship hundreds to stores in the Metroplex."

"So we can't place the guy conclusively at the scene." Chad had lost his earlier excitement, and Sarah knew he was only expressing the disappointment they were all feeling.

"But to show he could've been there would be pretty damning in addition to some other physical evidence," McGregor said. "What about the wire?"

Sarah considered correcting him, but Roberts beat her to it. "It's not called wire. The proper term is string. Piano string."

"I'll try to remember that," McGregor said with a trace of sarcasm. "Now can we get on with it?"

Roberts winked at Sarah, then assumed a more serious expression. "We haven't done much with the strings yet. Decided to follow the fiber thing to its conclusion since it seemed so promising. But the preliminary tests on the strings weren't too hopeful.

"The ones your guys brought in from the suspect's place were pretty rusty. At first I thought no way there could be a match. Then I talked to that piano guy Kingsly turned me onto. He told me how strings can clean up and be restored with solvents and oils. We're looking at the strings used on the victims again to see if there's any trace evidence of these chemicals."

"What are your chances of actually matching the strings?" Angel asked.

"Pretty slim." Roberts took one of the donuts and munched while he talked. "The piano guy said the only significant difference between strings would be metal fatigue. Or some of the copper on the bass strings could dull over the years. Since the suspect's piano is so old, it could have some fatigue. But we don't have the equipment to test it. We'll have to send it out."

"Where?" McGregor asked.

"I talked to some professor at UT Dallas. In the geology department. He says he can do it."

"Okay." McGregor nodded. "But protect the chain of custody with your life. I can just see some slick defense attorney getting mileage out of the possibility the wires that professor tested could've belonged to anyone."

"What about the wire cutters I found in the guy's car?" Chad asked.

"No go." Roberts shrugged apologetically. "They didn't cut the strings used in the murders."

"Okay," McGregor said. "We'll go back out there and pick up any tool that could possibly cut a wire. We'll test them all until we find a match."

"You want us to do it tonight?" Sarah didn't relish another evening of digging through the dirt in that garage.

McGregor shook his head. "I'll send some patrol officers over. Their presence might even spook the guy into doing something incriminating."

"What. We're not scary enough?" Sarah asked.

That drew a chuckle from Chad and a glare from McGregor.

# CHAPTER TWENTY-SIX

Sarah thought she'd relish a quiet evening at home with nothing more strenuous to do than pet Cat. But after a quick dinner of macaroni and cheese and a half hour of playing with Cat as he chased a yarn ball around, she was bored and restless.

And the kitten didn't even have the courtesy of staying awake to keep her company. He was snuggled in his favorite corner of the sofa, and she had the long evening stretching before her.

It might have almost been better to have joined the treasure hunt in Hammel's garage.

Before that wild thought drove her to actually doing it, Sarah called Paul, who said he would love some company.

Hanging up, Sarah's intellect tried to convince her this idea wasn't any better than the one concerning the garage, but she never did listen to the voice of reason.

She also didn't listen when the voice told her to avoid going into Paul's bedroom when she arrived at his apartment.

It was like an instant replay of her previous visit, and as instant replays go, Sarah didn't find it half bad.

Luxuriating in the afterglow, Sarah thought about how nice it would be to actually spend some time with Paul, time that wasn't hurriedly snatched from work. The case could be wrapped up in a couple of days. Then maybe she could take some time off.

"Paul?"

"Hmmm?" He ran his fingers up her belly and across the

swell of her breasts.

"What would you think of us going away together next weekend if I finish this case?"

"I'll be in Atlanta then. Got an audit to run."

"How long will you be gone?"

"Couple of weeks." Paul's tone was so matter of fact it was almost emotionless, and Sarah couldn't fight the wave of irritation.

"And when were you going to tell me? The day you left?"

"I really hadn't thought about it." He removed his hand and her body felt chilled where it had been.

"So I'm not very high on your priority list?"

Paul rolled over and sat up on his edge of the bed. "I thought we'd agreed to take this relationship slow and easy?"

Sarah looked at the tousled covers, rich with the scent of their recent activity. "I'm sorry. I didn't realize I was the only one who thought we'd passed that point the last time I was here."

"All we've done is start to explore the physical possibilities."

"Obviously." Sarah threw the sheet back and slung herself out of bed.

Paul stood up and faced her. "What's that supposed to mean?"

"You don't seem too eager to explore anything else."

Paul shook his head and turned toward the bathroom.

Feeling an urgency not to let it end this way, Sarah crossed the room quickly and put her hand on his back. "Please don't walk away from me."

His muscles stiffened beneath her touch. Then she could feel his shoulders slump. "Paul?" She forced the anger into a corner. "What is it?"

It took a moment, but then he sighed. "I don't want to be in a controlling relationship."

"Is that what you think I'm trying to do?"

Paul merely stood there, still and silent.

"I'd just like to know more about you," Sarah said. "From the moment we met you've been such a mystery. And that's certainly added to the appeal. But we've got to get beyond the jokes and what we enjoy in bed. Relationships are about so much more than that."

"Funny. That's what Gretchen used to say."

In his moment of silence, Sarah wanted to ask him who Gretchen was, but some instinct told her not to. Then he continued, "At first I thought it made good sense. We'd get to know each other so we could understand and be sensitive to individual needs. But that's not the way it works."

He stopped again. A myriad of new questions swam in Sarah's mind, but she knew the wrong one could close the floodgates. Perhaps any question would. She caressed his shoulder, hoping the gesture would convey her concern.

"She didn't really want to know me at all," Paul said quietly. "She wanted to redesign me like one of her houses. Out with the old. In with the new."

Sarah realized that her initial estimation had been right about the decorating. But she had to wonder why he continued to live here when everything must be a painful reminder. Was it a form of self-punishment? Or was he just too wounded to leave? Either option didn't hold much promise. She didn't need a bird with a broken wing.

Paul turned and faced her. "I didn't tell you that because I want your sympathy. You just need to know why I value emotional independence."

Sarah stood in the middle of the room, stunned. He'd said it, then walked into the bathroom as if his words carried no more import than where he preferred to do his shopping.

Unable to stop the tears, Sarah grabbed her clothes and

pulled them on. When Paul came out of the bathroom, a look of concern crossed his face. "Sarah? You're crying."

A bizarre inclination to laugh hit her. Of course she was crying. What did he expect?

He crossed the room and touched one of her tears with his finger. She pulled away from the contact.

"I didn't mean to hurt you."

His voice rang with such sincerity she forced herself to look at him. Distress radiated from his eyes, and for a moment she wondered if she was in the middle of some wild nightmare. Didn't he realize how cruel his words had been? How deep they had cut?

Obviously not. And that was the greatest mystery of all.

"I have to go." Sarah stepped around him and headed toward the door.

"You're not . . ." His voice faded as if he was having trouble with the question. "Can we see each other again?"

Sarah stopped but didn't turn around. "I don't know. Maybe we should both think about what it is we want out of this. And what we're willing to put into it." She opened the door. "Call me when you get back from your trip."

On the way home, Sarah thought two or three times about stopping for a drink, but she couldn't get the tears turned off long enough to do it. Each new wave of pain tore at her heart and flooded her eyes. How could she have been so stupid?

Good sense had tried to tell her not to step into the treacherous waters of a physical commitment, knowing for her it carried an emotional one as well. All the modern ideology about equality would never alter that basic difference between women and men. And she knew that.

Parking her car across the lot from her apartment, Sarah got out and realized that sometime in the past forty-eight hours the heat wave had broken, and she hadn't even noticed it. The breeze that touched her face was actually cool, so she decided to get her jogging gear and go for a run. If a problem couldn't be solved, it could at least be successfully avoided.

Most of Saturday it looked like they might be able to hang on to the case. The trouble was, Angel still didn't know how she felt about it. If Hammel was the killer, he deserved to be punished, but something about the zealous pursuit of him bothered her.

She knew the other detectives were coming from years of experiencing the frustration of cases not being solved. Not to mention the heat burning McGregor from the suits upstairs. But the evidence they had was flimsy, and it looked to her like they were trying too hard to give it substance. Even Chad had been whistling when they finished the last interview with people who worked with Hammel.

Most of them supported what the boss had said about Hammel's strange behavior, and Chad had acted like it had some great significance. As far as Angel could see, it didn't mean shit.

Driving back to the station for the late-afternoon briefing, Angel considered voicing her concerns to Chad, but the memory of yesterday held her back. No way was she ready to get into a discussion about racial issues again. Especially not with someone who probably wasn't even close to sharing her views.

"I don't know how else to do this, but come right out with it."

Chad's voice startled her and Angel glanced over at him. Whatever he wanted to say apparently wasn't going to be easy. He gripped the steering wheel tightly and chewed at the corner of his lip.

"What is it?" she asked.

"Do you have some kind of problem with Sarah?"

Angel quickly averted her face.

"Hey, I'm not immune to what's been going on. The tension's been so thick you could spread it on bread and eat it."

"That's none of your business."

"It is if it affects the job."

"But it hasn't."

"Are you sure about that?"

Angel glared at him. "Do you have a specific complaint?"

"Trouble like this can't be measured that way. It's something intangible that pushes people further and further apart. Pretty soon the distance is so great they can't find their way to the other side."

His words rang so true Angel had a hard time maintaining her anger. Since the fight she'd asked herself a hundred times a day whether the gulf was too wide to ever be closed. She'd avoided the other more pertinent question. What was she willing to do to close the gap?

Turning her face to the window, she realized she could no longer pretend that she didn't care. In the beginning, she didn't even have to pretend, but now things had changed. They were still two distinctly different people, but somewhere in the past weeks they had become a unit. And if she were really honest, the problem of racism belonged as much to her as to Sarah.

For all of her talk of enlightenment and broader viewpoints, she still harbored a slight mistrust of whites that flared at the most inopportune moments.

Chad reached across the seat and touched her shoulder. "I didn't mean to upset you."

Angel gave him a faint smile. "You didn't. Just made me think about some things I'd been avoiding."

"I don't know what the trouble is. Hell, I don't even *want* to know. But you can't just ignore it."

They drove for a while in silence, and Chad kept his hand on her shoulder. She found the presence comforting.

After pulling into a parking space by the station, Chad silenced the rumble of the engine, then turned to her. "I don't suppose this is a good time to ask you out?"

Angel laughed. "Are you nuts?"

"I don't know. Maybe." He picked at a scrap of paper on the seat between them. "I know this is lousy timing. But hell, the timing's stunk since we first met. If I wait until it's right, we could both be dead and buried."

"That could happen sooner than you think if we don't get inside for that briefing."

"So you aren't going to answer?"

Angel paused with one hand on the door handle. "I know this is going to sound pretty lame, but I really am on an emotional overload right now. Is another week or so going to matter?"

"I guess not."

Angel could tell he was trying really hard to mask his disappointment, and she felt a twinge of remorse. He was a nice guy who deserved someone who wasn't going to jerk him around like this. Briefly, she considered telling him that, but decided that might actually make the wound bleed.

"Come on," she said. "It's not like it's forever."

She was rewarded with a smile.

The small conference room overflowed with the personnel McGregor had assembled for the briefing. Sarah was squeezed between Grotelli, who reeked of garlic, and a young patrolman, who obviously thought heavy doses of cologne made a good antidote to body odor. If this wasn't over soon she was going to pass out.

She saw Angel come through the door, Chad following behind her. With no empty chairs available, they leaned against the wall, and Sarah was glad she'd gotten here early enough to get a seat despite the unpleasant odors.

"Okay, people," McGregor's voice boomed from the front. "Let's hear what you've got."

A young dark-haired guy in uniform spoke up first. Sarah listened as he gave a precise accounting of Hammel's time from leaving the station last night. "Eleven thirty-five, suspect arrived at residence via patrol car. Remained inside until seven A.M. Suspect emerged and entered his car. Drove directly to UPS processing center . . ."

Sarah's mind drifted after she realized there wasn't going to be anything significant from the surveillance. She shot a glance at Angel, hoping to catch some sign of change, but the woman avoided the attempt at eye contact.

The pen Sarah was doodling with gouged a deep crevice on her notebook. She tore the page out and wadded it up. A childish temptation to throw it across the room flitted across her mind, but she resisted. Not that it wouldn't feel good, but did she really want her fellow officers to see her acting like a three-year-old?

She forced her attention back to the reports, but they had little effect on her dismal mood. A cross-reference of phone records showed no connection between any of the victims and Hammel. Doodling again, Sarah faced her first real doubt that he was their man.

Roberts walked in, stirring a wave of anticipation that followed him as he weaved his way through the tables to the front of the room. He carried a manila folder, but not a smile.

"The results of the metal tests," Roberts said, handing the folder to McGregor.

"Thought the professor wasn't going to do them until next week," McGregor said.

"Curiosity got to him."

Watching the exchange, Sarah realized Roberts had brought bad news. Otherwise, he would have charged into the room, waved the folder triumphantly, and announced, "We hit the jackpot."

All this other stuff was just a delaying tactic.

Roberts finally got to the point. "The strings didn't match."

McGregor worried his chin with his fingers for a moment, then made a vague gesture of dismissal to the seated officers who slowly filed out in staggered groups. Only the three primaries remained.

Flinging the report on the table, McGregor paced from it to the wall and back again. Then he reached out and swept the papers to the floor. "Goddam! Fucking son of a bitch!"

Sarah waited long enough for the intensity to burn off his anger before intruding on it. "We were on the right track, Lieu. We'll just have to go back to those old cases and find the right guy."

# CHAPTER TWENTY-SEVEN

Angel tried to chase the thought away. She had been successful in her efforts to do that last night when it had first come to her, but she couldn't keep it at bay this morning.

It had started after the two fruitless hours they'd put into digging through files before deciding they were all too tired to be effective. She was driving home when her mind asked the question, "Why haven't you considered Alfred?" The thought had startled her so she'd slammed on her brakes in reflex, raising an angry honk of protest from behind.

A long telephone conversation with her mother and the power of fatigue had aided her efforts to avoid the idea last night. But the morning offered no convenient distractions until she went outside.

Carrying her coffee, Angel sat in a lawn chair and watched a mockingbird flit from a limb of the mimosa to a fence post and then to the top of her gas grill. He eyed her warily, poised for flight if she posed a threat, and Angel held herself still. The bird was a frequent visitor to her backyard, and she enjoyed his curiosity as he danced across the top of the grill, studying her with one black, beady eye. Sometimes he even answered her whistles, but he was more cautious today.

When the bird flew away, the action seemed to signal her mind to start thinking again. To consider Alfred as a suspect, she also had to wonder why she had avoided the possibility for so long. He had as much motivation as Hammel. As much access to the malls. Could it have been this repressed suspicion that she had been reacting to the other day, not the way the case was shaping up against Hammel?

Sighing, Angel drained the rest of her coffee, then stood up. She wasn't going to find any answers sitting here. They were all supposed to be taking a day off. "Start fresh on Monday," McGregor had said. But now that Angel had let the worry into her consciousness, there was no way she was going to forget it.

At the station, she was relieved to see that Sarah and Chad had taken the reprieve seriously. Nobody else commented about her presence as she made her way to her desk. There, in the pile she'd designated as not possible, she found the case file on Stacy's death.

Angel cleared a space on top of her desk and opened the file. A chill touched her arms lightly as she reviewed the information, reconnecting with facts she'd forgotten. Like how belligerent Alfred had been to the officers after the first year passed with no arrests. Several times he had needed to be forcefully removed from the station and only avoided arrest at the benevolence of Burtweiler who couldn't bring himself to charge the man.

Another twinge of conscience assailed her as Angel realized Alfred shared all of the factors that had made them consider Hammel. Had she compromised the investigation because of personal feelings?

She slammed the folder back on her desk and twisted her swivel chair back and forth, setting up a rhythm to help her think. Had there been a moment when she'd overlooked a suspicion? The events of the past few weeks played through her mind like a video until she finally gave it up as a waste of time. She could beat herself up all she wanted to, but it wasn't going to change anything. It would be far more productive to figure out what to do now.

Should she override departmental policy and investigate this on her own? There was always a danger of a case getting out of hand when there was a personal connection, and Angel knew she could be risking a lot. But she also hated the idea of Alfred going through the scrutiny by strangers, especially if he came up clean.

She really wanted him to come up clean.

Driving to the familiar house, Angel experienced a mixture of dread and melancholy. She'd been back rarely since Stacy's death, but each time she returned the memories of good times tugged at her.

Stacy had not been her best friend. That role had been reserved by Lola who'd moved to California shortly after graduation. But the circumstance of the friendship between parents had brought the two girls together frequently.

Betty, a plump woman in her mid-fifties with her salt and pepper hair cut short, opened the door to Angel's knock. After a moment's scrutiny, a smile played across the woman's face. "My goodness. Where've you been keeping yourself, girl?"

Angel returned the smile. "Busy with work."

"Your mama told me you got promoted a while back." Betty opened the door wider so Angel could step in. "How is she, by the way?"

"Much better. She's home now and should recover completely."

"There has to be some luck for somebody."

Angel wasn't sure if she heard a wistful note in the woman's voice, or if she was just projecting her own state of mind.

"Well, it certainly is nice for you to come for a visit," Betty said, ushering her into the living room. "Or did something else bring you?"

Suddenly faced with the moment, Angel didn't know how to begin. With a stranger it would be easy. But opening a line of questioning with this woman who had baked her cookies and applauded the shows that two young girls had created left her mentally scrambling. "Is Alfred home?"

"No. He said he had something he needed to do this morning."

"Must have been important for him to miss church."

"I don't know. He didn't tell me." A cloud of concern passed over Betty's face. Then she gave a little shake of her head. "How about some coffee? Just made fresh."

"That would be nice." Angel welcomed the reprieve from her purpose. This needed to go slowly for her benefit as well as Betty's.

Listening to the muted sounds from the kitchen, Angel walked over to the piano and trailed her fingers across the highly polished walnut. The Kimball, bought new almost fifteen years ago, if she remembered correctly, was as out of place as a Monet in a beer joint. She could imagine all that Betty and Alfred must have sacrificed to buy this treasure for their daughter.

"You want to play?" Betty asked. "It hasn't been touched since Stacy died."

Angel turned. "Maybe I shouldn't then."

"Nonsense." Betty put the tray with coffee and cookies on the low table in front of the sofa. "I've missed the music."

"I'm not sure what I did could be called music."

Betty smiled and gestured toward the piano. "Go ahead. It'll be fine."

Angel lifted the lid and touched the keys lightly in a ragged C chord. She was relieved to hear each note strike. Maybe she was wrong. She hoped to God she was wrong. But the hope died in the third chord with a dull thump.

"That's odd," Betty said. "Wonder what's wrong?"

"One of the hammers might be stuck." Angel quickly closed the lid, hiding her trembling hands at her sides before turning to the woman. "I think that happens when a piano just sits."

"Alfred will have to look at it."

Angel forced herself to move to the sofa instead of running out of the house. She sipped her coffee, trying to concentrate on what Betty was saying, but her mind kept fixating on missing strings and the implication she could no longer ignore. As soon as she could politely do so, she stood up to leave.

"It was so nice to see you," Betty said at the door. "I'll tell Alfred you stopped by."

Angel started to tell her not to, then stopped. Betty would probably tell him anyway. She was too much like Angel's mother not to. An unusual request attached to an unexpected visit could rouse some suspicions that were better left sleeping.

In the car, Angel fumbled the key in the ignition and the Cavalier's starting mechanism screamed in protest. Duty echoed the scream in her head. She knew she had to do the right thing, but God she didn't want to. They were friends. This wasn't supposed to happen with friends.

Slamming the car into drive, Angel tore away from the curb with a screech of rubber. The emotional war waged its battles within her, and Angel drove aimlessly.

After half an hour, she realized she was near the dojo. Maybe her subconscious knew what she needed better than she did. Grabbing the gym bag she kept packed in her trunk for just such an opportunity, she walked through the doors.

A cloying odor of sweat greeted her along with a wave from Randy who was watching two young boys spar. Several other kids practiced patterns, dancing across the mats in a symmetry of motion. Angel wondered if all the adults had stayed home today.

She didn't want to spar with Randy. He outclassed her by too much, but she also outclassed the kids. Neither match up would be fair.

Stepping into the locker room to change, she was pleased to see Danielle. "Are you getting ready to leave?" Angel asked.

"No. Just got here." Danielle pulled her long hair up into a ponytail.

"Interested in a workout?"

The girl turned to give her a surprised look. "Sure."

"Okay. I'll be out as soon as I change."

A few minutes later, Angel snapped the chin strap on her helmet and returned to the gym. Danielle was already on a mat stretching, and Angel joined her for the warm-up. Then they stood, bowed deeply, and faced off.

Danielle made the first move with a spin-heel kick that almost caught Angel off guard, but she ducked under it, poking a jab to Danielle's stomach followed by a backhand to her jaw. A sudden flurry of punches drove Angel to the edge of the mat, and she side-stepped, managing to land one feeble blow to the side of Danielle's head.

It didn't take long for the sweat to run in rivers down her back, and Angel fought for concentration. Either Danielle had improved immensely since their last pairing, or Angel had no business sparring in her current mental condition.

Suddenly, Angel staggered under the force of the front-snap kick to her chest.

"Break!" Randy called out, and Angel was vaguely aware of the girl stepping back.

Struggling to recover the breath that had been knocked out of her, Angel leaned over and put her hands on her knees. She could hear the soft pad of Danielle's feet on the mat, then a hand touched her shoulder lightly. "You okay?"

"Yeah." Angel stood up and rubbed the area just below her collarbone. "But I'll probably have a bruise."

"I'm really sorry." Concern clouded the girl's blue eyes. "It surprised me as much as it did you. I hardly ever get through your defenses."

"Maybe I've missed too many workouts."

"Johnson," Randy called out again. "Get your head into the program or get off the mat."

Angel pulled herself rigidly to attention. "Yes, Sir!"

Randy acknowledged her compliance with a slight bow, and Angel returned the protocol.

"You want to continue?" Danielle asked.

"Better not." Angel took her helmet off and wiped the ridge of sweat on her forehead. "Sorry."

"That's okay."

In the locker room, Angel turned the shower as hot as she could stand it and let the soothing warmth drum on her body. The war was over. She knew that. Personal loyalty had surrendered to duty.

She thought she should feel relieved that the battle no longer raged, but she felt nothing. Numbness pervaded every pore of her body and her heart was an empty vessel.

The feeling persisted while she got dressed and walked back to her car. Part of her wished for the earlier turmoil to return. She had to get some energy from someplace to make it over the next hurdle.

Angel raised her finger to push the doorbell, then lowered it. Indecision drove her down to the end of the sidewalk, then back toward the door. Just do it. Isn't that what the commercial says? She jabbed the bell, her heart thudding as she waited for a response.

When the door opened, Angel found her mouth too dry to speak. Surprise seemed to root Sarah to the floor, and Angel squirmed under the intensity of the woman's gaze. Finally, Sarah broke the thundering silence. "Yes?"

"We need to talk."

Sarah regarded her for another moment. "What about?"

"The case."

Sarah stepped back, opening the door wider for Angel to enter. She wiped her sweaty palms on her jeans and waited for Sarah to give some indication that they could move past the entryway. She didn't. She leaned against the opposite wall, folded her arms across her stomach and stared at Angel with an unreadable expression.

"I think I found another suspect." Angel could see a glimmer of excitement flash in Sarah's eyes, and she knew she could stop worrying about being thrown out.

"Who?" Sarah asked.

"Alfred."

"Your friend?"

Angel nodded, unable to speak.

"How did you reach this conclusion?"

Sparing her words, Angel recounted the events since this morning. If she stared at a spot just above Sarah's head, she could pretend she was just giving a report. Keep it cold and clinical.

"I can't believe this." Sarah moved into the adjoining living room, and Angel had no choice but to follow. "Now *you're* considering a black man as a suspect?"

Angel fought a surge of anger. "Okay. You're entitled to one cheap shot."

Sarah turned and Angel was afraid this time *she* was going to get slapped. But Sarah just stood there. Angel took another deep breath. "Listen. I'm sorry about that whole business." She paused, waiting for some signal from Sarah.

None came.

"I know I was way out of line," Angel finished lamely. "I don't know what I was thinking."

Sarah watched a myriad of emotions play across the other woman's face and tried to talk herself into being big enough to accept the apology. But she wanted to be small. She wanted Angel to admit to being more than out of line. She also still fought an urge to even the score.

Professionalism broke the impasse.

"Come and sit down," Sarah said, gesturing to the sofa. "And tell me again what you've got."

Listening to Angel, Sarah noted the similarities between Alfred and Hammel. They could possibly get a warrant and do an instant replay of Friday. When she suggested that, Angel shook her head. "Not yet."

"Why not?"

"Because I'd like to see if we can get a little more before we start dragging him through hell."

"Because he's your friend?"

"Yes."

Sarah had to admire her honesty. But it didn't mean she had to go along with it. "And you expect me to just agree to this?"

"No. I'm asking."

"Oh, right! This is the part where we're supposed to kiss and make up." Sarah stood abruptly, startling Cat who bounded over the back of the sofa. "You've got some nerve."

"I said I was sorry."

"Sorry don't cut it!"

The silence ran deep, and Sarah paced, feeling like her insides were attached to a rubber band that someone was twisting.

"What do I have to do?"

Angel's soft plea brushed Sarah like a feather, and she turned to regard the other woman. The anguish was clearly written in the dark, troubled eyes, and Sarah couldn't bring herself to add to the pain. "Okay," she said flatly. "Where do you want to start?"

"Right after Stacy died, Alfred used to spend a lot of time at an Outreach Center. A lawyer there even helped him with a civil suit against mall security. The head guy over there might know something helpful."

The afternoon heat threatened to overpower the air conditioner that was valiantly trying to serve its purpose. Angel pushed the regulator to *high* and hoped for the best.

Sarah sat silently beside her, and Angel erected a mental barrier to her concerns over what the woman might be thinking. It was enough that she'd agreed to come. Whether the trip would be fruitful was a different question.

Angel nosed the car into the parking lot at St. Paul's Episcopal School and turned off the engine. The sprawling, well-kept building stood in sharp contrast to the slow decay of the neighborhood in South Dallas, and Angel knew that the appearance held as much importance as what went on inside.

She could remember Headmaster Bellows emphasizing that truth to the assembled students the first day of every school year. The child who'd been happiest in shorts and a T-shirt hadn't understood. But the woman who'd excelled in the rigors of the police academy had finally seen the connection. It had a little bit to do with pride, but a whole lot more to do with personal discipline.

Angel opened the door, and Sarah followed her into a large meeting room. In one corner, two old men huddled over a checkerboard at a small table. Not far from them, a couple of pre-teen boys played a rowdy game of foosball. Several elderly ladies sat in a cluster of easy chairs, talking and laughing while their hands were busy with quilting.

A large, very dark man, who could have been a lineman for the Cowboys, approached with a broad smile. "What can I do for you . . . ?" His question faded as his smile changed to one of recognition. "Angel Johnson? Well, I'll be. What brings you out here?"

"I'm afraid it's official business." Angel nodded to Sarah and introduced her. "We need to talk to you about Alfred."

Bellows's smile gave way to a look of concern. "Is he in trouble?"

"We don't know yet. But we're interested in his recent activities. Has he been here in the past few weeks?"

"Yes, he has."

"Did you notice anything unusual about him?"

"Just the fact that he was here was unusual in itself. After we failed with that civil suit a couple of years back, he didn't come in much at all. Then he started showing up a few months ago."

"Was that the same business you were talking about before?" Sarah asked Angel.

Angel nodded and Bellows continued, "He was real excited about finally having someone to blame for what happened to Stacy, but the suit was thrown out before it ever came to trial. A judge ruled there was no liability."

"And how did Alfred react?" Sarah asked.

"He was angry at first. But then he seemed to accept it. I encouraged him to put it all behind him and get on with his life. I checked with his wife a few times after that, and it appeared that he'd taken my advice."

"Does that still hold true?" Angel asked.

A troubled look crossed his face as Bellows turned his attention to her. "I don't think so." He gave a slight shake of his head, then added quickly, "Not that there's been anything specific, mind you. But he's somehow colder now."

"What does he talk about when he's here?"

"Nothing. Hardly talks at all. He's come in a couple of evenings wanting to use a phone. Said his wasn't working."

"Did he use this one here?" Angel pointed to the phone on the wall.

"No. He wanted privacy. Asked if he could use my office."

"Could we see it?"

"Sure."

Sarah let Angel precede her as they followed Bellows into a long hallway. She listened with half her attention as he explained that he frequently lets people use his office phones. "Most folks don't like talking their business out there where everyone can hear."

Another sound intruded on the conversation, and Sarah cocked her head to listen. There was something familiar about it. Music. Where had she heard it before? She stepped away from Bellows and Angel, following the music to the other end of the hall.

Opening the door to the main body of the church, the melodious sounds engulfed her and Sarah looked around the dimly lit room, but she still couldn't pinpoint the source.

She entered and walked down the main aisle until she realized she was moving away from the sound. She turned and raised her eyes to the balcony where pipes stretched to the ceiling behind a woman seated at an organ.

The door opened again and Angel stepped in. "Sarah, what are you doing in here?"

"Listen."

Sarah watched the realization sweep across Angel's face. Then her partner turned to her with a look of desolation.

Knowing how hard it was for the other woman to accept each new piece of damning evidence against her friend, Sarah buried her excitement and kept her tone neutral. "We'll check the phone records. Just to be sure."

Angel didn't respond. Sarah walked over and lightly touched her arm. "We need to go to McGregor with this."

"I'd like to bring him in myself." Angel pushed the door open and stepped back into the hall. "He'll be home this afternoon. I can do it quick and easy."

"Not alone you don't."

"I don't want him to get hurt. We show up in force, no telling what could happen."

"Nothing's going to happen."

Angel shook her head and started to stride away. Sarah grabbed her partner's arm and pulled her to a stop. "I don't want to have to pull seniority here."

A wariness in Angel's eyes told Sarah that something else was going on. "Are you afraid to let me come with you?" she asked.

The expression didn't change.

Sarah shook her head in exasperation. Were they going to spin in this same circle forever? "I guess the choice is yours," she said. "Either you're going to believe me or not."

Sarah waited an eternity for some response. Finally Angel simply nodded.

It was a start.

"Did you get the number from Bellows?" Sarah asked.

Angel nodded again.

"Okay. Let's go."

# CHAPTER TWENTY-EIGHT

Specks of dust drifted like glitter sprinkled on the rays of late afternoon sunshine streaming through the front window. Alfred pulled the drapes, wrapping himself in darkness as he contemplated his life and the gun in his hand. It was over. At best it had been a futile attempt, and now it was over.

Angel knew. Otherwise she wouldn't have been here this morning. And she'd come back for him soon.

Turning from the window he walked on trembling legs to the piano and ran his hand across the keyboard, a thunk of hammer against wood reminding him of the strings that were missing. What would Stacy have thought of his using her piano as the instrument of her revenge?

The question stilled his restless fingers, and a deep bass note faded into silence. He'd never thought of that before. He'd never even stopped to consider whether she would have wanted revenge.

He pictured her in the last memory he cherished. The remembrance was so strong he could almost see her here now, sitting at the piano, eyes closed, tips of white teeth visible as she chewed her lip in concentration.

Her soul had belonged to music, and he'd loved to listen to her improvise with twelve-bar jazz, letting her fingers express her feelings. The music had rolled softly and gently around the small room.

Today, straining to catch an echo of what it used to say, Alfred knew the answer to his question. Slowly, tears brimmed in his eyes then followed each other in warm paths down his cheeks. They dropped with soft splats on the worn ivory and Alfred carefully wiped the keys before closing the lid.

The room was bathed in shadows and he made his way back to the sofa by instinct rather than sight. He sank into the soft depths, raising a squeak of protest from ancient springs, and tried to figure out if there was any redemptive value in this whole sorry mess.

The revenge hadn't been for Stacy after all. It had been for him. Maybe Betty had been right all along, saying he was too obsessed about it. He needed to let it go.

*But they killed my little girl,* he wailed silently. *And the bastards got away with it.*


Betty flicked the light on with her elbow then dropped the bag of groceries on the counter. She hated doing the shopping on Sunday. It wasn't the way to keep holy the Sabbath. But the thought of trekking down supermarket aisles on her way home from work never appealed to her either. And Saturdays. By the time she finished the cleaning, she was too tired.

She could force herself to get up a half hour earlier in the mornings to do some of the housework, but she was a tired old woman who valued her sleep too much. Besides that, Alfred got home from work before she did. Why couldn't he do some of the chores?

She strained to see if she could hear the TV in the living room. That would mean Alfred was still home. Hadn't disappeared as he'd been in the habit of doing lately.

She didn't know where he'd been going, or what he'd been doing. But it had bothered her in a way she didn't like to think about. Some sense of something not being quite right, but it scared her to try to figure it out. So she just kept pushing it out of her mind.

That had worked real well until Angel had come by the other day.

Betty pulled two boxes of cereal out of one of the bags and walked to the cabinet. She glanced at the open doorway to the living room. The fact that no light came through didn't mean Alfred wasn't home. He often sat in the dark, drinking his beer and watching the evening news. But today she didn't hear the muted sounds of broadcasting or the faint electrical hum that was a trademark of their old set.

Intrigued, she went to the doorway between the two rooms, just making out the vague form of her husband on the sofa. "You 'bout ready for some supper?"

He didn't answer. Nor did he acknowledge her presence, and a prickle of unease brushed her skin like a light breeze. "It's not good sitting here in the dark." Betty moved toward the lamp.

"No light."

The harsh words and his sudden movement stopped her cold.

Then when her eyes adjusted to the gloom, she could see he had a gun. Her first impulse was to scream, but she stifled it. Better to not appear alarmed. "Alfred. What are you doing?" She fought the darkness for some expression on his face that would take the sting out of her fear. "You put that up right now."

When he said nothing, turning the weapon in his hands as if contemplating possibilities she didn't even want to think about, Betty acknowledged what she'd forced herself not to even consider these past few weeks. The reasons for Alfred's odd behavior. His unexpected absences. The haunted look in his eyes. The nights he crept out of bed when she pretended to be sleeping, and she could hear the wrenching sounds of his distress from the bathroom.

"Oh, Alfred. What have you done?"

Pulling the plain Buick to a stop in front of Alfred's house, Angel told herself they were doing the right thing. But what if we're wrong?

You're not wrong. You just want to be.

Sarah gave her a reassuring nod. Then the women got out of the car, following the cracked ribbon of cement to the front door. The button for the bell was covered with a piece of tape, so Angel reached out and pounded on the wood, dislodging chips of peeling paint that drifted lazily down to settle on her shoes.

No response.

She knocked again, calling out, "Alfred? Betty? It's me, Angel. Can I come in?"

A gruff, masculine voice responded, "No!"

The finality of that single word caused the hairs on the back of Angel's neck to stand on end. This wasn't going to be good. After exchanging a nervous glance with Sarah, Angel called out again, "Alfred? You okay in there?"

Betty's voice broke into the ensuing silence. "He's got a gun."

"Oh, shit!" In one fluid motion, Angel drew her weapon and flanked the right side of the door. Sarah was her mirror image on the other side.

"Now what?" Sarah asked.

"You call for backup. I'll see if I can talk to him."

Angel watched Sarah step off the side of the low porch and start making her way toward the car, ducking low to be out of the line of any possible fire from the windows. Then Angel turned to the door. "Alfred, listen to me. We don't want anyone to get hurt. We just need to settle this now."

"Go away."

For one brief instant Angel was again torn between friend-ship and duty. "You know I can't do that, Alfred."

The only sound she could hear was the buzz of a katydid heralding the arrival of dusk. Then Sarah stepped back on the porch and handed her a cell phone. "Thought you could try this. It works in the movies."

Angel found reassurance in Sarah's manner and flashed a grateful smile as she took the phone.

The sudden peal of the telephone ripped the silence apart and startled them both. The incessant noise created a state of near panic in Alfred, and he looked wildly around. Watching him, Betty felt a tremble of fear. The ringing could drive him over the edge. "Should I answer it?"

"No."

The harsh noise continued, each ring jangling her already frayed nerves. "Please, Alfred? It's not going to stop."

Finally, he made a vague gesture that she interpreted as a sign of assent. She walked to the phone and cast the room into the relief of silence. Swallowing her nervousness she said, "Hello," then listened for a moment. "I don't know. I'll try."

Glancing back at Alfred, she spoke hesitantly, "It's Angel. She wants to talk to you."

He shook his head, and even in the darkness, Betty could read the resolve on his face. "He won't. Angel . . ." Her voice broke. "Please don't hurt him. He don't mean no harm."

Angel closed the phone with a loud snap as patrol cars rounded the corner with sirens blaring. Dogging the first patrol cars were two trucks with the familiar side-panel announcement: SWAT TEAM.

Sarah glanced from the approaching vehicles to Angel. "We'd better do something before the war breaks out."

"That's great. You're going to get my fucking head blown off just when I'm beginning to like you."

"Alfred's not going to do that. He's your friend."

"I wish I could believe that."

"What's our choice?" Sarah nodded to the SWAT trucks now stopped about a hundred feet from the house. "Just leave it to them?"

Angel eyed the men pouring from the back of the trucks with enough firepower to take out an entire army battalion. She returned her eyes to Sarah's steady gaze. "What did you have in mind?"

"Work your way around back and see if you can get in. I'll try to talk my way in the front. Who knows? Maybe one of us will get lucky."

"And what if he blows your fucking head off?"

"No." Sarah shook her head. "No one dies in this one. Understand?"

Angel nodded and stepped off the porch.

Sarah took a deep breath and moved closer to the door. "Alfred. Listen to me. I'm Angel's friend. We want to help you."

Silence.

"You need to put the gun down and come out. There's no other way."

More silence.

The seconds ticked off loudly in McGregor's head as he watched Sarah, willing her efforts to work. The last thing they needed was a blood bath. A harsh shout from inside the house sent her scurrying away from the door and McGregor tensed. God, he didn't want to storm the place but this standoff couldn't continue forever.

Sarah gave a wave of reassurance, and McGregor remembered to breathe again. Lloyd, the SWAT Commander who took his military training seriously, sidled up to McGregor. "One of my snipers says he has a clear shot. Give me the word and we'll take him out."

"No."

Lloyd gave an exasperated snort. "You think those females can resolve the situation?"

McGregor considered correcting the guy's attitude, but figured he didn't have time. "The perp's still contained, isn't he?"

"Yeah. But for how long? At least let me get on the horn and tell him what he's facing out here." Lloyd swept an arm to indicate the sharpshooters strategically placed behind vehicles facing the house.

"Oh, yeah, that'll go a long way toward maintaining calm." McGregor made no attempt to hide his sarcasm, and Lloyd seemed to swell with barely contained rage.

"Then I'll have to call the Chief."

"Fine. But until she says otherwise, I'm in charge. And we're going to let the women do the job."

Angel wiped the sweat from her palms, then gripped her weapon again as she sidled along the kitchen wall. She paused at the edge of the doorway into the living room where the harsh illumination from the kitchen ended. She didn't dare turn out the light. Not if she wanted any element of surprise. But if she rounded the corner, she'd present a perfect target.

Straining to hear, words began to take distinct shape in the murmuring from the other room. She recognized Betty's voice, pleading with Alfred to give himself up.

"I can't. You just go ahead and leave. You don't have to pay for this, too."

"But I will. Every day of my life without you. I had no choice with Stacy." Betty's voice rose to a shrill pitch. "But you're damn well not going to take this choice away from me."

"What can I do?"

The plaintive quality of his voice tore at Angel. He was a beaten man. If she didn't neutralize this right now, he'd take the only option he thought he had.

Steeling her nerves, Angel stepped around the corner with her weapon raised. "You can give me the gun, Alfred."

Her heart pounding, Angel faced the darkness, feeling the heat of tension all around. Where the fuck is he?

Angel re-created the room from memory and turned the barrel of her gun toward the sofa. Its bulk started to take shape as Angel's eyes adjusted. There, in the shadows, was Alfred.

"Don't make me use this," she cautioned.

The moment froze as Angel steadied her aim and Alfred took a deep, shuddering breath.

"Alfred, please. Let me turn on the light," Betty finally said. "Then we can talk like decent folks. Not hiding here in the dark."

Alfred didn't answer so Betty turned to Angel. "Is that okay?"

Angel nodded, moving slightly to keep Betty in her peripheral vision. The woman walked slowly toward the floor lamp and switched it on, bathing the room in a soft, yellow glow.

Sarah's voice called from the front, "Everything okay in there?"

"Yes," Angel answered, not taking her eyes from Alfred. "We're fine."

Angel waited for the man to make some move or say something, but he just sat there, staring at the floor. Feeling the tension pulse through her body with each beat of her heart, she calculated her chances of rushing him.

Slim to none, she finally concluded, wondering how long this impasse could go on. Her arms ached with the effort of straight-arming her weapon and she had an overwhelming urge to pee.

Finally, Alfred turned to look at her, his face ravaged by torment. "Do you trust me, girl?"

The question surprised her and for a moment she couldn't answer. She looked down the barrel of her gun and saw his eyes bright with fear and purpose. The revolver in his hand wavered ever so slightly.

"I asked you a question."

"Yes, Alfred. I trust you."

"Then let me do this my way."

"And what way is that?"

"You don't make my wife a widow."

Angel could hear Betty's sharp intake of breath and risked a quick look at her before responding. "And what do I get?"

The answer, when it came, was slow and deliberate. "You get to walk me out of here."

Sarah felt her nerves jumping in little spasms all over her body. The sweat running in great rivers down her sides was as much from the strain as the heat. She'd heard nothing since the light had come on and her imagination played several scenarios through her mind. None of them held much appeal.

She knew it was only a matter of time before the restless stirring behind her erupted into a bloody effort to end this madness. And she couldn't let that happen. She had a promise to keep. The breath she hadn't even realized she was holding came out in a loud whoosh when she heard Angel's voice, "Hold fire. Officer coming out."

Sarah backed away as the front door opened, then froze when Angel stepped out, Alfred right behind her. Sarah started to raise her weapon, but Angel stopped her with a single word, "Don't."

Sarah froze again, looking at Alfred to gauge his intent. His eyes flicked nervously from her to the impressive array of officers and vehicles behind her.

He was still a ticking bomb that could go off any moment.

"Lieutenant," Angel called out. "Alfred's ready to give himself up."

Seeing Alfred holding Angel like a piece of armor diffused any relief McGregor might have felt. Something wasn't right.

"If he's giving himself up, why isn't the fucker in cuffs?" Lloyd asked.

McGregor shot him an angry look. "How the hell should I know."

"One of my guys can still take him out."

"No." McGregor turned back to the tableau on the porch, cupping his hands around his mouth. "Alfred. Put your hands on your head and step away from the officer."

"He wants to talk to the press first," Angel called out.

"What? You can't agree to that," Lloyd said.

"Shut your mouth." McGregor kept his eyes riveted on Alfred, trying to find an option. Could they rush him? Distract him? Take him out without risking Angel? Rejecting each possibility, McGregor jumped when a female voice spoke beside him, "Let me go out there."

McGregor whirled to face Bianca. When the hell had the press arrived? "No way."

"He trusts me. He'll talk to me."

"Talking's not such a good idea right now."

Cutting off any further argument from her with a sharp motion of his hand, McGregor faced his dilemma again. What would Alfred do if his request wasn't granted?

As if sensing the question, the man on the porch raised a gun and pointed it at Angel's head. "I ain't got nothing else to lose," Alfred shouted. "Either way I make a statement."

McGregor felt a stir of movement beside him. Before he could react, Bianca stepped around the hood of the car pulling her cameraman with her.

"Get back here," McGregor yelled.

Bianca kept on walking.

McGregor kicked the wheel of the patrol car. "Goddam son of a bitch!"

Angel watched the reporter approach. What the hell was she trying to prove? Sarah was still in her line of sight and Angel could see the puzzlement cross her partner's face. Oh, God, don't do something to blow this now.

The gun brushed the side of Angel's face, a light touch of cool metal, and she realized with deadly certainty that Alfred would pull the trigger if he thought he had to. Promises tend to lose their potency in the heat of panic. She gave her partner a look that she hoped conveyed a calming message.

The reporter stopped at the curb, a few feet from the empty Buick. "Alfred, do you remember me? Bianca Gomaz? Channel Eight news? You can make your statement to me."

Angel willed herself to believe it would be okay. Alfred would say his piece and they'd all walk out of here. But her gut didn't buy it.

"I want everybody to hear it," Alfred said.

"They will," Bianca assured him. "We'll broadcast every word."

When Alfred started to speak in a faltering voice, his words brushed Angel's cheeks in soft spurts of air. "I know what I done ain't right. But I thought it was the only way. Nobody paid for my little Stacy," his voice broke. Then he took a ragged breath and continued. "Some punks killed her to get money for drugs . . ."

Listening to Alfred detail his vain attempts to find vindication, Angel relived the agony of grief and anger with him. Since she'd started to suspect him, a little part of her had understood the why. She hoped a jury would understand enough to keep him from the death penalty.

"I ain't proud of what I did," Alfred said. "But the innocent keep dying. Somehow I had to make people see. Make them care."

He paused to take another breath and Angel could feel the thud of his heart against her back.

"Now I see it wasn't the smart thing," Alfred said, his voice stronger now. "But when you're desperate it looks like the *only* thing. And it's not just me that's desperate. All those people are dying and it's got to stop. Poor black folks can't make it stop. But the ones with power can. And they better start before it's too late.

"That's all I got to say."

Angel watched the reporter start slowly backtracking, then felt the pressure of the gun against her head ease. She quickly looked to Sarah for some sign that it was okay to move. Sarah gave a slight shake of her head. Then Angel felt a flutter of breath against her ear as Alfred spoke in a soft whisper.

"Betty had nothing to do with this. Promise me nothing will happen to her."

Alfred seemed to be waiting for some sign of agreement, so Angel gave a slight nod. Then he said, "And tell her I'm sorry."

For a moment Angel wondered why Alfred made that last request. Why couldn't he tell Betty himself? Then she saw Sarah's eyes widen in horror just a split second before the explosion detonated in her ear.

Sarah lunged. She was too late to stop the action that blew parts of Alfred's head all over the white siding in a stark spray of red but in time to catch her dazed partner before she crumbled to the porch.

A cacophony of sound followed the gunshot. A high-pitched keening from inside the house. Bianca's voice screaming, "Roll tape. Roll tape." The drum of running feet closing the distance. All this registered unconsciously as Sarah pulled her partner away from the carnage, murmuring, "You're okay. You're okay."

The petite body trembled in Sarah's hands and she didn't envy Angel the nightmares that would come when the shock wore off. The woman's entire back was sticky and wet with the remains of one Alfred J. Thomas.

Later, after the paramedics had checked Angel and sent her home with her brother and a sedative and after the coroner had stated the obvious and released the body for transport, Sarah saw Bianca still hustling around filling reels of tape.

Marching over, Sarah held one hand in front of the lens and spoke to Bianca. "Stop the filming. Now."

"I don't have to."

Sarah turned to the cameraman. "Turn the fucking machine off."

He did.

Sarah whirled on the reporter. "Anything for a story, huh?"

"I was only trying to help," Bianca protested.

"Maybe if you hadn't been so willing, he'd still be alive." It pleased Sarah to see a shadow of uncertainty cross the reporter's face. Of course the woman didn't realize. She probably never even thought about the potential consequences of her actions. "Telling his story was the only thing Alfred had to live for."

"But it's over now," Bianca said, mustering a bit of her usual bravado. "Wrapped up all nice and neat. No more prolonging his agony or the state's."

"Tell that to his widow."

# Chapter Twenty-Nine

Angel wanted to feel comforted in the presence of her family, gathered here like a retrospective of years past when some occasion drew them together. She had a lot to be thankful for. She was still alive. Her mother was recovering well. The case was closed, and she'd even gotten a commendation out of it.

But she still felt like shit.

Every night she relived the terror on that porch and woke up feeling the wetness of Alfred's blood on her back. No matter how many showers she took, she could never scrub away the memory.

The family gathering was ostensibly billed as a belated celebration of her mother's homecoming. LaVon had called a couple of days ago to suggest it. But Angel knew the gesture was motivated to a large degree by a big-brother effort to heal another hurt. Only this one went much deeper than a scraped knee.

LaVon had brought all the fixings for banana splits and had sequestered himself in the kitchen where he'd been happily whistling and clanking for the past fifteen minutes.

"No tellin' what that kitchen is gonna look like," Martha said from the couch where she was propped up on pillows.

"Maybe he'll be a good boy and clean up after himself," Angel offered.

"That's a joke."

"I'll do it."

Angel looked at her father in surprise. Did he even know how?

"Now, Gilbert," her mother said. "I'm sure Angel wouldn't mind."

"What? Haven't I been doing a good enough job since you came home."

"It's not that. It's just . . ." Martha fidgeted with the afghan across her knees. "You never had a mind to do stuff like that if there was a woman handy."

"And how long have you nagged me about that?"

Angel listened, watching the interplay between her parents with interest. Was it her imagination, or was there a new level of tenderness between them? Well, that wasn't such a big surprise, considering. But Daddy being domestic?

The arrival of LaVon with the banana splits interrupted her musings. She accepted hers with a grateful smile and savored the first rich, sweet bite of chocolate ice cream dripping in strawberry sauce.

Never having been much of a drinker, she contemplated the recklessness of drowning her sorrows in a nightly sweet-fix. Or was that as destructive as drinking? Yeah, you idiot. You could end up looking like a blimp.

LaVon settled on the floor across from her, his back resting against the sofa. "So," he asked. "You still thinking about quitting the force?"

Angel choked on her ice cream and shot him an angry look. His innocent smile told her that everything had been calculated, down to and including where he sat, so she couldn't avoid the shocked look on her mother's face.

The little shit. She'd told him that in confidence.

"Angel, honey. Certainly you're not thinking that because . . ." her mother seemed to have trouble saying the words.

"You can't quit."

The statement rang with such authority; Angel looked at her father to see if he really thought he could still order her around.

"It's my life. I'll do what I want."

"Fine. If that's the way it has to be." Her father paused to take a bite of ice cream. "But it's a damn shame."

"What does that mean?"

"It means," he said, looking at her over the rim of his bowl, "that you're too good at what you do to quit."

A week ago she would have treasured the long awaited affirmation, but today it fell flat against the deep ache of pain. When she spoke, her voice was a soft whisper. "I wasn't good enough to keep Alfred alive."

Her father rubbed the bristles on his chin with stubby fingers. "Alfred was gonna do what he did no matter who was there. It was his choice and nobody's fault."

Angel wanted to believe that. She needed to believe it. Part of her had known from the moment it happened that Alfred had taken the only way of out his dilemma that he could see. But another part of her played the eternal what-if game. What if she wouldn't have agreed to his request? What if she could have found a way to disarm him? What if . . . ?

"Have you talked to Betty?"

Her mother's question broke the web of self-recrimination that was choking her. Angel shook her head, remembering the funeral. The unexpected rain had added a fitting touch to the tragedy. She'd wanted to tell Betty how sorry she was. She'd wanted to fulfill her promise to Alfred and tell her how sorry he was. But her shame and guilt had held her to the fringes of the crowd and chased her away before the first handful of dirt cascaded over the casket.

"Well, you should," Martha suggested. "You both need it."

"So this is supposed to fix me now?" Angel directed the question and her irritation at LaVon. "Tell me a few nice things and everything's okay again?"

"No one can fix you but you," LaVon locked her in a look of intensity. "If you want to."

Sarah shifted her weight in the chair, wondering why she'd even come. *Because your life is shit. And you'd better get it together before you don't have one.*

Doc Murray sat across from her, his face kindly with bushes of eyebrows over soft brown eyes and a mouth that smiled easily.

They'd been at it for almost a half an hour, with short bursts of talk shot into the long stretches of silence that he seemed more comfortable with than she was. It didn't feel like they were getting anywhere. But what the hell did she know. She wasn't used to going to shrinks.

"So you felt like you should have stopped it?" Murray asked.

"I didn't *feel* like anything," Sarah snapped. "It was my job. Perps are supposed to be arrested and stand trial."

"So it pisses you off that you didn't have control?"

"No. It pisses me off that someone had to die."

"Like John."

Sarah didn't answer.

"And that kid."

"That doesn't have anything to do with it."

"Really?"

Murray let a painful silence fill the room. Sarah's instinct told her to let it be, but she lost reason in a rush of emotion. "None of them should have died," she said softly. "I should have prevented it."

"You feel like you were responsible?"

"I didn't say that."

"Then what are you saying?"

"I don't know."

It was Sarah's turn for silence and Murray finally stepped in. "What was your relationship to John?"

"We were partners."

"That's all?"

"What does that mean?"

Murray arched a bushy brow, and Sarah couldn't believe it. What was he? Doctor Sigmund-Murray Freud?

She shot out of her chair and leaned across his desk. "Okay. You want to know the intimate details of our relationship? I'll tell you. Yeah, partners are close. Closer sometimes than spouses. We're like two sides to the same coin. And we always know if we look behind us, the other one is there. It's trust, asshole. The intimacy of trust."

"And you broke that trust."

His words were like ice water on her anger and she had to choke another emotion back. She whirled away before he could glimpse it in her eyes.

"I only say that because every other cop who's come in here after losing a partner feels the same way. It's a terrible burden to carry."

The sentiment beckoned. If she turned and went to him would he wrap her in his arms and comfort her? She fought the temptation, standing rigidly in the middle of the room.

"So what about your new partnership?"

Sarah shrugged.

"Are you going to leave Angel out in the cold?"

The question turned her around to face him. "What does that mean?"

"You won't be much good to her if you don't get these other issues solved."

"And that's psycho-babble for what?"

"Get your shit together."

"But what if she doesn't want to be my partner?"

"Why wouldn't she?"

Sarah's answer struggled past the lump in her throat, the words barely a whisper. "Because I promised her no one would die."

There. They were back to square one and he could take her through the whole litany again. But he didn't. He framed his pursed lips with his fingers and regarded her with a sympathetic expression.

"What?" she said. "The good doctor is speechless? You don't have an opinion?"

"What I think doesn't matter. It's what you think and what you have the courage to do."

Sarah drove through the familiar neighborhood, paying little heed to the dying daylight that dappled the trees. Doc Murray's words played through her mind like a mantra, "You've got to put the past to rest."

He'd suggested her current mission, and she wondered if some magic was supposed to happen. She would knock. The door would open. And everything would be okay again.

Fat chance, Sarah thought, accelerating and turning the corner for the tenth time. That only happened in fantasy.

*But what's the alternative? If you don't do this, you'll always be perched on the edge of that precipice. And one of these days you'll fall.*

Resolute, Sarah made another right turn and headed down the block again. Easing to the curb, she turned off the engine and rolled down the window.

Distant sounds of suburban life drifted on the warm breeze, the whir of a lawnmower, the tinkling laughter of children at play. Then the low steady hum of rollerblades on concrete grew to a crescendo as a skater neared, then whizzed past the car.

Taking a deep breath of air scented lightly with honeysuckle,

Sarah wondered if the pastoral scene was too good to be true. It could be a setting for a vintage Cappra film where people lived in serene simplicity and nothing bad ever dared to happen. But it did. Tragedy struck indiscriminately, and no place, no person, was immune. That was reality.

Sarah opened the car door and got out, heart pounding and palms dripping. What if they weren't home? She couldn't decide if that would be good or bad.

Squaring her shoulders, Sarah walked to the front door. Breaking her earlier fantasy, she rang the bell instead of knocking. The heavy wooden door muffled a trill of sound, and Sarah waited. Finally footsteps, then the door opened.

Jeanette, her long dark hair pulled back in a ponytail, stood there. Sarah noted the strain of grief in the hollows of the eyes facing her, and a rush of emotion threatened her breathing.

*I can't do this. It's too hard. How can she not blame me?*

"Sarah."

It took a moment for the word to settle the storm in Sarah's mind and she forced herself to meet Jeanette's eyes. They were soft and liquid with tears. No sign of accusation.

Sarah took a deep breath to stop the wild beating of her heart and stuffed trembling fingers into her jacket pockets. "Can I come in?"

Jeanette nodded.

# ABOUT THE AUTHOR

A diverse writer of columns, feature stores, short fiction, novels, screenplays, and stage plays, **Maryann Miller** has won numerous awards including being a semi-finalist in the Chesterfield script competition with the adaptation of *Open Season*. Her articles and short stories have appeared in regional and national publications, and the Rosen Publishing Group in New York published her nonfiction books for teens, including the award-winning *Coping with Weapons and Violence in School and on Your Streets*. A novel, *One Small Victory*, was released from Five Star Publishing in June 2008. *Play It Again, Sam* was a July 2008 release from Uncial Press as an e-book. Other experience includes extensive work as a PR consultant, a script doctor, and an editor. She is currently the Managing Editor of Winnsboro Today.com, an online community magazine. Visit her on her Web site maryannwrites.com and on Facebook and Twitter.

When not writing, Miller enjoys acting, directing, doing puzzles, quilting, and playing "farmer" on her little piece of heaven in East Texas.